Y0-CAA-030

Out of the Mist

Also by JoAnn Ross
in Large Print:

A Woman's Heart
Blue Bayou
Magnolia Moon
River Road

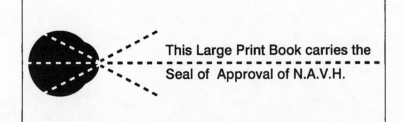
This Large Print Book carries the
Seal of Approval of N.A.V.H.

Out of the Mist

JoAnn Ross

WHEELER
PUBLISHING

Henderson County Public Library

Copyright © 2003 by The Ross Family Trust
Stewart Sisters Trilogy: Book 1

All rights reserved.

This book is a work of fiction. Names, characters, places and
incidents are products of the author's imagination or are used
fictitiously. Any resemblance to actual events or locales or persons,
living or dead, is entirely coincidental.

Published in 2004 by arrangement with Pocket Books, a division of
Simon & Schuster, Inc.

Wheeler Large Print Romance.

The text of this Large Print edition is unabridged.
Other aspects of the book may vary from the original edition.

Set in 16 pt. Plantin by Christina S. Huff.

Printed in the United States on permanent paper.

Library of Congress Cataloging-in-Publication Data

Ross, JoAnn.
    Out of the mist / JoAnn Ross.
        p. cm.
    ISBN 1-58724-529-9 (lg. print : hc : alk. paper)
    1. Motion picture producers and directors — Fiction.   2. Great
Smoky Mountains (N.C. and Tenn.) — Fiction.   3. Scots —
United States — Fiction.   4. Scottish Americans — Fiction.
5. Highland games — Fiction.   6. Resorts — Fiction.   7. Clans
— Fiction.   8. Large type books.   I. Title.
PS3568.O843485O97 2003
    813′.54—dc22   2003061291

To Jay

Gale Garp

As the Founder/CEO of NAVH, the only national health agency solely devoted to those who, although not totally blind, have an eye disease which could lead to serious visual impairment, I am pleased to recognize Thorndike Press* as one of the leading publishers in the large print field.

Founded in 1954 in San Francisco to prepare large print textbooks for partially seeing children, NAVH became the pioneer and standard setting agency in the preparation of large type.

Today, those publishers who meet our standards carry the prestigious "Seal of Approval" indicating high quality large print. We are delighted that Thorndike Press is one of the publishers whose titles meet these standards. We are also pleased to recognize the significant contribution Thorndike Press is making in this important and growing field.

Lorraine H. Marchi, L.H.D.
Founder/CEO
NAVH

* Thorndike Press encompasses the following imprints: Thorndike, Wheeler, Walker and Large Pr int Press.

Acknowledgments

With gratitude to my clever journalist son, Patrick, who came up with the origin of Robert the Bruce's coronation brooch. Also, thanks to Andrew Lenz, whose Web site offers a font of information about piping, who generously took time to respond to my E-mails, and who will hopefully forgive any liberties I've taken in the name of creative license.

1

It was dusk — too late for sunset, too early for stars. Ian MacKenzie had expected at least another hour of daylight, but night was coming fast to the Smoky Mountains. Making matters worse was the storm blowing in from the west. Slate-gray clouds rolled across the rounded mountaintops; thunder rumbled ominously in the distance.

Before being talked into this damn fool scheme, he'd been on his way to Monte Carlo, where he'd planned to spend the next two weeks sailing and romancing supermodels and princesses.

Instead, he'd come to this remote mountain borderland between North Carolina and Tennessee to catch a thief. The plan was to reclaim his family's property, by stealing it back if necessary.

Then, his duty done, his conscience cleansed, he was heading to Monaco to begin making up for six long months of celibacy.

The sky darkened like a black shawl settling over the mountains. The dashboard thermometer revealed that the temperature outside his rental car was plummeting, and ominous drops of rain began spattering the windshield.

"This is insane." Ian had been saying that ever since he'd landed in Washington, D.C., from Edinburgh, by way of London. He'd then climbed aboard a commuter jet at Dulles International Airport to Asheville, North Carolina, where he'd rented a car for this final leg of his journey.

The Hertz rental agent had told him Highland Falls was approximately sixty miles from Asheville. "As the crow flies," she'd said as she handed him back his credit card. "It's a bit longer by road."

That was proving to be a vast understatement.

The wind picked up; the rain began to slant. He hadn't passed another car for at least an hour and it had been nearly that long since he'd seen any of the small cemeteries, with their worn gravestones grown over with rambling honeysuckle and blackberry briars, or the weathered cabins tucked into the protective, fog-shrouded hollows.

Beginning to suspect he'd taken the wrong fork ten miles back, Ian considered turning around. The problem with that idea was that he'd undoubtedly end up getting mired in the mud. Besides, he hadn't come all this way to give up because of a little squall. He was a Scot, accustomed to miserable weather.

Thunder shook the mountain and rumbled

from ridge to ridge, and soup-thick fog reflected the yellow beam of his headlights — which was why Ian didn't see, until it was too late, the storm-swollen creek that had overflowed its banks. Clenching his jaw, he plowed ahead.

His relief on getting through the torrent rushing across the narrow road was short-lived when the engine coughed . . . then shuddered to a stop.

"Damn." He slammed his fist against the steering wheel. "Damn Duncan MacDougall's black heart."

Ian twisted the key in the ignition.

Nothing.

"And damn the bloody Stewart clan. Every bloody last one of them."

Forcing himself to wait a full thirty seconds — during which time he also cursed the rock-hard Highland stubbornness that had maintained the Stewart and MacDougall feud for seven hundred years — he tried again.

Still nothing.

Rain streamed down the windshield in blinding sheets as he turned on the dome light and studied the map. If it was at all accurate, he was approximately a mile from his destination.

"Hell — barely a decent jog."

Giving the car one last chance to redeem itself, Ian tried the ignition again. When the attempt proved futile, he jammed the keys into his jacket pocket, grabbed his duffel bag from the back seat and began marching up the road, cursing into the wind.

★ ★ ★

"Well, what do you think?"

Lily Stewart glanced up from the uncooperative computer that had already crashed three times tonight, and took in the redhead twirling in a blaze of glitter.

"I don't believe I've seen so many sequins since you dragged me to that Elvis impersonator convention in Memphis." Her aunt's scarlet sweater was studded with red sequins and crystal beads, and the short red leather skirt displayed firm, stocking-clad thighs. "You're certainly showing a lot of leg tonight."

"If you've got it, flaunt it."

Ruby rings blazed, and diamonds flashed as the fifty-something former chorus girl fluffed her cloud of firecracker-bright hair, several shades darker than Lily's strawberry blond. "I'm not tryin' to be subtle, baby doll. Ian MacKenzie is showing up tonight with his video cameras, and you know what I always say: too much —"

"Is never enough." Lily had heard the motto innumerable times while growing up. Zelda Stewart was part Auntie Mame, part Dolly Parton. She was also the closest thing to a mother Lily, who adored her aunt, had ever known. "I never have understood how you manage to walk in those ice-pick heels."

Lily had been seven years old when she'd broken her ankle falling off her aunt's skyscraper-high gold platform sandals while playing dress-up with her two sisters. That was the day she'd realized she'd never be the glam type.

"Practice, my darling niece, practice." Zelda performed another spin Lily suspected not many supermodels would have been able to pull off on the end of a runway. "So when is this Scotsman who's going to save our collective butts due to arrive?"

"I don't know. He's already late."

Since confirming that his plane had landed at the Asheville airport more than three hours ago, Lily had begun to worry he'd been delayed by the storm. Even worse was the possibility he'd taken a wrong turn and gotten lost. She'd grown up on tales of people who'd disappeared into these mountains, never to be seen again. Wouldn't that start the annual Highland Games off on a lovely note? She could just see the tabloid headlines now: "Oscar-winning documentary director disappears deep in *Deliverance* country."

"And I don't think he's coming here to save anyone's butt."

Lily couldn't figure out why the filmmaker *was* gracing Highland Falls with his famous presence and unlike everyone else in her family, she wasn't certain Ian MacKenzie's out-of-the-blue announcement that he was considering documenting the town's Highland Games was a good thing. His work, while technically brilliant, showed a dark and pessimistic view of the world that always left her feeling depressed.

13

"It's just as the cards predicted," Zelda claimed. "We desperately needed an economic savior, so the gods sent us MacKenzie."

Lily, who didn't share her aunt's faith in the well-worn deck of tarot cards, didn't respond as she booted the computer up again.

"I did a scrying before I came down here." Lily also wasn't certain what her aunt saw when she gazed into her collection of crystal balls gathered from all over the world, but Zelda's predictions had proven correct more often than not. "The past months, the crystals have been filled with thick, dark clouds, but this afternoon they were rising."

"A positive sign." They could certainly use one.

"Absolutely. And there was a bright spot right in the middle, like the sun breaking through, which means an improvement in finances. Ergo, having Ian MacKenzie show us off to the world is bound to bring in more tourist dollars."

"I suppose so." It was certainly what everyone, from her father and Zelda down to Jamie Douglass at the Tartan Market seemed to be counting on. Too many hopes and dreams were being laid on the shoulders of one stranger.

"Did you see the piece *Biography* did on him last week?" Zelda asked.

"I caught a bit of it."

Liar. She'd been riveted to the screen for the entire hour. Of course, her only interest had been in discovering whatever scraps of informa-

14

tion she could about the notoriously reclusive director. She'd barely noticed, and then only in passing, how sexy his butt had looked in those faded jeans with the ripped-out knees, which she doubted had been intended as a fashion statement.

Zelda sighed. "Such a tragic past the poor man's suffered. No wonder he's chosen to document the dark side of life. My first thought, when I saw that clip of him walking in the fog on the moors, was that he'd be a natural to play Heathcliff in a remake of *Wuthering Heights*. Not only is he gorgeous, in a dangerous, 'gone to the dark side of hell and lived to tell about it' way, that Highland hunk is going to put us on the map."

The thick, towering front door burst open. One look at the very large, wet male silhouetted by a bright flash of lightning revealed that Zelda had at least nailed the dangerous part.

His lean, rangy body, the shock of black hair glistening with raindrops, the strong, firm jaw and broad shoulders and long legs, made Lily think of an ancient warrior wielding a claymore in the midst of battle.

Dressed from head to toe in black, with the storm raging behind him and the wind howling like a banshee, the man definitely lived up to his Dark Prince of Documentaries description.

All those photographs and video clips on *Biography* hadn't done him justice. Ian MacKenzie's lived-in face was all planes and hollows, decidedly masculine, but starkly beautiful in a way that Lily, who'd spent twenty-nine years plagued by the description of being the perky Stewart sister, found eminently unfair.

Her assessing gaze locked with eyes that were swirling shades of gray, as stormy as a winter sea. As she was unwillingly pulled into those fathomless depths, Lily dearly hoped that the violence depicted in his films wasn't echoed in this scowling Scotsman who didn't remotely look like anyone's savior.

2

Though Ian was in a filthy mood at having to slog a mile through the mud in a needle-sharp rain, he was stunned by the Stewart home. He'd read about the castle dubbed by locals as Stewart's Folly. Knowing Americans' penchant for hyperbole, he'd expected a mock-Tudor manor house with a turret or two.

But this was no mere manor house. The massive, castellated block of limestone was bathed in hidden spotlights, creating the incredible silhouette of a fantasy castle against the storm-dark sky. Nothing was left out; there were battlements, arrow slits, pointed Gothic windows, and square Norman towers at all the corners.

The inside was even more impressive. An entire forest must have been leveled to panel the walls and barrel-vaulted ceiling of the huge entry hall, which looked as if it had been designed to welcome visiting royalty. The room boasted two towering fireplaces, both tall enough for a man to stand in.

Above the mantel at the far end of the hall hung the Stewart crest: a winged pelican feeding its young, with the motto: *Virescit vulnere virtus.* "Courage grows strong at a wound." If that were true, then John Angus Stewart would be a great deal more courageous by the time Ian left America.

In contrast to the surrounding darkness, the room was ablaze with light from dozens of Venetian chandeliers hanging from the high ceiling.

"Good evening."

The young woman behind a wide desk a few feet inside the doorway smiled a welcome that didn't quite reach her eyes. Eyes, he noticed despite his seething irritation, that were a soft moss green that unreasonably reminded him of a mermaid.

An unruly mass of chin-length strawberry-blond curls framed an old-fashioned peaches-and-cream complexion. There was a sprinkling of freckles across the bridge of a nose that could only be described as pert.

Ian usually went for dark and sultry women; this one, clad in a loose, lightweight forest-green sweater over bark-brown jeans, reminded him of a wood nymph, which should have prevented the quick, unwelcome tug of attraction he couldn't afford.

"Welcome to Highland Falls, Mr. MacKenzie."

She rose and came from behind the desk, moving with a fluid grace he usually associated with taller women, and extended a hand. Her nails were neat and tidy, in contrast to the pale skin of her hands that looked as if she'd tangled with barbed wire and lost. "We've been expecting you."

He surprised them both by skimming a finger across one of her scraped knuckles. "That looks nasty."

The impulsive touch created a spark he couldn't excuse as static electricity since they were standing on a slate floor. He knew she'd felt it, too, when her eyes turned wary and she backed up a step.

"It's just a little scrape from a chisel. I spent the morning carving."

His sketchy research, which was all he'd been able to accomplish when dragged into this scheme, had told him that Lily Stewart ran a local art gallery and sometimes filled in here at Stewart Castle, the family home, which had been turned into an inn for those seeking luxury in remote surroundings. He'd read nothing about her being an artist.

"Wood or stone?" he asked.

"Wood." A slight sigh ruffled her bright bangs. "I've already failed miserably at stone and was hoping wood would be more forgiving, but haven't seen a single sign that's going to be the case."

She seemed more resigned to the idea than disturbed by it. Her smile, which brightened her eyes, echoed the warmth from the flames crackling in the fireplace, heating up places inside him he'd put into deep freeze years ago.

"You've no idea how discouraging it is to be the only member of my family without talent."

"Talent's an intangible thing."

"That's exactly what I told my art teacher when I was studying in Italy, but I'm beginning to suspect that he may have been right when he said that my lessons were a waste of both our time. Not that any time spent in a land which boasts the best art, pasta, wine, and ice cream in the world can be considered a waste.

"I should have known better than to begin in oil, since that's my father's medium, but I had this schoolgirl fantasy of us working together side by side in his studio. Somehow I'd fooled myself into overlooking the little fact that I hadn't shown any flair for painting and my teacher only let me stay in his class if I promised not to tell anyone I'd ever studied under him. Since that was an obvious failure, I thought I might try watercolors, which is why I went to Italy. I assume you've been there."

It wasn't exactly a question, but since she'd finally paused for breath, Ian responded. "I have."

"Then you know the light's terrific. Especially in Tuscany, where it's as if the painting gods created the light especially for watercolors. Unfortunately, that didn't work out, either: my pastoral scenes were Grandma Moses primitive without the charm.

"I've worked my way through chalk, mixed medium, collage; I even tried glassblowing for a very short while in Murano, and attempted

20

sculpture in Rome — which is where I failed stone — and proved hopeless at every one.

"My sister Lark writes songs as easily as she talks, and sings up a storm, but I can't even carry a tune. I am able to write a decent thank-you note, but my other sister, Laurel's, investigative reporting has triggered more than one congressional committee. My grandfather's World War II photographs are in the Smithsonian, my grandmother Annie was a fabulous watercolorist when she was painting, and her sculptures have gained her a new audience. Father's work is in museums all over the world, and my aunt" — she gestured toward the other woman in the room — "writes brilliant novels."

"My niece has an unfortunate tendency toward exaggeration."

The voice, which broke in when Lily Stewart paused for breath, was rich and husky. Ian turned and was nearly blinded by the light sparkling off all those sequins.

"She's also biased," the woman decreed. "My little mysteries are clever and commercial, but hardly brilliant. Tennessee Williams was brilliant. F. Scott Fitzgerald, Tolstoy, and Flannery O'Conner were brilliant. I'm merely mildly talented." She smiled up at Ian. "In case you haven't figured it out, I'm Zelda Stewart."

Ian nodded. "I recognized you from your book jackets, Ms. Stewart."

"Oh, you must call me Zelda, darling." She fluffed her fluorescent hair. "All my friends do

21

and I have the feeling we're going to become very close friends." She swept a measuring look over Ian. "You remind me of my second husband. Dark, dangerous, with a sexy edge. Why" — she patted a creamy breast framed by the plunging neckline of the scarlet-as-sin sweater — "all I had to do was look at him and I'd go weak in the knees. Not to mention other, more vital, body parts."

"We were concerned you'd gotten lost." Lily deftly cut her off. "I called the airport hours ago, and they confirmed your flight had landed, but when you didn't arrive, I began to fear the worst."

"I ran into complications."

"Oh." She paused, obviously waiting for him to elaborate. "Well," she said cheerfully, when he didn't provide details, "all that matters is that you're here now. Your suite is all ready for you."

"I'm surprised you have a suite available at such short notice. What with Highland Week coming up."

"We're booked to the rafters. But coincidentally, something opened up."

"Lucky me."

Ian had been on the receiving end of luck — both good and bad — enough times to believe in it, but something in her voice wasn't ringing quite true. Along with being a thief, she was also a liar. And not a very good one.

She waved off the American Express card he held out to her. "No charge."

22

"I can't do that." His tone, while polite, assured her it would be pointless to argue. "If I accept a free room, I risk accusations that I went soft on a subject."

"I can't believe anyone could ever accuse you of being at all soft," she said in a mild way that had him unable to decide whether he'd just been complimented or insulted. "We're only talking about games, Mr. MacKenzie. Bagpipe competitions, some caber tossing, ballad singing. It's certainly not in the same category as a war tribunal."

"That's just as well, because I've already filmed a war tribunal."

"I know. It was riveting. As was the film you made about the police murdering those homeless boys in Rio. I went through nearly a box of tissues when I saw it at an art theater while I was living in Florence. Which makes me wonder," she pressed on, "why you'd want to come here in the first place."

"I felt it might be time for a change of pace."

"Well, the games are certainly a world apart from your usual topics," she agreed. "Shall we collect the rest of your bags from your car?"

"That can wait for morning, since I've got all I need for tonight and my car is a mile down the road."

"Oh, dear." Concern darkened her expressive eyes. "You had an accident?"

"A flooded engine."

"Ah." She nodded, obviously relieved.

23

Ian couldn't remember when he'd last seen anyone whose every thought was broadcast across her face. He found it an odd character trait for a thief. Then again, if every international jewel thief and smuggler looked the part, they'd all be in prison, and Interpol, Customs, and the FBI theft unit would be out of business.

"We'll have someone retrieve the car first thing in the morning. It'll surely be dried out by then." She pushed a huge leather-bound book across the carved wooden counter. "If you'll just fill out the register, we can get you settled into your room."

"You don't use a computer?"

The heavy furniture, the velvet-draped Canterbury windows, the tapestry wall hangings of hunting scenes, and the stone floor were nice touches, but a handwritten register was carrying this ancient-castle motif a bit too far.

"Usually. But the storm keeps taking it out, so I don't really trust it." Her smile, this time meant to reassure, returned. "We mostly use the book as a backup record, since people who stay here expect things to be old-fashioned. Not that you need worry, Mr. MacKenzie. We may look like something from the fourteenth century, but we have all the modern conveniences."

She plucked a huge key from the rack on the wall. "We've put you in the tower suite in the Tennessee wing."

"Tennessee wing?"

"Early borders were fluid around these parts,"

24

she explained. "Andrew Stewart began building this house shortly after the American Revolution. The story goes that while he was in Massachusetts he became friends with Paul Revere, who enjoyed his whiskey and gifted him with a few silver pieces. Being a canny Scot who didn't let friendship or emotion get in the way of business, Andrew sold them to buy the land. Somewhere along the way, a surveyor made a mistake that wasn't discovered until the walls were three-quarters laid.

"There were three choices: draw new borders by snaking a line around us, make my ancestor tear down the stones on one side of the line — which, given Andrew's tenacity and temper wasn't any choice at all — or simply allow the house to straddle the line and be in both states.

"Since we're rather isolated here, the latter was what was decided, and things went along well enough until the Whiskey Rebellion in 1794. That's when the family sided with the states fighting against federal taxation."

"Don't forget when we were part of the state of Franklin," Zelda broke in.

Lily let out a peal of laughter. "I was trying to keep this brief." She drew in a breath. "Okay, the short version is that North Carolina tried to give this part of the mountains to the federal government, who didn't want us, so that didn't last very long. The town and the distillery, which is still operating, are legally in Tennessee. As is most of the private part of the house.

"My aunt Melanie and her daughter Missy live in the North Carolina wing. Aunt Melanie's one of the Lancasters, who've been part of Charlotte society forever, and feels closer to her roots there."

The light from the fire crackling in the fireplace brought out a shimmering ring of gold around her pupils. Ian was thinking that it was good for both of them that he liked long, leggy brunettes with dark eyes and slow, sultry smiles, when a dimple deep enough to drown in creased her smooth cheek and made him reconsider.

"We don't often put guests on the Tennessee side, but since that tower has the best views of the valley, not to mention glorious sunsets, I thought you'd enjoy it. It's one of the largest bedrooms in the house and was recently redone."

"I'm not particular." Not intending to spend any more time in this remote mountain community than necessary, Ian had no interest in sunset views.

"Of course you're particular," Lily's aunt declared. "Anyone can tell, from watching your films, that you're a man who cares about every detail." She gave him another slow, thorough once-over. "Some might even call you obsessive, but there's no way you're going to put anything out there in the world with your name on it if it isn't perfect."

"That's a fairly accurate analysis." She also could have figured it out from that damn biography he'd never authorized.

26

Unfortunately the A&E producer hadn't been put off by his refusal to cooperate, which was how Ian — a man who'd always been more comfortable looking at life through the distancing lens of a viewfinder — had ended up on television screens all over America.

"I've picked up a bit of knowledge of men over the years," Zelda said. "I'll know more after I do another reading, now that your energies are here in the house." Her eyes, which were a darker green than her niece's, narrowed with speculation. Accustomed to being the observer, Ian didn't enjoy having the tables turned on him. "Our little festival will undoubtedly prove a refreshing change from all those depressing topics of torture and murders."

This from a woman whose recent book had included a brutally realistic description of medieval battle? Yet it was true that death — most particularly that of innocents — had always been a recurring theme in his films. "This project's still up in the air. I have no way of knowing if there's anything here that'll make a story."

"Well, we'll just have to make sure we give you plenty of inspiration."

"I wouldn't want you to commit murder on my account."

Zelda Stewart's appreciative laughter was rich and warm. If he'd been twenty, hell, ten years older, he might have been interested.

"For a time I fantasized doing away with my sexy second husband, who had all the morals of an alley cat," Zelda mused. "But I got even with him." Her reminiscent smile was quick and a little bit evil. "I had him drawn and quartered."

Ian nodded. "*Clansman*, the first book in your Highland Rogues series."

Zelda's eyes brightened with pleasure. Like her niece, she didn't bother to conceal emotion. "You've obviously done your homework."

"I always do. You've written ten books in the series and sales have increased with each succeeding title. The last one hit the *New York Times* list and there's talk of a movie deal in the works."

"Readers do so love men in kilts." She smiled lustfully. "Particularly when the stories are spiced up with time travel and murder. As for the movie deal, it's currently in option hell. If it ever does get made, I'd love Russell Crowe to play William, but the studio hotshots are thinking more along the lines of Heath Ledger, who is admittedly a very handsome young man. Emphasis on young — apparently it all comes down to demographics. Youth must, after all, be served. But I will insist on Liam Neeson for his father."

"Good casting," Ian said agreeably, suspecting that Zelda Stewart was more than a little accustomed to getting her own way.

He'd picked up one of her books at a duty-free shop in Singapore a few years ago, and while he'd found the mystery well crafted, there was too much romance in the story for his taste.

And the time-travel aspect definitely required more of a suspension of belief than he was capable of. One of the reasons he'd chosen to make documentaries was that as a realist, he preferred fact over fiction.

"Your description of everyday life in the thirteenth century was very engaging." He may not be known for his manners, but he liked Zelda Stewart's brassy attitude and believed in giving credit where credit was due.

"You're not the only creative person who believes in research." She fluffed the cloud of flame-hued hair again. "You wouldn't have been looking into my background if you weren't seriously considering making the film."

"Perhaps I was considering making a documentary on how a girl raised in the Appalachian hills left home at seventeen to be a showgirl, then went on to become a best-selling novelist."

"Wouldn't that just bore audiences to tears? And I wasn't exactly a showgirl. I only danced in the chorus line."

He skimmed a look at her still-slender thighs, revealed by an outfit that was way over the top for a rainy evening at home. Even if your home happened to be a castle.

"You still have the legs to prove it," he said.

She fluttered her lashes in a decidedly Southern-belle manner. "Are you sure you don't have Southern blood, darlin'? Because you definitely know how to flatter a girl."

"It's not flattery if it's true."

Zelda Stewart was a spectacular woman, the kind who, like the fine whiskey the family had been making here for over two centuries, improved with age. She was also managing to smooth out some of his ragged edges roughened from the storm.

"Well?" a deep voice boomed out, echoing off the walls. "Have you heard anything from the MacKenzie?"

John Angus Stewart, "laird" of Stewart castle and an artist whose energetic, oversized paintings managed to make Jackson Pollock's work appear almost sedate, marched toward them, the heels of his ghillie brogues striking against the stone floor. The robust stride, flaming red beard, and barrel chest large enough to have its own zip code, all contributed to his powerful, robust appearance.

"The MacKenzie's arrived," Ian said mildly.

"And high time, too." Lily's father stopped in front of Ian, and bear-paw hands that looked more suited to wielding a battle-ax than a paintbrush went to his hips. "We expected you three hours ago."

"I was delayed by the storm." He refrained from suggesting that if Stewart wanted people to show up punctually, he ought to pave the damn road.

"What kind of bloody Scot allows a little rain to get in his way?"

"Daddy." Lily placed a slender hand on her

father's brawny forearm. "Mr. MacKenzie is a guest," she reminded him mildly.

"Well, of course he is." He deftly switched gears. "It's miserable damn weather out there, and it doesn't help that Andrew Stewart bought land on a hill that's as steep as a mule's face. You'll be wanting a wee dram of Highlander's Pride to warm you up." He opened a massive cabinet behind the counter and took out a bottle of the whiskey that had made the Stewart family wealthy.

"They say the proper amount to pour into a glass is two fingers," he said as he poured the whiskey into four cut-crystal old-fashioned glasses. "Fortunately, I've got large fingers." He added a small splash of water from a bottle. "Opens up the flavor," he said as he handed one glass to his sister, another to Lily, the third to Ian, and kept the fourth, which he lifted.

"May we be healthy, rich, and happy. And may our enemies know it. *Slainte!*"

He and Zelda tossed back the whiskey as if it were water.

The whiskey exploded on Ian's tongue and made his eyes water. Only steely pride kept him from choking.

During his travels, he'd drunk *aguardiente* made from distilled sugar cane in Peru, *arak*, an insidiously strong distilled rice liquor in Bali, and *masato* from fermented yam in South Africa. The one thing all three drinks had had in common was that they were lethal. They certainly hadn't been as sophisticated as Stewart's. Nor as strong.

"When the conglomerates began buying up the industry, my father had two choices: to sell out or change direction. He wasn't about to surrender the Stewart heritage, so he stopped producing whiskey for the masses and concentrated on the connoisseurs. Highlander's Pride is one of only two uncut, unfiltered, straight-from-the-barrel whiskeys available in America today," the older man boasted. "It's guaranteed to put hair on your chest. This particular batch was brought in at one hundred twenty-six proof."

Which worked out to sixty-three percent alcohol. No wonder it had flamed in his throat.

"Seems that it might be better as sipping whiskey," Ian said mildly.

Now that the flames were dying down, he could concentrate on a smooth aftertaste of vanilla, apple, caramel, spices, and smoke. He also realized that Lily Stewart had only taken a sip before putting the glass aside.

"You could be right," the older man agreed cheerfully.

But sipping, Ian considered, didn't allow you to test a man's mettle. Ian figured he'd gained points by not choking.

"We'll go slower on the next ones," John Angus said.

"I appreciate the offer, but I've come a long way and would prefer to get settled in."

Eyes the color of midnight over the moors darkened beneath rust-hued brows. "It's not like a Scot to turn down good whiskey. And this is superb whiskey. My father poached the master distiller from Scotland."

"He obviously knows his job, because it's excellent." Ian also knew that the distiller wasn't the only thing James Stewart had poached from Scotland. "As for being Scots, I haven't thought of Scotland as home for a very long time." If home was where the heart was, he didn't have one. Which was fine with him. It was also none of Stewart's business.

"I suppose that explains why you've lost the burr from your voice. Hell, man, I've never lived in the mother country, but my heart's in the Highlands and I'm a Scot through and through. Blood tells."

"So they say." If there was one topic Ian didn't want to get into, it was that of blood and family ties.

"We'll talk in the library." It was more command than suggestion. He could have been a thirteenth-century laird ordering a lesser baron to go raiding with him. "We'll discuss the film you'll be making over a few more glasses of Highlander's Pride."

"As I told your sister and daughter, I'm not certain there's going to be a documentary."

By not committing to anything, he'd be free to leave on a moment's notice once he'd completed his mission. Ian silently cursed Duncan again for getting him involved in all this bloody intrigue.

The older man's beefy hand swatted away his words. "Of course there's going to be a documentary. Do you realize that twenty million Americans claim Scots ancestry?"

"Yet the American government's census only shows five million." Ian had, indeed, done his homework.

"Who are you going to believe? The government or those millions of people who are proud of their heritage? You've got a ready-made audience of twenty million even before you start counting all those people who *wish* they were Scots. Have you ever seen a hundred pipers and drummers marching across a field?"

"I can't say that I have."

"It's a spectacle that'll send a chill up a grown man's spine and a tear down his cheek." John Stewart poured himself another two fingers, then splashed in a bit more. "I've shot some video myself — at last year's games — and put it on our Web site. It's not professional quality, but it gets the idea across."

He shot Ian a sly look over his shoulder. "No telling what a man with your talent could make of such a grand show."

"Daddy." Lily's voice was edged with a soft warning. "Mr. MacKenzie has come a very long way. He also got drenched in the storm. I imagine he'd like a nice hot shower and some rest."

Stewart's wide brow furrowed and he looked inclined to argue. Then his thoughtful gaze shifted from his daughter to Ian, then back to Lily.

"Good idea," he decided. "Why don't you show our guest to his room, Lily." His smile was guileless but a glint of determined mischief danced in his eyes.

Ian had seen that look before. It was the look of his grandfather's Westie, right before the dog grabbed onto the postman's trousers and refused to let go. It was also the look Duncan got in his eyes whenever he'd parade some local girl in front of his grandson in hopes of ensuring a MacDougall heir.

"We'll talk in the morning." Stewart picked up the bottle and took it with him as he left the room. His sister wished Ian a good night, then followed.

3

"My father," Lily said dryly, "has a mind of his own."

"Nothing wrong with that."

"Mmm." She didn't sound entirely convinced. "You did very well on the whiskey test. I was going to warn you ahead of time, but then you and Zelda began talking about her book and the opportunity got away from me."

"The day a MacKenzie can't handle a little whiskey is the day all my ancestors start spinning in their graves."

When Lily reached for the duffel bag, his hold on it tightened, creating a brief tug-of-war. "I've got it."

"It's no problem. Stewart Castle believes in pampering its guests."

"I said, I can handle it."

"Fine." She paused a beat. "Mr. MacKenzie?"

"It's Ian."

"All right. Ian." Rosy lips curved. "You're still holding my hand."

"So I am." He didn't like the strange prick of regret he felt when he released it.

Although his career required he deal with surprises on a continual basis, Ian had never liked them. He definitely did not like distractions. Lily Stewart, winsome international jewel thief, was turning out to be both.

Assuring himself that he was just wiped out from jet lag and the long drive, he flung his bag over his shoulder, then fell into place beside her, shortening his stride to hers as they walked across the huge room and up a wide staircase carved with flights of birds and swirling festoons of fruit and flowers.

"This is extraordinary." He brushed his fingertips over the banister that had been polished to the sheen of silk. "Was it brought in from France?"

"Actually, it was carved right here on the premises."

He knew his face, usually professionally inscrutable, revealed his surprise.

"Most of the woodwork was done locally. You'd be amazed at some of the carvers who make these mountains home. While I may not have any talent myself, at least I can get pleasure by surrounding myself with the work of local artists in my gallery."

"Do you display your father's work?"

"Only the rare reprint. He has an amazing amount of energy lately that's been coming out in his art. Zelda insists he's doing the best painting of his life because all his chakras are finally aligned properly, and while I'm not so certain I believe that, I am happy for him. I'd love to represent him, but Firefly Falls Gallery is a small place and his canvases probably wouldn't fit in the door. They've gotten quite oversized."

"Like his ego."

"He possesses a strong streak of self-confidence," she allowed. "Which I suspect is necessary in any artistic person." Her wide, generous lips tightened and the sudden passion swirling in her eyes gave her the look of an annoyed nymph. "Even documentary makers."

So she wasn't all sugar, but a little spice as well. *"Touché."*

A small gilt-cage elevator was located on the second floor. Lily's scent, fresh and sexy at the same time, bloomed around them in the intimate, confined space as they rode up two floors to a set of narrow spiral stone steps. Ian followed her up the staircase leading to the tower room, feeling not an ounce of guilt for enjoying the view of her pert ass.

The tower room was a cozy and colorful garden of chintz. Botanical prints hung from wide ribbons on the flowered walls, and the green Wedgwood pitcher and bowl on a marble-topped stand were relics of a less comfortable time. A fire crackled a warm welcome. While no expert on art, even Ian could recognize the painting over the bed, of a wooded waterfall surrounded by wild rhododendron, as one of Annie Stewart's watercolors.

"This was my grandmother's room until recently," Lily divulged. "She said the view inspired her. But then it became difficult for her to make it up and down those uneven stone steps.

"Her vision has become blurry from glaucoma, so she lives on the first floor now. She wanted to be here to greet you when you arrived, but a sight dog she's been waiting for just unexpectedly became available when someone above her on the list canceled, so she's been away at school in Piney Flats learning to work with him. She'll be back day after tomorrow, so you can meet her then. If you're still here, that is."

"Why do I get the impression you'd just as soon I not be?"

"To be perfectly honest, I haven't made up my mind." She paused in the act of closing the draperies and looked out into the storm. "It must seem overwhelming at times."

"What?"

"Possessing the power to change the world. I'd think that'd be a very heavy burden to carry on one man's shoulders."

"It probably would be, if I believed I had that power. To be honest, I doubt I change a damn thing."

She turned back toward him. "Then why do you do it?"

"To shine a spotlight on inequity."

"And to tell the world the truth?"

"At least my take on it."

She looked a little concerned again. "Well,

then, I'll have to hope that your take on our games isn't so negative that you'll be cruel."

"I'm never unnecessarily cruel."

"Yet some reviewers have said that you can be honest to the point of cruelty."

So he wasn't the only one who'd been doing his research. "They've said that. But perhaps it's the behavior I'm documenting that's cruel."

"I wonder which came first," she murmured.

He arched a brow.

"Does that attitude come from your work, or do you choose such grim subjects because you're drawn to revealing the dark side of the human spirit?"

"I've never given it any thought. I merely film topics that interest me."

She tilted her head and looked up at him. "I'm finding it hard to believe you're the same individual who made that sensitive film about the victims of that terrible serial killer."

He'd had to fight for that one, since Finn Callahan, the FBI Special Agent handling the case, had initially refused to speak with him. Finally, pressured by the victims' families, who wanted the film made as a memorial to their loved ones, Callahan had allowed him twenty-four hours' access. It'd been just dumb luck that Ian had been there the night Callahan cracked the case.

"No one who knows me would ever call me sensitive." Callahan had called him an ice-hearted ghoul. Since the agent hadn't been the first to make that accusation, Ian hadn't been offended. "I merely have a knack for hitting people's emotional hot buttons."

"That talent doesn't make me any less ambivalent about your film."

Lily had never been convinced the documentary would be a good idea. Now that she'd met Ian MacKenzie in person, she was even more uneasy about his motives.

"You seem to be in the minority. Your aunt's definitely in favor of it. And your father's been writing me letters trying to get me to cover your games since before I won my first Oscar."

"I know."

"Yet you seem surprised I'm here."

"We're not the type of story you usually cover. Besides, I'm not certain that being put into a worldwide spotlight is the best thing for my family or Highland Falls." Even though, due to dwindling income from the distillery, the constant maintenance and repairs on a house that was quite honestly a money pit, along with that problem her father had gotten into last year with the IRS, they badly needed the publicity.

"Spotlights do have a way of bringing things out into the open. Revealing secrets people would rather keep hidden."

When he moved toward her slowly, deliberately, it set her nerves jangling. There was something in his deep, rough tone Lily couldn't quite discern.

Sarcasm? Resentment? Anger?

"Is that what you're planning to do?" He was so close to her she had to tilt her head back to look up at him. Her pulse kicked up a beat. "Expose all my family's secrets?"

The corner of his mouth quirked as he hooked his thumbs into the front pockets of those wet jeans and rocked back on his heels. "I haven't decided yet. Do you have that many secrets?"

The hint of a smile did nothing to soften a face that, while gorgeous, was lacking in any kindness. His jaw was darkened by a day's growth of beard; his eyes managed to be remotely cool and unnervingly intense at the same time. Just as his voice was both rough and silky.

Mesmerizing. That was the word, she decided, while the rain hit against the leaded windows and the wind wailed across the hilltops.

Even as she was drawn into his gaze, Lily sensed a steely, invisible barrier between them. Had all the years spent documenting man's inhumanity to man created that detachment? Or was the ability to disengage himself emotionally what had allowed him to choose such harsh subject matter in the first place?

Realizing he was waiting for an answer, she dragged her mind back to his question. "Anyone who lives in a small town is pretty much an open book."

He narrowed those flinty eyes. "Then why don't you want me here, when it's so obvious that your aunt and father do?"

Even as the unsettling blend of anxiety and attraction swirled inside her, Lily held her ground. "Let's just say that I'm uneasy with how you might portray the heritage revival of a community that goes back two hundred years. After all, our Highland Games represent a return to the clan system that ended with the defeat of Bonnie Prince Charlie's Highlanders in 1746."

"Not all Scots came to America because they lost a battle."

Didn't the man have an iota of national pride?

"And the repression following the Jacobite Risings wasn't the first time the Highlanders suffered," he pressed on. "Your own Stewart clan tried to weaken the clan chief's power with the Statutes of Iona, nearly a hundred and fifty years earlier. They forbade firearms, required the children to be sent away to the Lowlands to be educated in English, banned the bards —"

"I'm well aware of the history of both the country and my family." She lifted her chin and met his gaze. There was no way he was going to make her feel responsible for what some distant ancestor did in 1609. "I'd also hate for you to make a documentary suggesting that the games began only as a tourist attraction."

"Actually, they began as a War Bonds fundraising effort in New York in 1941."

"Technically you're right," she conceded. "But they're still an ancient tradition that's been fought for, even died for, and never relinquished, even when the games had to be performed in secret. They're our bond with those across the water. And a way to honor all those immigrants who crossed the sea so that future generations, like my family, would be free to celebrate who and what they are."

"Nice speech." He clapped slowly. Sarcastically? "But your reenactors aren't Scots. They're Americans."

Definitely sarcastic. "Well, of course they are. Loyal, law-abiding, tax-paying Americans who eat apple pie and get teary-eyed singing 'The Star-Spangled Banner' at baseball games. But somewhere, deep in their hearts, they're still also Scottish men and women."

Since her father had roped her into planning the annual festival, Lily had begun to consider it more of a bother than a connection with the past, but she still got misty-eyed at the kirking of the tartan that kicked off the games.

"My family takes the games very seriously, Mr. MacKenzie. I'm not going to stand by and let you make fun of them or hurt them in any way."

"That's very admirable." His obviously false smile was as cold and dormant as a February garden.

Refusing to be cowed, she shrugged. "It's just the way families are."

"Not every family. And if you're referring to that so-called voice of the blood, I will point out it's never been scientifically proven."

"Proven or not, it exists for many people." She was surprised a man who'd gained fame and fortune delving for truth appeared to be so closed-minded. "As you'll see if you decide to stay."

He might be the most fabulous-looking man she'd ever met; he might also be one of the most talented. But if he did agree to make his film, they were clearly going to have to work on his negativity.

Enough was enough. She'd had a trying day, and she no longer had the patience to put up with this ill-humored Scot. No matter how out-rageously sexy he looked in those wet black jeans.

"You're still wet and I'm keeping you from that shower. The bathroom's right through there —" She pointed toward the arch of a barrel vaulted-doorway. "We had the plumbing completely redone last year, so the water actually flows, rather than trickling as it usually does in old houses." The work had also cost a fortune.

"Since people come here to get away from the outside world, we don't have phones or televisions in the rooms. There are phones in the great room and the library, and whoever's on operator duty will take messages.

"You'll find brochures for several attractions in the great room, and any of the staff on duty will be happy to help you make arrangements for things like tickets to the games. Naturally, you won't be expected to pay for them. We serve breakfast in the gathering room downstairs from six-thirty to nine-thirtyish or ten."

"That's a little vague."

"If a family shows up ten minutes after closing, the cook isn't going to deny them an omelet or scones. The kitchen has closed for the night, but if you'd like a sandwich, there was some leftover roast beef from tonight's dinner —"

"I don't need anything."

His tone was curt, dismissive. Lily felt the heat rise in her cheeks and damned the way she'd never been able to conceal her feelings.

"Fine. I'll leave you to your unpacking, then." She kept her eyes on his to prove to them both that she could. "Good night, Mr. MacKenzie."

Lily left and closed the door behind her, ridiculously grateful for the thick oak plank door between them.

4

It was a cold March day. A stiff spring breeze blew over the cattle-dotted meadows and woodlands that had been ravaged by the punitive raids of Edward Plantagenet, king of England.

If Edward's intent had been to take the fight out of the Highlanders by destroying the most hallowed spot in all Scotland and by absconding with the revered Stone of Destiny, the symbol of Scotland's sovereignty, he'd miscalculated. The people had immediately begun rebuilding their ancient Pictish capital, and on this special day, a tent city had been set up along the river. Silken pavilions belonging to the lords and bishops shared space with the more rustic structures set up to house the merchants and craftsmen who'd traveled from all corners of the country, and with the canopied shrines of various religious orders.

Although the coronation of a king was a solemn occasion, after all the troubles the people had suffered, it was a joyous event, which accounted for the circus atmosphere of tumblers, musicians, players, races, and contests of physical strength and daring. The cattle pens

47

were filled; the horse lines vast, the trading brisk. Banners — ecclesiastical, heraldic, guild, decorative — snapped in the brisk wind. Although March was an unlikely time for an outdoor event in the Highlands, a bright benevolent sun was proof to all that God himself was smiling down on the coronation.

Further proof that the Lord was on The Bruce's side was the revelation that the stone Edward had stolen years earlier had actually been a false stone; a cesspool cover that had been cleaned and put in the real stone's place after the abbot had received warning of the raid. The true stone had been retrieved from its hiding place in a nearby cave.

Unfortunately, while no one mentioned it for fear of putting a pall on the occasion, no one could have missed the fact that most of the lords and bishops had claimed pressing matters which kept them from watching Robert the Bruce be crowned their king.

But The Bruce was not going to allow them to ruin what he'd been planning for, fighting for, for so long. His first coronation had occurred two days ago, when he'd sat on the stone and was crowned by the archbishop of St. Andrews. The countess of Buchan — who, born a MacDuff, possessed the hereditary right to crown all of Scotland's kings — had stolen her husband's horse and raced to Scone when she'd heard of the planned ceremony. She'd arrived too late, but since her participation brought the sanction of ancient tradition, it was decided that they'd repeat the coronation.

Clad in robes furnished by Bishop Wishart of Glasgow, secured by a silver brooch imbedded with a center crystal surrounded by pearls, Robert marched through the crowded church to the high altar on a flourish of trumpets, and seated himself once again on the stone. The sweet, high voices of a boys' choir rose like birdsong in air scented by incense from the acolytes' swinging censers.

There was more singing, more music, the droning Latin of the mass. The king was anointed with holy oil; then cymbals clashed when the countess of Buchan placed the slender gold circlet once again on his auburn head.

Trumpets flared again and every man, woman, and child rose to cheer as Robert was given the scepter, the Book of Laws, the great two-handed sword of state, and the great Lion Rampant banner of the king.

"God save the king!"

The cry was repeated throughout the day, riding like a wave over the tent city as the celebration continued with jousting, feasting, music, and dancing.

As the fires burned and the people rejoiced, Robert the Bruce accepted their fealty with a somber awareness that this day was but a brief respite in an ongoing struggle.

"God save my king." The lovely woman who also wore a gold circlet on her yellow hair smiled up at him. The friendly, familiar lust sparkling in her blue eyes made him feel more powerful than both coronations combined.

"God save my queen," he murmured, his lips nuzzling that silken skin behind her ear.

Even as desire ribboned through him, he couldn't stop thinking of the message informing him that the earl of Pembroke, newly appointed English commander in Scotland, had arrived at Carlisle to build a great army. Even worse, a furious Edward had sent the Prince of Wales to assemble a second army, and the old king who had bedeviled the country for so long was actually preparing to come north himself.

There would be much bloodshed ahead, but there was no turning back for any of them. Even Isabel MacDuff, who'd defied her husband and the English king, would not be able to return to her home.

Robert gazed up into the black sky; smoke from the fires rose over the land, blurring the friendly sparkle of stars and the reassuring glow of the moon. A shadow moved over his heart.

"By the rood, somehow I'll bring about a united, independent Scotland," he vowed to his God and to himself. *Or die trying. Which is a distinct possibility.*

"Of course you will," Elizabeth agreed.

"God save the king!" the boisterous crowd shouted yet again.

God save me.

5

Ian waited, listening to the sound of the elevator creaking its way back down to the first floor. Then he took his cell phone out of his jacket pocket and flipped it open.

The long lonesome wail of a train somewhere out in the fog took his mind back to another rainy day sixteen years ago.

He'd been standing at his parents' gravesite. It was a cold, foggy day on the windswept Scottish moors; the rain felt like chilled needles as mourners huddled together beneath somber black umbrellas.

Ian's gaze had been captured by the one man who hadn't sought cover, standing arrow straight a short distance away. He was a stranger yet his face was familiar, possessing Ian's own gray eyes and deeply clefted chin.

Now you come. Anger struck at Ian's heart like flint against stone. *Now that your daughter's dead and being buried in the cold hard ground.*

Had the MacDougall come to pay his respects to his only child?

Had he come to grieve her passing, along with his own coldhearted behavior that had

51

cost him nearly two decades of estrangement?

Or had he merely shown up to see for himself that the man who'd gotten the unmarried, teenage Mary MacDougall pregnant nearly nineteen years ago was, indeed, truly and surely dead?

Ian welcomed the hot flare of anger, which scorched away the shocked numbness that had settled over him the moment he'd received word that his father's brand-new Porsche had spun off that narrow, twisting road on the Greek island of Seriphos.

He'd been in a strange, disconnected state the entire five days he'd sat by his mother's hospital bed while searchers attempted to recover his father's body from the Mediterranean Sea. Somehow he'd managed to cut through the red tape and paperwork required to bring his parents' bodies to Scotland's Highlands, where his mother had been born and had always wished to be buried. A place that was so much a part of her life and heart, which was featured so in her tales of growing up, that the moment he'd driven past the stone Norman cathedral, Ian had experienced a sense of déjà vu, even though he'd never set foot in the medieval city before.

The man continued to stare at him. His eyes, which also resembled his daughter's — though Mary's had been a soft, warm, inviting gray — were cold and sharp as a falcon's.

Ian steadfastly ignored him to accept the words of condolence from his parents' many friends, words that sounded as if they were coming from the bottom of the nearby sea.

Gavin MacKenzie had never met a stranger, and Mary MacDougall MacKenzie had not only been a breathtakingly beautiful, stunningly talented actress, wherever they traveled, she'd opened her home to guests who quickly became fast friends. Ian could not recall very many evenings spent alone with his parents, just the three of them.

Since they'd both possessed roving spirits, Ian had experienced prayer flags in Tibet, the brilliant sun on white stone in Greece, the leggy grace of giraffes racing across the Serengeti. He'd grown up surrounded by some of the most creative minds in the world. But he'd never been to the Scottish Highlands, and he'd never met his maternal grandfather, Duncan MacDougall.

Until today.

He continued to shake hands, nod, and say what he hoped was the appropriate thing as the stream of mourners continued to pay their condolences. There'd be a supper, of course; he was expected to attend. Wanting to be alone with his grief, Ian would rather sup with the devil in hell than tolerate hours of well-meant stories about his parents' many acting roles and adventures. But in times of tragedy people seemed to feel the need to bond together, and in Mary and Gavin's world, talk had always been the coin of the realm.

"Will you be coming in the car with me, then,

Ian?" asked the raven-haired Irish actress who'd recently won acclaim for playing Joan of Arc at the Dublin Opera House.

"I'll be along in a while, Nora." His gaze drifted from her pretty blue eyes to those intense flint ones. "I've something to take care of first."

"Would you be needing some help?"

"I will not." The denial was quick, and more curt than intended. Her pretty face fell; her cheeks turned as pink as if he'd physically slapped her.

Damn. He hadn't meant to hurt her. Ian trailed a finger up one of those flushed cheeks and wondered if the warmth was coming from his seething anger or her own inner fire.

She was a remarkably responsive woman; ten years older than his own eighteen (which was admittedly a bit old to play Joan, but she had the good fortune to have features that would allow her to play the ingenue for at least another few years), she'd initiated him into sex two years ago in her suite at Paris's Hôtel de l'Abbaye while performing in *Romeo and Juliet*. Gavin and Mary MacKenzie had played the Capulets; she'd been cast as Juliet.

At night she made audiences attending the Théâtre de la Huchette weep with her portrayal of the innocent, fate-doomed teenaged girl. During the day, she'd taught him things about the female body that most men could go a lifetime without discovering.

There'd been no promises made, and when the curtain went down the final time six months later, they went their separate ways. But the bond they'd established that summer had never ended, and on those occasions when their paths would cross — which they often did, the theater being such an insular world — they'd end up back where they first began. In bed.

Until last night. Ian knew she'd been disappointed that he hadn't opened the adjoining door between their hotel suites.

"Go along, Nora," he said, gentling his voice. "I'll catch up with you at the hotel."

She followed his glance to the scowling MacDougall. "Your mother would want you to be kind."

He wasn't that surprised she'd guessed who the man was. There was, unfortunately, no mistaking the family resemblance.

"She had eighteen years to return. If she'd wanted me to have anything to do with him, she would have introduced us herself."

"It wasn't as easy as that." She dragged a beringed hand through her slick slide of hair, which sparkled with mist from the falling rain. Even the memory of those silken waves spread across his bare thighs failed to arouse a body that felt as numb as his brain.

"She refused to go home without your father. Unfortunately, Duncan MacDougall had banned Gavin from his home."

The story of the Highland feud, the pregnant

daughter thrown out into the cold, the young couple banished for life, was the stuff good theater gossip was made of.

"My parents were happy together." Of that, Ian had not a single doubt.

"I've never seen a couple more suited," she agreed. "Gavin being so dashing and larger than life, and Mary being such a lush, warm, and loving earth goddess, with a talent I would have envied if I hadn't adored her so."

Tears welled up in her china-blue eyes. Ian hoped like hell he wasn't going to be treated to one of her crying jags. Nora Burke was not nicknamed Sarah Bernhardt for nothing; everything she did was exaggerated and emotional. Which had made her an exceptional bed partner.

"I'll allow him to pay his condolences, for her sake," he decided. "But if he's here to make amends for his behavior, he'll be finding out that he's come too late."

Her tear-glistened eyes narrowed as she gave him a long judicial look. "You're a good son, Ian MacKenzie. And you're going to grow up to be a great man."

"I'm already a man." He was of legal age, after all. "As you, of all people, should know."

"Knowing how to give a woman multiple orgasms does not necessarily mean you've reached manhood. Though it's quite a fine start," she said fondly, with a wicked sparkle returning to her eyes. "What I'm trying to say, darling, is that you have your entire life ahead of you. You've still got to explore your options, to decide whether to write, as you're thinking of doing, or follow your parents onto the stage.

"Having experienced a great deal more of life than you, I feel the need to warn you that you've got a strong streak of the MacDougall stubbornness in you — which, if used for good, can get you far. But if you allow it to control you, rather than the other way around, you could end up as alone and bitter as that old man over there."

It was not often she pointed out their difference in age. The fact that she did so now was proof of how serious she was. "You're sounding a bit Dickens, love. Should I be expecting a visit from the Ghost of Christmas Future next?"

"Don't be sarcastic. It doesn't suit you." She skimmed the back of her hand down his wet cheek. "And your mother wouldn't appreciate it. Mary was my dearest friend on earth, and it was many a night I spent listening to her unburden her heart with tales of your grandfather's harshness and unbending ways." She cupped his chin in her fingers and held his mutinous gaze to hers. "She wouldn't want you to be falling into the same trap."

"I won't ever be anything like him."

Looking back on that day now, Ian recalled meaning it.

"It's glad I am to be hearing that." Her smile had bloomed like the sun coming from behind the low-hanging clouds. "I'll see you back at the hotel, then. And we'll lift a glass of champagne to your parents, who are undoubtedly head-lining in heaven."

Nora left, leaving Ian alone in the cemetery with this grandfather he'd never met. Had never wanted to meet.

They stared at each other, the gulf between them seeming as wide as the North Sea. Finally the man pushed away from the tree and began walking toward him.

"So ye'd be Ian," his rough voice said. The Scots burr was strong enough to inflate a set of bagpipes, suggesting that he'd spent his entire life in this remote place.

Duncan MacDougall was tall, long-legged, and rangy, and, surprisingly for a man who'd never had to work in his own fields, appeared to be all lean muscle and sinew, without an ounce of superfluous flesh on his frame. Such raw physical strength could, Ian supposed, appear threatening to some people.

"I'd be Ian MacKenzie." Refusing to be in-timidated, Ian stressed his father's name. That name that supposedly had been banned from ever being spoken beneath a MacDougall roof.

"The burden of carrying on the MacKenzie name may have fallen on yer shoulders," the man had said. "But the blood flowing through your veins makes you half MacDougall."

If a transfusion could have rid Ian of the MacDougalls' damn blood, he would have done it in a heartbeat. Because if Duncan MacDougall was grieving for his lost daughter, he was doing a damn good job of hiding it. The man appeared even colder than the wind that was swooping down from the ancient, snow-topped mountains, turning the rain to sleet.

"You determined that I'd never belong to your family when you disowned your daughter and threw her out of your house without a penny."

"The girl got herself pregnant."

"Would you have preferred her to have an abortion?"

They glared at each other, both all too aware that she'd been carrying Ian when her father had shut her out of his home and his life.

"Abortion's a sin, as she was well brought up to know. She also learned in the kirk each Sunday that premarital relations were sinful — but she wasn't all that worried about her immortal soul when she let that itinerant actor plant his bastard seed in her."

Ian's hands clenched into fists. "You're lucky you're an old man." Years later, Ian would realize that Duncan had only been in his fifties, but to Ian's eighteen he'd seemed as ancient as Moses, with his white hair and long white beard. "Or I'd kill you for speaking that way about my mother."

" 'Twas wrong of me to refer to ye that way," the older man surprised Ian by allowing. "No man is responsible for his beginnings."

"I don't give a damn what you think of me. It's your daughter you owe an apology. For that, and more."

The cleft chin shot forward. "She said she

59

didn't want my support. Said her MacKenzie would take care of her with all the money he'd be making from his acting." He'd spit the words out as if they had a bitter taste.

"My father did take care of her. A damn sight better than her own father did, from what she told me."

That was a lie. His mother, loving soul that she'd been, had never said a negative thing about her father.

"MacKenzie wasn't taking such good care of my daughter when he was driving like a bat out of hell and killed her."

The accusation hit like a shower of stones. Hearing the thought that had first passed through his own mind, only to be immediately censored, shook Ian. "He swerved to avoid a drunken driver who'd cut the corner too wide and was headed straight toward their car." In what Ian had considered the cruelest twist of fate, the drunken heir to a shipping fortune had escaped without so much as a scratch to either his Alfa Romeo or his body.

"If they hadn't been on that road, the accident wouldn't have happened. The girl had a good home growing up. After she took up with your vagabond father, she lived in hotel rooms."

"A home is more than rocks and mortar. She may not have lived in a manor house, but she never failed to make any place a home, whether a rural country inn or a five-star Paris hotel."

"She was nae reared for that sort of life. How

do you think I felt, knowing that my only daughter was living like an itinerant Irish traveler when she could have been a lady?"

Rage was no longer a white-hot flame; instead a sheet of ice flowed over Ian's aching heart. "You rotten son of a bitch," he said through clenched teeth. "If you had even half a brain or heart, you'd know that Mary MacKenzie was a lady to her fingertips."

He gestured toward the crowd of people who'd stopped on the road lined with limousines and taxis, and were watching them with undisguised interest. Obviously Nora hadn't wasted any time spreading the news of his grandfather's arrival.

"And she had more friends and people who loved her than you could ever imagine."

Though he'd always suspected all those friends hadn't quite filled the hole in her heart caused by her estrangement from her father. And he'd throw himself off the nearby cliff before admitting that the last thing she'd said to him, while lying in that hospital bed, was that she prayed her death might finally bring her father and son together.

Ian had never denied his mother anything, and he'd never wanted to disappoint her. So he was extremely grateful he didn't believe in an afterlife, because he hated the idea of his mother watching down from some heavenly cloud, saddened by how this meeting was doomed to failure.

"How many people do you think will show up to see you laid in the ground?" Ian asked. Since it was a rhetorical question, he didn't wait for an answer. "I'm Ian MacKenzie." He jutted out his chin. "And as far as I'm concerned, any remote connection I might have with the MacDougalls died with my mother on Seriphos."

He turned on a booted heel and stalked away. He did not look back.

The hell with it, Ian now thought, sixteen years later. He flipped closed the phone and began to strip off his rain-sodden clothes. Let the bastard sweat for a few hours.

6

Lily was propped up in a tester bed with her aunt's latest book. Usually the stories of the robust, time-traveling, murder-solving Scots Highlander swept her away, but tonight her mind kept wandering to Ian MacKenzie.

She was surprised and unnerved by her reaction to the man. After all, she'd certainly had her share of boyfriends growing up. And in Italy, she'd been flattered by all the attention from the swaggering men with flashing dark eyes, suggestive smiles, and chauvinistic attitudes. Granted, by her second week there, after her bottom became black-and-blue from pinching fingers, she'd come to the conclusion that hitting on anything female was built into the Italian male DNA.

But then she'd made a classic mistake: she'd fallen for a man who introduced her to a jet-setting lifestyle of yachts and parties and fancy hotels she'd only seen in movies before. And after Dante had died in a tragic accident, she'd discovered that she'd been not his true love, as he'd so often told her, but the clichéd "other woman."

She'd grown up a lot during her Italian odyssey. It had made her more worldly, and much more accustomed to dealing with men with sex on their minds. Not that there was anything wrong with sex, so long as you didn't confuse it with love — which she'd been on the brink of doing with Dante.

So she should certainly be able to handle one surly Scots filmmaker. But there'd been that strange moment, when their hands had first touched, that she'd wondered how his hand would feel on her body.

Deciding to put the problem of Ian MacKenzie aside for now, she'd just returned to the book when there was a knock on her door.

"Lily?" her father's voice boomed. "Are you awake?"

"Yes."

He didn't wait for an invitation, just strode through the doorway. When he threw his huge body onto a brocade chair, Lily held her breath hoping that it would hold. "I need your help."

Now there was a surprise, Lily thought dryly; she was always the one her father turned to when he got himself into one of his jams. Why couldn't Laurel, the firstborn, have his problems dumped on her once in a while? Or Lark?

Because her sisters had cleverly escaped Highland Falls, while Lily had returned like a homing pigeon after Dante's horrific death and her father's skiing accident. In the beginning, she'd planned only to stay long enough to make sure her father was back on his feet. But that had been three years ago, and she was still here.

"What's up?" she asked, returning her wandering attention to her father.

"I'm in desperate straits."

So what else was new? Most mountain men were fairly low maintenance; John Angus Stewart was not. Every event was high drama. A cold was never common, but the worst in the history of medicine, verging on life-threatening pneumonia at the very least.

A single word of praise from a critic was a five-star rave review that should be etched into stone for prosperity, the slightest criticism, a dagger directly to the heart that could send him into a funk for weeks. It never rained on her father's life; it poured.

"Let me guess." She reached into the drawer of the bedside table and took out a package of M&M's from her stash of emergency chocolate. "Your new painting is too big to get out of your studio." Last year he'd created a triptych that had required tearing out the western wall of his studio in order to send it to the New York SoHo gallery that had first claim to his works.

"It's worse. And it's not about me."

Well, that was certainly a first. She popped a red M&M into her mouth. "It's not?"

"Well, not entirely."

"I see." That was more like it. Like so many artistic people she'd met over the years, her father could be horrendously egocentric. At an early age, she'd come to accept this behavior as creative temperament.

"It's about Jenny."

"You've broken up?" Not surprising — though his romance with the young dollmaker had lasted longer than any of the others. Her father was not an easy man. She chose a yellow, then a blue.

"Of course we haven't. Didn't she tell you? We're in love."

"She mentioned it the other day, when she brought in some new dolls to sell on consignment, but I thought perhaps . . ." That the idea had been a product of Jenny's wishful thinking. Lily drew her knees to her chest and wrapped her arms around them. "Your track record isn't exactly stellar in the romance department, Daddy." That was certainly an understatement.

"This is the real thing, Lily." His voice was unusually muted. "I haven't felt this way about a woman since your mother."

Lily told herself she should be glad her father was happy. It wasn't that he'd ever lacked female companionship. He was a very virile, larger-than-life man imbued with a bold, artistic personality, and since he always stayed at the gallery owner's apartment while in New York, she'd suspected that there was more than just the art business going on.

But in the twenty-nine years he'd been a widower, she'd never — not once — gotten a hint that any dalliance might be the least bit serious.

"That's really lovely," she said, meaning it. If nothing else, he'd have someone else to cater to his whims. "So, what's the problem?"

"Jenny wants to celebrate my ancestry by getting married in the chapel during the Highland Games."

"That certainly sounds like a grand affair," she allowed, picturing several hundred Scots-American clansmen in tartans crowded into the castle's small chapel.

"It should be a humdinger," he agreed.

"It's also very soon."

"There's no point in wasting time. I'm not getting any younger."

He was also thirty years older than the prospective bride, which made the couple about the same emotional age. "I don't understand the problem."

"The girl isn't Scots, and she's never been to the Highland Games."

"Then this should be a terrific first-in-a-lifetime experience."

"She's afraid she'll screw things up."

Lily did her best to duck the ploy she saw coming at her like a hammer throw. "Well then, you'll just have to show her the ropes, won't you?"

"Now, you know I'd love to do that, darling. But I have a showing in two months, and if I don't get some paint thrown onto the canvases that are piled against the studio wall, I won't make my deadline."

"You're not the only person with deadlines."

People came to the games prepared to spend money, and it was imperative that the displays in her gallery encouraged participants and spectators to take memories of Highland Falls back home with them. Along with Christmas, which had gotten a huge boost when she'd put her inventory on the Internet last season, the games could determine whether she ended the year with a profit, or drowning in red ink.

"Lily," he pressed on as if he hadn't heard her, "if I don't get those paintings to New York, I won't get paid and we'll all be out on the street."

While her father's paintings brought in a great deal of money, he hadn't inherited the Scots gene of thriftiness. Then there was the unpalatable discovery that the accountant who'd been doing his taxes for nearly a decade had been secretly depositing her father's quarterly tax payments in an offshore bank in the Caribbean. He'd disappeared last year with his secretary and was now undoubtedly lying on some tropical beach and sipping mai tais, while his clients scrambled to pay not only their tax obligations, but the punitive interest, as well. And she didn't even want to think about this year's property tax bill, which she doubted Andrew Stewart had considered when he'd built this sprawling American castle.

"I've got the IRS on my back, and developers are breathing down my neck," he said. "Land values are going up, which makes property taxes go right up with them. And do you have any idea what it costs to keep this place going?"

"I know all too well."

It had been her idea, after the tax debacle, to turn Stewart's Folly into an inn to try to stop the monthly budget from bleeding red ink. Thanks to being the main sponsor of the town's Highland Games, they were actually beginning to turn things around, but building a reputation as a resort took time. Which was why her father and Zelda were counting on Ian MacKenzie's film to show them in a flattering light.

"Surely you don't want me to be the Stewart who loses the family home?"

"Would that be so bad?" Lily asked. "That recreational properties company representative who was here a few months ago promised that if they took over the hotel part of the castle, the Tennessee wing would stay a family residence."

"I'd rather burn the place down than have our home taken over by some money-grasping, soulless financial corporation." He was pacing now, long strides that ate up the polished wooden floor.

"Here's the thing, Lily love. I hate to admit it, but my work was getting stale. It had lost its vitality, its power. Then I fell in love with Jenny, and everything turned around. I feel thirty years old again. I'm doing the best work of my life, and it's because of her. I owe the girl — which is why I'm willing to give her anything she wants to stay in Highland Falls."

"And she wants marriage?" Lily asked dubiously.

"She does indeed. As do I. Which brings us back to my dilemma. She needs help with the wedding arrangements."

"There must be wedding planners down in Asheville or the Tri-Cities." The east Tennessee mountains were dotted with picturesque wedding chapels, including the Highland Honeymoon Hotel and Chapel right here in town. "I wouldn't begin to know how to plan a wedding."

"Don't be difficult. You know very well that you had your own wedding all worked out when you were seven years old. Your dress, the music, even down to what the bridesmaids would be wearing."

Lily was surprised; she hadn't thought he'd been listening. "That was just a schoolgirl's romantic fantasy."

He nodded his leonine head. "That's precisely what Jenny wants. A fantasy."

Then let the damn dollmaker create her own, Lily thought with an uncharacteristic flare of irritation.

Jennifer Logan had arrived months ago to sell her dolls at one of the South Appalachian craft fairs, and seemingly had been convinced by both the spectacular scenery and John Angus Stewart to stay. Lily hadn't paid much attention to her father's flirtation with the woman young enough to be his daughter, even when they'd set tongues wagging by getting engaged. Engagements were one thing; marriage, on the other hand, was a huge responsibility requiring consideration, tolerance, monogamy, and the ability for long-term commitment. All qualities that John Angus Stewart was not known for.

"Your grandmother obviously can't be expected to do it." He pressed his case with the persistence of an aluminum-siding salesman. "Zelda would turn it into a carnival, with bodybuilders in kilts driving the bride to the chapel in a chariot, and your aunt Melanie is probably going to be unhappy enough to hear I'm remarrying — not that I'd want the Southern *Gone With the Wind* extravaganza she'd undoubtedly insist upon. Which leaves you the only person I can trust."

"I'll see what I can do," Lily said with a rippling sigh.

"You'll be terrific." He framed her face between his bearlike hands and kissed her cheek, the beard he grew every year for the games scratching her skin. "I told her you'd get together to discuss ideas over lunch tomorrow."

"I've got a lot to do tomorrow."

"You've been working too hard lately. It'll be good for you to take a break." He skimmed a paternal hand over her hair. "All work and no play makes Lily a dull girl."

That matter settled to his satisfaction, he left the room with a remarkably sprightly step, leaving Lily to wonder, as she'd been doing a great deal lately, if she had indeed become dull.

Not dull, she decided as she dug into the bag of M&M's again. Just predictable.

But now Ian MacKenzie had stormed into her life, she was responsible for coordinating the games, and she'd been roped into pulling off a wedding in two weeks' time. On top of running the gallery.

At least the next fourteen days weren't going to be boring.

7

Ian woke to the sound of cows lowing in the distance. He pushed himself out of bed, opened the heavy draperies, and gazed out over the breathtaking scene of the valley below and the seemingly unending hills, veiled in the soft blue haze that gave the Great Smoky Mountains their name.

He opened the window and drew in a fresh breath that cleared his mind even as it soothed his senses. Birdsong threaded its way through a forest of spring-green trees and, beyond what appeared to be a croquet lawn, a silver creek rambled across the castle property, tumbling over mossy rocks.

If he'd come here for R and R, he'd be sorely tempted to stay. Unfortunately, his unwilling quest had nothing to do with either rest or relaxation.

Reluctantly, he picked up his cell phone and dialed the number he'd refused to call for years.

"It's about time," a deep Scots burr growled. "When ye didn't call last night, I began to worry you'd backed out."

"A MacKenzie never welshes on a deal."

There hadn't been any contact between Ian and his grandfather for a decade after the funeral. But obviously the old man had kept track of him, because five years ago, when he'd landed in prison during a coup on a small, remote Caribbean Island, the old skinflint had actually opened the MacDougall coffers and tried to grease the political wheels to get Ian out. When that hadn't worked, he'd hired mercenaries to fly a helicopter in for a daring midnight rescue.

The rescue team — made up of former American and British commandos — broke him out of prison in a hail of gunfire and took him to Scotland, where doctors were waiting to reset the bones broken during the new regime's attempt to force Ian to admit he was not really a filmmaker, but an MI6 agent on an assassination mission.

Since it was difficult to stalk away while in traction, he'd ended up spending three months at the MacDougall manor house, recovering from his wounds and near starvation.

Realizing that his grandfather had probably saved his life, Ian had managed to somewhat overcome his resentment, especially since it was blatantly obvious that although Duncan claimed he'd only been ensuring that the MacDougall name lived on, the old man was actually attempting, in his own gruff way, to atone for past sins. While they'd never be close, some fences had been mended.

"It wasn't easy getting here. A mountain storm was dumping rain like piss from a wellie."

"What kind of Scotsman gets put off by a little rain?"

"That's funny. Stewart said much the same thing when I finally arrived last night. Did the two of you get together and practice your lines?"

"I've not spoken to any thieving bastard Stewart for nigh onto six decades."

"And people accuse the Scots of holding grudges."

"It's nae a grudge. 'Tis the way of things. So, did ye get a chance to look around?"

"The place was pretty much shut down when I got here last night. And it's still early. I'll start checking things out after breakfast." Though he could undoubtedly search the Stewart castle for a lifetime and still not find all the hidden nooks and crannies.

"Did ye meet the girlie?"

"Yes. And I think you might have gotten your story wrong. She doesn't seem like a thief."

"Women never show their true faces to a man. Mata Hari didn't look like a spy, either. Is she bonny?"

"I suppose some might say so."

When Ian had first taken her hand, he'd been struck by a sudden, wicked urge to touch her all over. With his hands and his mouth. His sleep last night had been filled with hot dreams that, even recalling them now, had an immediate effect on his body. This hard-on had been plaguing him ever since he'd imagined rolling around with Lily Stewart in the meadow outside the tower window.

"She also doesn't seem that eager to have me here."

"Of course she's no' eager. Wasn't she canny and brash enough to somehow get the Mac-Dougall brooch out of the country, even with the additional security at airports these days? No doubt she's expecting us to try to steal it back again."

"There's no way she could connect me with the MacDougalls."

"Aye. That's true enough," the old man said matter-of-factly, giving no hint as to his feelings. Duncan MacDougall held his cards close to his chest. Another thing he and his grandfather had in common.

"You're a fair handsome lad, what with your mother's knife-edged cheekbones and your father's mouth." It was the closest thing to a compliment his grandfather had ever given his father, which suggested the lengths the old man would go to win Ian's cooperation. "Bed the lass, Ian. Get her to tell you what she's done with the brooch, and get it back."

"You've been watching too many James Bond movies. What makes you think I can seduce her into showing me the brooch?"

"If you can't, you're no true MacDougall. We've always had a way with the ladies."

If Duncan MacDougall had had better luck with one particular lady, Ian wouldn't be here.

"There's another problem. She was also quick to point out what I already told you: that I don't cover soft subjects."

"There's nae a soft MacDougall in the clan. You have to do it." Duncan pressed his case on what suspiciously sounded like a wheeze. "If not for your clan, in memory of your dear mother."

"If I were you, I wouldn't be bringing my mother into this conversation."

"She was a MacDougall before she was a MacKenzie."

The old man's mind was still sharp as a tack, and he was as sly as a fox.

"Dammit, Duncan." Ian raked a hand over his hair. He'd thought it was a cockamamie idea to begin with; now that he was actually here, it was looking impossible. Which, since he was not accustomed to failure, was really pissing him off.

"That brooch is ours, Ian. It's been ours since it was taken from The Bruce himself as he fled from defeat at the battle of Dalrigh."

It had been in 1306 when the MacDougalls had attacked Robert the Bruce in revenge for the king's murder of his rival for the throne, John Comyn, a nephew of the MacDougall clan chief — but the old man still talked about that day as if it were yesterday. Having spent too many years filming what too-long memories and centuries-old feuds cost the world, Ian refused to be impressed by that argument.

"I'm not sure I even believe that story," he said. "But if it was taken from him, the brooch belonged to The Bruce. When he failed to have a male heir, his daughter married into the Stewarts. So technically it's Stewart property." Though the old man already knew this, Ian wanted to press his case one last time before throwing in the towel.

" 'Tis the spoils of war," Duncan insisted stubbornly. "Nae different from all those treasures the Vatican keeps in its vaults from the Crusades."

"The Stewarts and the MacDougalls have been stealing the damn thing back and forth from each other for nearly seven hundred years. Why don't we be the ones who decide to let the matter stay in the past, where it belongs?" Ian suggested.

"Having made all those films about war crimes, ye, of all people, should know that those who forget the past are doomed to repeat it. The brooch belongs to the clan. And since I'm not as spry as I used to be, it's up to ye to be reclaiming it."

"Why do I get the feeling this latest theft has become personal?"

"Theft is always personal."

"Granted. But the brooch isn't the only thing James Stewart absconded with."

"I don't know what ye'd be talking about," Duncan snapped, signaling he knew exactly what Ian was talking about.

"I'm referring to your fiancée — who ended up a Stewart bride."

"That was sixty bluidy years ago," Duncan growled. "What would be making ye think I even remember her name?"

"Seems it'd be a bit difficult to forget the name of a woman who left you standing at the altar in front of the entire village."

"Her elopement with the Stewart was nothing to me." Duncan's tone was unconvincing. "I was only doing me father's bidding when I proposed to the lass. He wanted to join her land with ours."

"Which you managed to do anyway, after her old man died without any heirs who wanted to farm rocks, allowing you to pick it up for a song. As for the lass, if you didn't want to marry her, you should be grateful to Stewart for taking Annie MacFie off your hands."

What must it feel like, to have both your fiancée and your daughter run away from you? Of course, Duncan had driven his daughter away. Ian suspected much the same thing had happened with the woman who'd ended up being Lily Stewart's grandmother — a woman who was still living somewhere in this sprawling Stewart's Folly.

Frustrated, he crossed a forbidden conversational line. "Some men might not have found it a hardship to be married to Isabel MacGuire," he said, feeling oddly protective of the grandmother he'd never met. Duncan had married the widowed storekeeper ten years after having been jilted. "She was a beautiful woman." The photograph his mother had taken with her from Scotland had shown a lovely woman with a widow's peak, lively dark eyes, and a warm, engaging smile.

Ian was surprised when he heard a deep sigh on the other end of the line.

"Your grandmother was a bonny lass," Duncan allowed. "And loyal and faithful as the day is long, unlike that other, who had the sticking power of a butterfly, flitting from flower to flower. Which I suppose I should have expected, her bein' an artsy-fartsy type and all. 'Twas just as well things worked out the way they did. What in the bluidy hell would I want with the kind of female who could be lured away by a man just because he happened to own a damn castle?" he demanded, suggesting he still hadn't put the event behind him. "And not even a real one."

"It may not go back to ancient times, but the stones it's built from are real enough. And it's certainly decked out better than most restored ones I've seen."

"Rub it in, why don't ye," the old man muttered. "So when do you think ye'll find it?" Duncan asked, bringing their conversation back to its original track.

"I've no idea. This is a huge place and I wouldn't begin to know where to look for it. Since, unlike so many of my MacDougall ancestors, I'm no thief."

The critics occasionally accused him of too *much* honesty, which Ian had always considered an oxymoron. Like too much sex.

"Get the lass to show it to ye," Duncan repeated. "And it's not thievery to be reclaiming stolen property. Raiding is a fine old Scots tradition; one that's unfortunately fallen into disfavor over the years."

"Over the centuries, you mean."

"Don't be such a stickler for details. It'll make a fine story. May even win you another of those fancy gold statues to put on your mantel."

"I don't have a mantel." Like his parents, he preferred hotel rooms. They were more convenient and required no commitment. "If I do decide to go along with this plan, there's no way I'd include the theft in any film. I also don't think anyone's going to believe that I'm actually here to make some feel-good documentary about a bunch of Americans dressing up in kilts and throwing telephone poles, pretending to be Scots."

"They're cabers, as ye should well know. And would ye be forgetting that ye started out with soft issues?" the old man reminded him. His first documentary had garnered attention at the prestigious Cannes and Sundance film festivals.

"Those were home movies. I never intended them to be turned into a film, until that producer showed up and wanted them for *his* documentary. I figured if the MacKenzie family laundry was going to be aired in public, the least I could do was try to control what people saw."

He'd turned the Hollywood guy down and bank-rolled the project on a shoestring himself, personally choosing every frame, including those that revealed his parents' flaws. Even at twenty, he'd been a stickler for the truth.

"They'll believe you because every last one of the Stewarts have always believed that every bit of dirt on earth was put there for them, and they'll jump at the chance to be in the spotlight and show off the brooch."

"The daughter doesn't seem that enthusiastic. If she can sway the others' opinions over to her side —"

"Pah. If they weren't all puffed up with pride, why would they have built that bluidy castle in the American mountains?"

Ian couldn't argue with that reasoning. This castle, as magnificent as it admittedly was, was also as ridiculous an idea as the feud.

"I'm an old man, Ian," Duncan said, on a suspiciously phony wheeze. He'd looked the picture of health just five days ago. His eyes had been a clear and purposeful gray, and while he might have lost a few inches of height over the years, he seemed as spry as ever. As they'd trekked across the rolling fields dotted with white and black sheep, his gait had been as long and as determined as when he'd crossed the cemetery fifteen years earlier. "An old man who doesn't want to die knowing that I was the one who cost the MacDougalls our brooch."

"You're shameless."

"Then ye'll go through with it?"

Ian cursed. "I'll try. But I'm not promising anything."

"You'll succeed." The satisfied tone suggested Duncan had not expected any other outcome. "You're a MacDougall, after all."

"A MacKenzie," Ian murmured to dead air. Having won the little battle of wills, Duncan had immediately hung up.

Ian decided to take a shower and get some breakfast, then he'd decide what the hell he was going to do about the fact that he, a man who'd gone to prison rather than reveal his sources, was being quite effectively emotionally black-mailed.

8

Jennifer Logan didn't look like anyone's idea of an older man's "trophy wife." Her wispy, honey-blond hair was pulled back into a loose braid that fell halfway down her back, her T-shirt was over-sized, her jeans baggy. The only thing vaguely eye-catching about her were the fluorescent purple toenails revealed by her Birkenstocks.

"I really appreciate your having lunch with me, Lily," she said in a soft, almost breathy voice as the waiter filled tall glasses with iced tea. "Especially since I know how the idea of your father remarrying after all these years might be difficult for you."

"I'm happy that he's happy," Lily said truthfully as she dug around in her bag for the little sugar packets she'd brought along to the Happy Cow restaurant.

While she had nothing against the vegetarian restaurant that had been Jennifer's choice, she'd learned long ago to bring her own sweetener. The Happy Cow did not believe in processed foods of any kind.

"But I'll bet you'd rather he be happy with a woman his own age."

Lily stirred a spoonful of sparkling white granules into her tea. "To be perfectly honest, by the time I was six, I realized that none of the women my father brought home were exactly stepmother material. I also noticed they didn't last long." *Oops.* "Not that I'm predicting that for the two of you."

"Too bad you don't carry crystal balls in your gallery," Jennifer said with the sweet, open smile that Lily suspected had first attracted her father. It literally lit up her plain face, making her look as though someone had turned on a lightbulb inside her. Her eyes, as china blue as those of one of her handmade dolls, sparkled with a bit of wry humor. "You could predict our futures, like your aunt Zelda."

"Zelda doesn't exactly see the future all nicely laid out. From what I've gathered, it's more a signs-and-symbols sort of thing. But even if crystal balls were an exact science, I'd just as soon not use one myself."

Jennifer braced both elbows on the table, linked her fingers together, rested her small, pointed chin on them, and eyed Lily speculatively. "I wouldn't want to know what the future holds, either. It makes life more of an adventure."

Although she'd been selling this woman's dolls in her gallery for the past six months, Lily realized that she didn't know anything about her father's fiancée. Which was odd, in a way, since in a town as small as Highland Falls, everyone

85

minded everyone else's business. No one had private lives, since secrets were too good not to be shared. No one but Jennifer, who'd remained distant, working alone out in that mountain cabin on her dolls, which everyone agreed were wonderful examples of old-time Appalachian craft that you didn't see much of anymore.

Lily realized she didn't even know how Jennifer and her father had met. She also wondered what, if anything, her father knew about the woman he planned to marry.

"I know how it is, not to have a mother," Jenny offered, almost as if she'd read Lily's thoughts. "Mine ran off when I was still a baby."

"I'm sorry. So you grew up with your father?"

"No. He and my mother never married, but I always knew who he was. So after I graduated from high school, I took a bus from Eugene down to San Francisco to meet him. I figured, now that I was on my own, and didn't represent a possible financial burden, he might be interested in meeting me."

"What happened?" Lily loved stories; hearing them and telling them.

"He took me to a steak restaurant for dinner and told me, in a very nice way, that he had a family — a wife and three kids — and although I seemed like a nice girl, it'd just be too difficult to explain me to them."

"That must have been hard to hear." Her father had many faults, but Lily could not imagine him responding in such a cold, hurtful way.

Jenny shrugged her slender shoulders. "It wasn't the high point of my life. But it did make me realize how fortunate I'd been that my aunt and uncle had taken me in, after my mom left for L.A. They always treated me as if I were their own daughter. In fact, I hadn't even known they'd adopted me until they sat me down and told me when I was six."

She managed a slight smile. "I probably didn't appreciate them as much as I should have. When I was much younger I had fantasies of my mother coming back, and that she'd marry my father and they'd have lots of children and we'd all live happily ever after, in this sort of Partridge Family way. But without the singing."

"I had fantasies about my mother coming back, too." As outspoken as she tended to be, Lily was surprised to hear herself revealing such an intimate secret to someone she barely knew. "Which, of course, was impossible." Though she thought she felt her soothing presence at times: a soft feathering of air against her temple, a warm, encouraging voice in her mind she knew wasn't hers.

"But the heart wants what the heart wants," Jenny said.

"Yes."

The ponytailed waiter appeared at the table. Lily ordered the brown rice and avocado salad while Jenny opted for the whole wheat mushroom crepes.

"I know the odds are that I'll outlive John,"

Jenny said once their orders had been taken. "But I've been reading a lot about winter-spring romances. Charlie Chaplin was thirty-five years older than Oona O'Neill, who was only eighteen when they got married, and they had more than thirty years together until he died. If John and I can have even half that time together, I'll feel blessed." She took a sip of tea. "Your father is a very special man."

"Another thing we can agree on." Lily drew in a deep breath and asked the question that had crossed her mind when Jenny had divulged the story about her childhood. "Look, this isn't any of my business, so you don't have to answer, but after what you told me about your own father rejecting you —"

"I'm not looking for a surrogate to fill some huge emotional hole in my psyche." Jenny's smile was serene. "Nor am I after your father's money. While I'll probably never be as wealthy as he is, my needs are modest and I make enough to live comfortably. I've also offered to sign a prenuptial agreement. An offer he refused, by the way."

Lily wasn't particularly surprised. If her father had paid that much attention to money, Stewart's Folly might not be in as dire straits as it was.

"Well," she said, as their lunches arrived, "as I said, I'm just happy that he's happy."

"I really do appreciate your coming to my rescue." Jenny put her hand on Lily's. For a woman with a modest lifestyle, the flawless canary diamond taking up so much of her ring finger seemed a bit excessive. "I don't know anything about planning a wedding."

"That makes two of us, so I guess we'll just have to muddle through together. What did you have in mind?"

"Something medieval Scots to celebrate your father's roots," Jenny replied without hesitation. "A celebration that will be the highlight of the games, and something people will still be talking about years from now. Something fabulous. But intimate and personal at the same time."

Less than two weeks to perform a miracle. "You know," Lily ventured, "I was reading this travel magazine in the waiting room of the dentist's office, and there was an article showcasing the hotels in Las Vegas. It's amazing the way they create entire worlds, zapping people back to the days of Egypt, or to New York or Paris. There's even one that has a medieval theme, with jousting and banquets and a wedding chapel. Perhaps —"

"I'm not eloping on the most important day of my life." The sudden sharp lift of her chin revealed the dollmaker wasn't nearly as fragile as she looked. "It's important to both John and me that we're married at Stewart Castle, with all his friends present to share in the celebration."

"Well, that's definite enough." Lily stirred more sugar into her tea. "Fabulous," she murmured. "But intimate." And probably impossible. "In just two weeks?"

"No problem. I've brought you tons of research material." As Jennifer reached beneath the tablecloth and pulled out a huge canvas tote bag filled with books and magazines, Lily took a long drink of her sweetened tea and wished it was something stronger.

Firefly Falls Gallery, located on a narrow street lined with leafy trees, managed to be bright and airy while packed with merchandise, from the hand-pegged heart-of-pine floors to the soaring beamed ceilings. Unlike most art galleries Ian had visited, this one hadn't opted for stark white walls to showcase a few expensive works of art.

Scenic watercolors of misty mountains shared wall space with shelves that had been painted a deep brick red to better showcase handwoven Cherokee baskets and quilts. A display of glass vases and bowls in the front bay window refracted the afternoon sunlight, splintering it into rainbows that danced on the ceiling.

When the small bell tied to the door announced Ian's arrival, Lily glanced up from arranging carved wooden animals on a sturdy hand-hewn oak table.

"Hi. Are you finding your way around town all right?"

He'd managed to convince himself that he'd imagined the warmth of her smile. But as her lips curved, he knew he'd only been lying to himself, to keep from thinking of her as an appealing woman rather than a family duty to be gotten over with as quickly as possible.

She was wearing a snug top of some stretchy silk material with swirls of sherbet colors which clung enticingly to pert breasts, and a pair of pink jeans that dipped below her navel. Last night's perky wood nymph now looked like something delicious that should be scooped into a sugar cone.

Unreasonably tempted to taste, he ran a finger around the rim of a blown-glass bowl the color of a clear mountain lake. "So far I've managed not to get lost." His physical reaction to her was disturbing. He knew getting involved with her would be nothing but trouble, but his damn body kept refusing to get the message. "Is this a Falconer?"

"That's right. You've a very good eye."

"I attended a showing in France last year." He'd been between projects, and had left the gallery with a leggy lingerie designer. "The brochure said he was very selective about where his works are allowed to be sold."

"Which makes you wonder why he'd allow me to handle any of his pieces in my little back-of-beyond shop." Her tone was dry, but her eyes were filled with humor. Toward him?

Ian was unaccustomed to having anyone — particularly women — laugh at him. "That depends. Have you met him?"

"Actually, I have."

"Then I'm not at all surprised." It would be hard to deny this woman anything. He picked up a small bottle he recognized as the glass blower's personal take on 1930s Venetian glass. "My mother had a collection of Art Deco scent bottles," he surprised himself by revealing. "I suppose they were highly impractical since we traveled a lot, but they were gifts from my father, celebrating the special occasions of their lives, and I think she treasured them more because they were from him than for their intrinsic value."

"That's sweet. And so romantic."

"Why am I not surprised you're a romantic?"

"Card-carrying and proud of it. Let me guess — you're not."

"Romance is merely an illusion based on runaway emotions. People believe what they want to believe at the moment. Then when everything comes crashing down around them, they wonder why they didn't see it coming."

"It's possible to get blinded by the idea of romance," Lily allowed as she dipped into a crystal jar and took out a Scottish toffee. It had certainly happened to her in romantic Italy. She held the jar out to him; he declined with a shake of the head. "I've a terrible sweet tooth, which has helped send my dentist's three children to college." She sighed blissfully as she chewed the sweet. "But there are worse vices. I suppose you don't believe in love, either?"

"You suppose right."

"I suspect that's because you've never been."

"And you have?"

"No, but that doesn't keep me from believing in the concept. I've come close. During my time in Florence, I fell passionately in love with the city and almost in love with a dashing Italian."

The idea of this all-American girl-next-door in the throes of passion was definitely playing against type. It was more than a little intriguing.

"Then it ended badly," he guessed. "And you grew up."

"It ended badly," she agreed. "He was killed in a boating accident on Lake Como. His hydroplane blew up during a race. One minute he was there" — she snapped her fingers — "the next, he was gone. *Then* I grew up."

Damn. It was rare that Ian felt guilty about anything. Maybe for an encore he could find a puppy to kick. "I'm sorry."

"So was I. To make matters worse, he turned out to be married."

"You didn't know?"

"Of course not!" She was obviously offended by the implication she might have an affair with a married man. "And my grand European romance may have been based on a lie, but sometimes romance *is* real. It sounds as if your parents are the second case."

She had him there.

"I just happened to be watching *Biography* when they did that show on you," she said when he didn't respond.

"It was unauthorized. They didn't get any cooperation from me. And what wasn't an exaggeration was way off the mark."

Now that he knew Lily had watched the damn thing, he was even more grateful the producers hadn't managed to find out about Duncan.

"Was the part about your parents' death true?"

"Yes."

"That must have been a terrible time for you."

Ian shrugged. "The accident was a long time ago."

"It still must be difficult. I never knew my mother — she died shortly after giving birth to me." She told him what he already knew. "But I still miss her. I imagine all children feel a huge hole in their hearts and their lives when they lose a parent. No matter how old they are at the time."

He wasn't about to admit how close she'd hit to the bull's-eye.

"Do you have family, at least?"

"No," he lied.

"That's so sad."

She touched his arm and those remarkably expressive eyes turned misty. Ian had always ruthlessly ruled his emotions; Lily Stewart seemed to be ruled by hers.

"Sometimes my family drives me crazy, but I can't imagine a world without them in it. Especially my grandmother, and Zelda, and my sisters." Her warm smile created a low, nagging ache of need.

Putting a bit of distance between them, Ian picked up a sunset-hued vase. "This is spectacular."

"Isn't it? I was thrilled when Saxon brought it to the shop last week."

"Saxon Falconer brought it here himself? Personally?" Apparently she'd not only met the reclusive glass blower, but they were close. How close? he wondered as something unrecognizable stirred inside him, curling around into a snakelike bundle of want and need.

"That's not so surprising, since he lives in these mountains," she said mildly. "He grew up here."

He knew his expression must have revealed his surprise when she laughed. "I told you we have a lot of talent here."

"It appears so. Is all your stock from local artisans?"

"Usually, but I always make sure I have a lot of Scots items on hand for the Highland Games." Cheerleader dimples flashed again. "Which gives me an excuse to go to Scotland once a year."

It was the first thing she'd said that dovetailed with what Duncan had been claiming. Ian picked up a small enamel box with a scene of

Stirling Castle painted on the lid. "So you've been there recently?"

"Three months ago. I spent ten glorious days touring the Highlands, visiting local artisans and museums and historical sites."

"You're a history buff?" He moved on to a display of pins and earrings shaped like the Scottish thistle.

"Not really, but there's so much history everywhere you go in Scotland, it's impossible not to get drawn into the old stories of wars and feuds. The tales read like fiction or a great play. I suppose that's why they've remained popular for so many centuries."

"That, and the fact that Scots tend to enjoy their feuds."

Her rich laughter rippled beneath his skin. Ian's flash of irritation at the idea that such a simple, ordinary thing as a laugh could affect him so easily evaporated as he spotted an ornate pin.

"That's a copy of a brooch that once belonged to Robert the Bruce," Lily said as he picked it up and studied it more closely.

It was identical to the one in the photograph Duncan had given him. The one he'd come here to find.

"Have you ever seen the original?" he asked casually.

"No, but I'd dearly love to." She skimmed a finger over the faux pearls surrounding the oval-shaped crystal set in silver. "According to

96

legend, a MacDougall tore it from The Bruce's cloak as he fled in defeat from a battle in the fourteenth century."

"The Brooch of Lorn," he murmured. "Wasn't it, in turn, stolen from the MacDougalls?"

"During the religious wars of the 1640s. There are rumors of it changing hands several times, but when I was visiting the MacDougall manor, I was told it was kept in a vault that only the clan chief is permitted to open."

She was either the most brazen liar he'd ever met, or she was innocent. He leaned closer.

"If it's kept under lock and key, how did this jewelrymaker know what it looked like?"

"There's a photograph of a former Mac-Dougall laird wearing it when he was visited by the queen of England, back in the fifties. The 1950s," she clarified. "The artist also worked from old sketches and descriptions of the battle in which it was supposedly taken."

She was no longer looking at the brooch, but up at him. Lord, she smelled fantastic. Like fresh air and sunshine. And temptation, dammit. A temptation he was determined to resist.

He was returning the pin to its velvet-lined, midnight-blue suede box when the bell on the door jangled violently, and a woman some-where between forty-five and sixty swept into the gallery. She was wearing a beautifully cut cream jacket and trousers, a silk blouse, and very good pearls. Her makeup had been ap-plied with a clever touch to soften the lines at the corners of her eyes, her hair had been expertly streaked, and her lips, tinted raspberry red to match her blouse, were pursed in a furious frown.

"Lily," she said, not seeming to notice the pheromones bouncing against all four walls like pinballs. "I've been looking all over creation for you."

"I've been right here," Lily said as she pulled herself out of her trance. Good heavens, she'd been right about Ian MacKenzie being dangerous. Just the way he'd been looking at her had made her tingle in places she hadn't even known she could tingle. "Trying to arrange all the new stock that just arrived from Scotland."

"This is far more important than any stupid Scots souvenirs."

If Lily was offended by either the snappish tone or the words, her noncommittal "Mmm" didn't reveal it. "Aunt Melanie, this is Mr. MacKenzie from Scotland, the man who may be filming our Highland Games."

"Well, I know that." The glance she swept over him was designed to make him feel like a peasant in the presence of the queen. "You, Mr. MacKenzie, just happen to be a very strong part of my problem."

"Aunt Melanie." Lily murmured a faint warning.

The older woman tossed her honey-blond head. "It's true. I've been having enough problems with Missy as it is. Ever since she caught wind of this documentary, she's been giving me nothing but trouble."

"Missy's always been such an agreeable girl." Too agreeable at times, Lily had often thought, though it would be hard to be anything less than acquiescent when you had the indomitable Melanie Lancaster for a mother.

"She *was* an agreeable girl until she got this ridiculous Scottish-heritage notion into her head. We're not even Scots, for heaven's sake. She comes from French and English royalty. You'll never guess what she told me this morning." Without giving Lily a chance to respond, she went on. "She's refusing to go back to Charlotte for the debutante ball."

"Horrors," Ian murmured beneath his breath.

Lily had to fight a smile from quirking at the corner of her lips. "I can see where you'd be upset."

"Upset?" Her aunt's voice had Lily worrying about her lovely display of Edinburgh crystal shattering. "Upset doesn't *begin* to cover what I'm feeling. It's bad enough your father is marrying a girl young enough to be his daughter. I can't imagine what this would be doing to my sister if she were alive."

"If my mother were alive, it'd be a moot point. Since they'd still be married."

"Hmmph. That's what you think."

Lily tossed up her chin. "That's what I know." She loved her aunt and would always be grateful that she'd come to Stewart's Folly to help raise

John Angus Stewart's three daughters, but there were times when she could be more than a little tedious.

"Well, that has nothing to do with my problem and we'll never be sure, will we? Do you have any idea how much her ball gown cost?"

"Missy's?"

"Of course Missy's."

"No." But she'd bet the gallery her aunt was about to tell her.

"A fortune. We bought it at Neiman Marcus in Atlanta. It's fit for a fairy-tale princess. The bodice is white satin covered with seed pearls, and the hoop skirt is white tulle."

"It sounds lovely."

"It's more than lovely; it's exquisite. I would have done murder for a dress like that when I was Missy's age."

Lily wasn't entirely sure her aunt was kidding. "People's tastes differ."

"But the dress is only one of my problems. She's refusing to make her debut because you've scheduled the junior level piper competition for the same day as the ball. There's no way Missy can compete, then make it down to Charlotte for the ball.

"The Lancasters have been coming out since the eighteenth century. They've been coming out in Charlotte for the past one hundred years. There's no way my daughter is going to be the one to break the tradition."

"She's been practicing the bagpipe very

hard." Even as thick as the walls of Stewart's Folly were, Lily had been able to hear the off-key droning of "The Scottish Soldier" reverberating from the North Carolina side of the castle for months.

"It's bad enough her father gave her those damn bagpipes in the first place!" It was close to a wail and once again caused Lily to worry about her crystal. "Sending her to that two-week school for her birthday last year put the icing on the cake. I know he did it just to spite me."

"I doubt that was the case."

Three years ago, Melanie's husband, declaring that he wasn't cut out for small-town life, had taken off with Bonnie Brewster, proprietor of Bonnie's Bonny Bonbons. Apparently free truffles weren't the only samples Bonnie had been handing out. They were currently living in Knoxville, and from what Lily had heard via the grapevine, he was too happy with his wife and newborn twins to want to spite anyone.

"I also suspect he did it because he's feeling guilty for not being more involved in his daughter's life."

"I suppose that's a possibility," Lily allowed.

"Of course it is. Well, if he'd wanted to be more involved, he shouldn't have run off with that candy-making slut." Melanie's eyes were blue fire. "Leave it to Charles to atone for his sins with a ridiculously expensive set of bagpipes. How on earth do I explain to her great-grandmother that my daughter would rather sound like a dying elephant than learn how to dip a proper curtsy?"

"I don't know." Lily was so in over her head.

"The answer is, I can't. And I won't. Because Missy is going to make her debut, even if you have to rearrange the schedule."

"I'm sorry, Aunt Melanie, but I can't do that."

"You'll have to. Because if my daughter doesn't make a proper debut, it'll be on your head, Lily Stewart."

She turned on a high heel and stalked out of the gallery.

9

"She seemed to take all that fairly seriously," Ian said.

"Too seriously." Lily sighed. "She's really not as shallow as she sounded."

"She's the aunt who lives on the North Carolina side," he guessed.

"Yes. We have this expression in the American South about steel magnolias —"

"I've heard it."

"Well, beneath that blond-belle exterior, there beats the heart of a true steel magnolia." With an unfortunate tendency to be tedious.

Ian was considering that if he did the film, the debut-versus-piping controversy could prove a nice touch, when the door jingled open again and a teenaged girl rushed in. Her cheeks were flushed and her eyes, behind her granny glasses, were red-rimmed, evidence that she'd been crying.

"Lily, you have to do something," she wailed. "Mother's being impossibly unreasonable."

"She told me about the debut," Lily said. "The gown sounds lovely."

"Who cares about a stupid ball gown?"

Missy's voice climbed even higher than her mother's had, and Lily wished she'd opted for more of that thick earthenware pottery rather than the crystal. "I never asked an entire village in India to go blind sewing on those stupid seed pearls. I don't even *like* seed pearls. I'm *not* coming out."

Missy fisted her hands on jeans-clad hips. "I hate the idea of being a stupid debutante! It's nothing more than a meat market, parading females in front of males to marry them off." She stamped her foot. "I'm never going to get married."

"You may change your mind about that."

"No. Every single one of my friends' parents is divorced. I'd rather become a lesbian than be cheated on by some man I made the mistake of giving my heart to."

Lily suspected the piping competition versus debut wasn't the only thing going on here. It couldn't be easy suddenly having two newborn half brothers you'd never met who got to live with your father full time, not just two weeks every summer and alternating Christmases.

"I think that might be a bit extreme."

"You don't understand, Lily." She pressed her folded hands against the front of a T-shirt that pronounced SAXOPHONES ARE FOR PEOPLE WHO CAN'T PIPE. "I was *born* to be a piper. It's not that I chose it. It chose me. When I discovered the competition was at the same time as that stupid ball I didn't want to go to in the first place, there was absolutely no choice. This is a new world, and piping isn't just for men anymore. Mother will just have to accept that the Lancaster women have a new tradition."

Demonstrating the same flair for dramatics as her mother, she flounced from the gallery, slamming the door behind her. The bell jingled a not-so-merry farewell; a framed black-and-white photograph of Loch Ness hanging on the wall slanted.

"Well, I've always said that conflict makes for good drama," Ian murmured.

With a laugh, Lily straightened the photograph. "And they say small towns are boring."

"Why did they come to you with their domestic spat?"

"They expect me to make it right, of course."

"Why?"

"Why, what?"

"Why you?"

Lily folded her arms. "Do you know, I've been asking myself that a great deal lately."

"Come up with any answers?"

"Not a one. But when I do, I'll be sure to let you know."

"I'll be waiting." He rocked back on his heels and rubbed the cleft in his chin. "I've made a decision about the film."

"Oh?" Her stomach tightened. Only twenty-four hours ago, she was hoping that Ian MacKenzie would decide the festival wasn't worth his time or his videotape. Now, despite the fact that he made her as edgy as a cat in a thunder-storm, Lily wasn't in any hurry for him to leave.

"I'm going to make it. Want to know why?"

"Because of its potential redeeming social value?"

"No."

"Because you can't wait to make fun of crazy Americans dressing up in kilts and attempting to get in touch with their roots by playing bag-pipes?"

"Not that, either." His usually flinty eyes had darkened in a way that reminded her a lot of those lustful Italians, and made her mouth go dry.

"You've gotten yourself caught up in Aunt Melanie and Missy's domestic drama, and can't leave without knowing which wins out — pipes or hoopskirts?"

"That conflict does have possibilities. But the reason I've decided to do it is because I've got to get your face on film."

Well. Lily let out a short, surprised breath. That was certainly not the answer she'd been expecting to hear. "Does that line work very often?"

"I have no idea, since it's not a line. Merely a fact."

Knowing she was playing with fire, Lily couldn't help asking with open disappointment, "Then you're not hitting on me?" It wasn't every day she put on makeup, and changed her clothes three times before finally opting for her tightest-fitting jeans, which weren't the most practical for shelving stock.

"Any woman who's spent more than a day in Italy should be able to recognize when a man's interested."

And he was. Lily could see the signs: the way his pupils flared as his eyes took a slow, leisurely tour of her that was more stimulating than the feel of some men's hands; the way his voice grew deep and rumbled like thunder over the blue-hazed mountains; the way his dark head had lowered until his full, sensuous mouth was a mere breath from hers.

Her curiosity had been killing her since the strange electrical charge that had shot between them last night when they'd shaken hands. Giving in to impulse, as she so often did, Lily lifted her arm around his neck. "Well, then, if you're going to be staying here for the next two weeks, we might as well get this over with."

She went up on her toes at the same time his head dipped.

Lily knew there was no way Ian MacKenzie's kiss could live up to the ones that had heated up her dreams last night until she'd awoken tangled in sheets she could have sworn carried his scent. After all, a kiss was just a kiss.

She was wrong.

Stunningly, mind-reelingly wrong.

Her brain was washed as clear as the Star of Edinburgh tumblers she'd dusted today; color as rich and dazzling as Saxon Falconer's blown glass flashed behind her closed lids.

She moaned, her hands fisting in the ebony silk of his hair, as he lifted her off the floor to deepen the kiss. Her breasts flattened against his chest, which was as rock hard as the mountains of his homeland, their bodies so close together she couldn't tell whether it was his heart pounding she felt, or her own.

His teeth nipped at her bottom lip, just hard enough to send desire surging through her like a bolt of lightning from a summer storm.

Someone trembled. Him? Or her? What did it matter, when she was so desperately hungry, and Ian so blatantly aroused? Knowing she'd had the same effect on him was an aphrodisiac in itself.

Was he actually turning her around and around? Or was that spinning, dizzying feeling just in her head? Lily heard a curse through the roaring in her ears, felt it against her ravaged lips.

Then she was somehow standing on her own two feet again, but since her legs felt as solid as water and the wooden floor seemed to have turned to sponge rubber, she wasn't ready to let go.

"I didn't know they had earthquakes in North Carolina." His voice was rough, his breathing ragged. He seemed as surprised as she was. His fingers were still pressing into the bare skin beneath her Lycra top.

"We're in Tennessee," she said breathlessly.

"Well, then, that explains it." His gaze was molten as it roamed over her mouth. "Are you always this impulsive?"

"About life," she said. "Not men. Especially men who make me nervous."

"And I make you nervous?"

"Absolutely."

"You *should* be nervous," he agreed. "In fact, you should probably run for the hills."

Lily suspected he was right. "Too late, since I'm already in the hills. And maybe you should, too."

His mouth quirked. "Maybe I should. But it damn well wouldn't stop me from wanting you."

Lily liked it that he was so truthful. She'd sworn, after Dante's widow had shown up at Lake Como, that honesty was going to be high on her priority list when choosing her next lover.

"I want you, too." There was no point in denying it, since that mind-stealing kiss had already given her away. "But it's too soon."

He surprised her by laughing at that; a rough laugh that sounded a bit rusty. His touch was strangely gentle as he ran a fingertip over lips still tingling from that dangerously explosive kiss she'd initiated.

"Too soon may have been if I'd taken you last night, when we were both tempted. But you will be in my bed, Lily Stewart. Sooner, rather than later."

The idea was all too appealing, but his male

arrogance was not. "Perhaps you're unfamiliar with American women, Mr. MacKenzie, but we tend to make up our own minds about whether we'll sleep with a man."

He flashed a grin as wicked as a devil's wink, as dangerous as a Highlander's blade. "I wasn't talking about sleeping. I was thinking more along the lines of making love to you."

"There's no need to use pretty euphemisms; you're talking about sex, not making love."

"You're as outspoken as you are impulsive."

She shrugged. "Would you prefer I lie and pretend I'm not attracted to you, so we can play games?"

"Games can have their appeal, with women who enjoy playing them. But I find your honesty rather charming. And no, that's not a line, and yes, I've had sex in mind since you lured me into that tiny little elevator with you."

"Next time you can walk up the stairs."

"Ravishing you on those back stairs has decided appeal. But I prefer the idea of taking you in that pretty little gilt cage, with your hands above your head, fingers gripping the bars, your legs tight around my hips."

The erotic picture flashed through her mind and flooded her already rattled senses.

Needing to occupy her hands to keep them from playing in the black silk of his hair, she picked up a glass witch's ball. "I may be impulsive, but I don't go to bed with men I don't know."

"Come to bed with me and we'll take care of that."

Her laugh exploded. "I was afraid you'd be a problem the minute you walked in the door."

"Believe me, darling, you weren't alone in that thinking. Because I knew you'd be trouble."

No one had ever referred to her that way, and Lily decided she rather liked it. It made her sound dangerous, like some film noir femme fatale. One of those women wearing a sexy, body-hugging dress, killer heels, and dark lipstick who'd sashay into some private detective's seedy office and get him mixed up in murder.

"This is where I remind myself that I've sworn off your type of man."

She'd dated more than a handful of bad boys when she'd been younger, realizing later that she'd naïvely believed she could change them. Since Dante she'd been more cautious, going out with a thirty-five-year-old CPA who'd done her taxes and seemed far more interested in her Schedule C than getting her into his bed, an engineer for TVA who was away most of the time inspecting dams, and most recently a banker immersed in genealogical research.

Sometimes she didn't know why she even bothered to date at all.

"You've *never* been my type," he said. "But that doesn't really seem to matter when it comes to rampaging hormones, does it?"

"No one can accuse you of not being brutally honest."

"It's simpler that way, between a man and a woman. And, as much as I want to explore the passion that is so obviously lurking beneath that American cheerleader exterior, what I originally meant is that I want you for my film. I want to put you at the center, have you introduce the various aspects of the games, explain their history, and tell a little bit about how Highland Falls and Stewart's Folly came to be."

"I'd think you'd want my father to act as narrator. He's far more passionate about the town, the games, and our home."

"That's precisely why I don't want him. Your father's too much of a presence, too larger than life. Even if he didn't come off as a caricature, no one in the audience would ever identify with him."

"But isn't that the point of a documentary? To introduce viewers to people and events they might not otherwise experience?"

"Of course. But they also need to be able to empathize. You're the quintessential girl-next-door; they'll feel comfortable with you."

"Comfortable." Although it wasn't in Lily's nature to pout, she did so now. "Like an old pair of slippers? Worn and boring?"

"Now who's being overly dramatic?" He looped his arms around her waist and drew her closer again, the gesture seeming natural. "After that kiss, you can't possibly believe I find you the faintest bit boring."

"No." The amazing thought that a man who

looked like Ian MacKenzie — a man who'd traveled the world, who was famous, and who, even without the sexuality that radiated from him like a summer sun, could probably have any woman he wanted — actually wanted *her,* warmed Lily from the inside out.

"Maybe you need a bit more convincing," he suggested.

"I don't think that's a good idea. This is, after all, a public shop."

"So hang up a Closed sign."

She was considering doing exactly that when the door swung open again with a jangle that was beginning to get on her nerves.

10

"I've been looking all over town for you, Lily," complained the man dressed in a city dark suit, white shirt starched as stiffly as his demeanor, and plaid bow tie.

"I've been right here," Lily said.

"I came by an hour ago and the door was locked."

"I was at the Happy Cow with Jenny. Actually, I was just thinking about you." While contemplating how boring her life — and the men in it — had become. "What did you need?"

"When I picked up my mail this morning, Doris Larson told me about your upcoming exhibition of pornographic photographs."

Lily had been expecting this. The sixty-year-old woman who ran the Highland Falls post office out of the back of the Tartan Market was the local town crier.

"They're not pornography, Donald, they're erotic photographs. And very well done. Caroline Campbell's going to be famous someday. I consider myself fortunate to be the first gallery to show her works to the public."

"The Highland Games are a family event. I

can't believe you're going to hang them for everyone to see."

"I do wish you'd give me some credit. I'm not planning to put them in the front window."

"I should hope not. I hear the models are naked."

"They're wearing tartans." Discreetly draped. Hers had certainly been. "Besides, even if they were stark naked, there's nothing dirty about a nude body."

"I'll second that," Ian agreed, thinking of one particular female body he intended to get nude as soon as possible.

The bow-tied, stiff-necked jerk spun his head toward Ian, acknowledging him for the first time. "I don't believe we've met."

"Donald, this is Ian MacKenzie," Lily said. "The filmmaker," she elaborated at his blank look.

He dismissed Ian's entire career with a wave of his manicured hand. "I don't watch a lot of movies. Any time away from the bank is spent working on my book."

"Ian, this is Donald Forbes, president of the Highland Falls Bank. He's writing a family history that goes all the way back to when Fergus of Forbes was made governor of Urquhart Castle in 1236."

"I've only worked my way back to when Alexander Forbes was killed fighting at King David's side in 1332. David, of course, was the son of

The Bruce. But I've every reason to believe there's a direct lineage to Fergus."

"Isn't that interesting?" Ian figured this guy with the pasty complexion and bow tie would get along great with Duncan. They could sit around wading through dusty old texts, reliving ancient battles while life passed them by.

They shook hands. Unsurprisingly, the guy's grip was as weak as his jaw.

"Ian's in town to make a documentary about our Highland Games," Lily said.

"Now that you mention it, I believe I heard something about that from Melanie. She's not happy about the scheduling of the piping competition."

"I know."

"I assured her you'd change it to avoid a conflict."

"Did you?" Her cool tone was a vivid contrast to the heat in her eyes. A heat that echoed the fires Ian had discovered burning inside her.

"Of course. She was very distraught. Someone needed to calm her down."

"My aunt isn't happy if she doesn't have something to be distraught about."

"Melanie Lancaster is an admirable woman, and one of the directors of the bank."

Which meant Forbes had to suck up to her, whether he liked it or not, Ian guessed.

"She's also going to have to live with disappointment, because it's too late to start juggling the schedule around now. It took months of committee meetings to fit everything in. As for the photographs, they're going to be exhibited at a private, invitation-only cocktail party before the ball. Ticket sales are all going to benefit local charities."

"Do these charities realize they're contributing to the coarsening of Highland Falls?"

"As a matter of fact, all the chairpersons have seen the photographs and found them very appealing and artistically relevant."

He shook his blond head with obvious disapproval. "There are times, and this is one of them, when I firmly believe your father made a mistake allowing you to go to Florence."

"As I've told you before, he didn't have any say over the matter since I was an adult." Not in the mood for a lecture, one she could probably recite by heart, Lily looked up with relief as the bell signaled a new customer.

"Good afternoon, Mrs. MacIntyre," she greeted the woman, with a bit more enthusiasm than warranted. "How lovely to see you. What can I do for you today?"

"Jamie can't find his garter flashes. We think he must have left them in the hotel at the Gatlainburg games. Would you have some in stock?"

"Solid or tartan?" Lily asked as she crossed the room to a row of wooden drawers that extended from the floor to the ceiling.

"Tartan, if you have them."

"I'm sure I do."

"So you make films," Donald said to Ian in an unenthusiastic effort at small talk.

"Documentaries. And you write books?"

"*A* book. I've been working on it for the past decade. Once it's done, I don't think I'll have the desire to begin another. Besides, by then it'll be time to turn my attention toward getting married and starting a family."

"Good idea. Got anyone in mind?" Ian asked absently as he watched Lily pull a small wooden step stool from beneath a counter. As she reached above her head to one of the higher drawers, her shirt rose up, revealing an enticing bit of flesh. Her pink jeans stretched tight against her shapely ass, creating an enjoyable pull.

"Since you asked, I do, actually." They both watched Lily offer the customer a choice between the modern red plaid tartan or the softer ancient blue and green. "And you're looking at her," Forbes said.

There were only two women in the shop, and Ian didn't think the banker was talking about the sixty-something customer with the salt-and-pepper hair.

"You're planning to marry Lily Stewart?"

"We've been engaged for quite some time. We plan to marry as soon as I finish my Forbes ancestral history."

"She's not wearing a ring," Ian pointed out as Lily rang up the garter flashes.

"It's unofficial," Donald conceded. "But we have an understanding."

As far as Ian was concerned, and from what he'd witnessed throughout the world, understandings were hardly worth the paper they weren't written on. And the way she'd kissed him sure as hell hadn't hinted at any commitment.

"You're a lucky man."

"That's precisely what I was telling Mother this morning."

Lily walked Mrs. MacIntyre to the door, waved her off, then returned to the two men.

"Business is starting to pick up, the closer we get to the games," she said. "Did you have some special reason for coming by, Donald? Other than to complain about Caroline's exhibit?"

"I was hoping I could convince you to see reason regarding the showing. However, since that appears to be an exercise in futility, I also wanted to tell you that I made reservations at the Misty Mountain Inn for seven o'clock tonight."

"Oh." How could she have forgotten their monthly dinner? Because Ian MacKenzie's kiss had wiped her mind as clear as the glass windows she'd polished this morning. "I'm sorry, but I've so much to do to get ready for the games and the wedding, and now that I've agreed to help Mr. MacKenzie with his film, I'm afraid I'm going to be tied up tonight."

Ian wasn't normally into kinky stuff, but he found the idea of Lily tied to the four posts of that tower bed more than a little intriguing.

"But I'd planned to read you my new pages after dinner."

"Don't let me interrupt your plans," Ian said before she could argue further. It was just as well; the kiss had been a mistake. "I've some calls to make and some details to take care of. Why don't you go ahead and have your dinner with Fraser —"

"Forbes," the banker corrected stiffly.

"Have dinner with Forbes," Ian said. "And we'll get together after you get home."

"I'm not sure when — or if — I'll be home tonight."

It was a challenge. Calmly and sweetly stated, but no less than if she'd tossed down a dainty velvet glove. Obviously she was not at all pleased that he wasn't going to duel the bow-tied guy for her time.

Ian rubbed his jaw, pretending to seriously consider the matter. "Don't worry about it. If you can't make time, I'm sure your aunt Zelda would love to show me around. And she'd definitely add some pizzazz to the project."

He knew Lily was fond of her aunt; he also suspected she'd consider Zelda too much of a loose cannon.

"Ten o'clock," she said in a tone that was close to snappish. "In the library."

"I'll meet you there."

The blond and dapper banker appeared oblivious to the tension swirling in the suddenly heated air around them.

"Well, I guess I'd better go make those calls. Since I'll be in town for the next two weeks, I suspect we'll be running into each other again, Forbes." He shot a look back at Lily. "I'll see *you* tonight."

As the damn bell jangled again, Lily couldn't quite decide whether to take his words as a promise. Or a threat.

11

Scotland, Abbey of Glendochart, July 1306

It was a rare, blindingly bright day in the Highlands. Clouds drifted serenely in a blue sky over
the peaks of the mountains, meadows were
abloom in fragrant blue heather, and the
summer grass was thick where clansmen, unaccustomed to fighting in a united cause, kept
wary eyes on each other as they washed bloody
bandages in the sparkling river.

The Bruce was not in a sunny mood. It had
only been weeks since his coronation, which
should have been the high point of his life. Instead, he'd already been defeated and injured
in a major battle at Methvren. His brother-in-
law had rescued him by pulling him onto his
horse, and barely conscious, Scotland's new
king had retreated ingloriously from a battlefield where hundreds of his soldiers lay dead
and wounded.

Most of those who hadn't died had ended up
in prison, in chains. Others — the more important earls — had been drawn and quartered.
Worse yet, the common people in whose name
he'd supposedly taken on this battle were dying
in the thousands in the ensuing reign of terror.

Overhead an eagle circled, riding the air currents; larks trilled, and bees hummed contentedly, buzzing from blossom to blossom. There'd been a time when any of those things might have brought Robert Bruce at least a moment's pleasure. But no longer.

Being king of Scotland was certainly bringing him nae pleasure. He was sick — not only from the shoulder he'd broken in the battle, but sick at heart. He was a fugitive hunted by both English and Scots throughout his own country, and while he'd been forgiven by his own bishops, the pope in Rome had excommunicated him for the sacrilege and sin of his February murder of his rival, John Comyn.

Not only had he failed to lead his countrymen to victory on the battlefield, not only was he unable to perform in bed with his queen, but he also could well be damned.

" 'Tis useless, I am," he muttered, glaring up at the sun-gilded clouds. "So why don't Ye take me, God, and send me to hell now? How many more men, women, and bairns must die because of Robert the Bruce?"

"Ach," a gentle voice above him said. "You're being too hard on yourself, Robbie."

If his wife could sneak up on him, what was to prevent some enemy from crawling through the grass and slitting his throat with a dirk? He should only be so lucky.

" 'Tis my fault all those men died at Methven, Elizabeth."

"You'd nae be the first king to lose a battle," she said mildly. After four years with The Bruce, she'd seen a great deal of savagery across this war-torn nation.

" 'Twas nae battle. 'Twas a bloody massacre. Pembrooke outsmarted me. And for that, good Scots died by the score. Because I failed them."

"A massacre it might have been. But you dinna fail them, Robert Bruce. Moubray did when he betrayed ye."

"I should have known," he said doggedly. It ate at him, gnawed at his gut until it felt rawer than his wounded arm. "I left the battlefield while my men were mowed down like sheep."

"Ye were carried wounded from the battlefield before you could be killed. So you could live to fight another day."

"I'm no warrior. And no true king."

"You're my husband." She splayed her hands on her hips. "And unless I was dreaming, I was crowned queen of all Scotland, which makes you my lord king. Or have ye forgotten having that holy oil put on your brow?"

"God doesn't anoint a murderer."

"Don't be saying such foolish things," she snapped with temper more suited to a redhead than her cool blond looks. He'd always liked that she was a strong, fiery woman, in bed and out; now he just wished she'd go away and let him brood in peace.

"Scotland needed one king. God chose that king to be you. Which is why, no matter what

Rome says, Comyn had to die. And ye had to be the one who did it."

She knelt down beside him and put her arms around his neck. "My husband is a strong and brave man. A man who nearly died risking his life for his people. A man strong enough to earn the fidelity of good men who've come to fight for the cause.

"That's who I married. And that's the man ye must be. If not for yourself, if not for me and your daughter, for all those loyal Scots." She waved toward the men lounging in the grass, at the valley, and the hills beyond, her gesture encompassing the country he'd sworn to make whole again.

He touched his lips to her forehead and felt a deep stir that was more emotional than physical. "What would I do, without such a warrior queen to have faith in me?"

"I'm nae a warrior," she said with false modesty. She was the bravest person — man or woman — he'd ever known. "Merely a woman who, if she does possess strength, receives it from her husband." She framed his face between her palms. "It was your strength I fell in love with, long before I knew your heart. A heart that's been as wounded as your arm. But ye have a strong body, a strong heart, and an even stronger will, Robbie Bruce. Which is why you're going to stop mourning and take up the fight again."

She was right, of course. As always. She was

also the only person he could truly trust in these dangerous times.

"Aye, I'll be taking up the fight and dealing once again with the English king. But first" — he pressed her down into the grass and covered her body with his — "I'll deal with my queen."

As always, being with Elizabeth energized him and made him feel as if he could take on a dozen Edwards. Unfortunately, the respite was far too short. They'd barely returned to the camp when a messenger came running up with the news that someone had betrayed him, giving away his hiding place, and the English were on the march.

Though he would have preferred making a stand, they were once again outnumbered, encumbered with women and children, and the enemy knew this land far better than he.

The only choice was to go higher into the barren mountains and hope to reach Loch Awe, the stronghold of his Campbell allies.

And so they were on the move again. Robert was riding through a small gorge, Elizabeth and his daughter Marjory, from his first dear departed wife, beside him, when he heard the unmistakable clash of arms over the roaring sound of the river rapids.

To the right was a steep hill of heather and stone, to the left the cliff dropped straight down to the river.

Trapped.

"Gather the women and the children," he told Elizabeth, "and ride back down the hill."

His queen did as he instructed, flying back the way they'd come, leaving the men facing the hoards of screaming Highlanders running down from the top of the hill at breakneck speed.

They were a sight to chill any warrior's blood. Many were clad solely in short kilts, others were naked, save for their boots. It was chaos. Madness.

The Bruce's men, astride their horses, didn't stand a chance as the Highlanders swarmed around them. There was the clash of steel against steel, the warriors on the ground slamming their claymores into chain mail. Terrified horses reared and were quickly gutted by the sharp blades of the enemies' dirks. Everywhere around Robert the mounts were falling, taking their riders with them to the ground, where they'd either be crushed by a ton of writhing, screaming animal or beheaded by a bloody battle-ax.

Because of his broken shoulder, Robert Bruce could barely lift his five-foot-long, two-handed sword, let alone wield it from horseback. Yet refusing to surrender, he stood high in the stirrups, making himself a target as he swung it in long slashes, left, right, left, right, again and again.

"A Bruce!" He shouted his battle cry. "A Bruce and Scotland!"

Naked Highlanders were falling like oaks, when suddenly one mighty swing wrenched his already torn shoulder. Gritting his teeth against the pain, The Bruce roared, threw the sword into the melee with his good arm, then drew his ax.

More Highlanders were coming up from behind; they were surrounded. He fought to turn his horse around even as he continued to wildly swing his ax while dodging the stabbing dirks, which fortunately continued to bounce off his chain mail.

Three of the Highlanders surrounded him, blocking his way, and he recognized one as a MacDougall of Lorn. The Lord of Lorn was married to a sister of Sir John Comyn, the man The Bruce had murdered, and murder was in this man's eyes as he practically pulled himself astride the horse in his attempt to drag Robert to the ground. Unable to maneuver in the teeming mass of men and horses and weapons, he only managed to grasp Robert's cloak. It tore away, taking with it the jeweled brooch clasp.

Gathering his men, the king formed them into an arrowhead formation, putting the women and children in the center, then charged through this new group of advancing Highlanders, shouting his war cry, swinging his ax, cleaving a wedge through the men who began to be crushed by the tide of horses.

In the end, he was left with a mere fifth of his total force of five hundred. He'd fought two battles since becoming king and lost them both. The problem was that Robert, a Norman lord and Celtic earl, had forgotten how to fight in this part of the world.

He'd regroup. Change his tactics. He'd survive on whatever the land provided, slaying MacDougalls — along with the MacFarlanes, MacNightons, and MacLachlans, clans allied to the MacDougalls and the Comyns — whenever the opportunity presented itself. The next battle, he'd win. And the next battle after that. And as many as it took until he forced the English to sit at a peace table and acknowledge Robert the Bruce as a sovereign king of all Scotland.

Oh, yes, he decided, as he dispensed with his chain mail armor, which only slowed a warrior down. And then he was going to retrieve his coronation brooch from whatever thieving MacDougall remained alive.

12

Once she'd closed up shop for the day, Lily made a three-way phone call to break the news of their father's upcoming nuptials to her sisters.

From her Alexandria apartment, Laurel suggested, "Order the bridesmaids' dresses two sizes too small. That way everyone will hate her and maybe she'll decide to leave town."

"Unfortunately, she wants us to be her attendants," Lily said. Jenny had dropped that little bombshell on her right after the stack of books.

"You're kidding." Lark, whom Lily had tracked down in Austin, was clearly less than enthusiastic at the prospect.

"She believes it'll be a bonding thing to bring the Stewart family together."

"We're already together," Laurel pointed out. "Lark and I may have left Highland Falls, but we all know there's no escaping Dad. *She's* the interloper."

"She seems nice enough."

"You'd probably say that about Jack the Ripper," Laurel said.

"She's probably just a bimbo after his money."

Lark's voice held a surprising amount of scorn. Lily couldn't recall her sister ever saying a negative word about anyone. Of the three of them, she was not only the most naturally creative, but like Lily, she'd also always viewed life through rose-colored glasses. Even during the most tumultuous personal times.

"She says she offered to sign a prenup, but Dad refused. He seems really happy."

"You mean his dick is happy. To most men, that's pretty much the same thing." Lark spoke to someone in the background, then said, "I've got to go. There's some damn problem with the sound system and they can't find Cody, surprise, surprise. Fortunately, we'd planned a short break in the schedule so I could cut some new songs, and the dates coincide with the games and wedding. Cody will probably hit the roof — not that I care — and since the new plane was delivered yesterday, I won't have to try to get reservations on such short notice."

"You bought a plane?" Lily asked. "Wouldn't it take a 747 to carry your band and all that equipment?"

Lily had always thought Lark's singing strength was her ability to connect one-on-one with her audience. Lately, at her husband/manager's insistence, she'd begun playing in stadiums with a show designed to bedazzle the thousands of people who'd paid big bucks to watch more and more elaborate special effects.

"It'd take a lot bigger one than the corporate

jet we bought," Lark agreed. "But the equipment and band are going to continue to go by road."

"Well, that should be more restful." Lily couldn't remember the last time her sister had taken a day off. Fame was definitely a dual-edged sword.

"Not really, since the reason Cody decided we should get it was so I could fit in more appearances."

"That doesn't make any sense," Laurel said. "How are you going to do a show without your band?"

"Not shows. Cody's been working with the label to set up publicity appearances: record store openings, CD signings, discount stores, live radio and TV interviews, that sort of thing. And he thinks I'll get more national press if I'm seen out in the clubs."

"You've always hated the club scene," Lily said. Lark was the most introverted of the Stewart sisters, which was why Lily still had trouble imagining her going on stage every night and singing before thousands of adoring fans.

"True. But like Cody says, sometimes a girl's just gotta do what a girl's gotta do." Her words were slightly slurred.

"Are you all right?" Lily asked. "You don't sound well."

"I'm okay. Just tired to the bone. And there's some other stuff going on that I won't bore you with right now, since you've got enough on your plate."

"We're sisters. If something is bothering you, it bothers me," Lily replied firmly.

"Not if you don't know about it."

"Lark?" Laurel's tone was suddenly the one Lily suspected she used when grilling a congressman on her political beat for the *Washington Post*. Of the three of them, Laurel had inherited their father's pit-bull tendencies. Plus, she could definitely be the bossy big sister. "What the hell's wrong?"

"It's not that big a deal." Lily could hear Lark's sigh on the other end of the line. "Just one of those marriage things. Which," she said, with a bit of the soft spunk which always surprised people when she pulled it out, "you wouldn't know about, Laurel. Having never been married yourself."

"I've never had bubonic plague, either." Laurel returned the comment with the same strong overhand she'd used to destroy her opponent back when she'd played on the Highland Falls high school tennis team. "But I know I wouldn't enjoy it. So, what's wrong?"

There was more conversation in the background.

"I've really got to run," Lark said. "Or all anyone will hear tonight will be microphone feedback squawk. I'll be home for the games and the wedding, if Daddy doesn't wise up in the meantime. We'll talk then.

"I'm coming, dammit," she called out to whoever was in the room with her. Lily would have had to have been deaf not to hear the stress in her voice. "Hang in there, baby sister. See you soon."

There was a click from the Texas end of the phone call.

"She sounded exhausted," Lily said to Laurel.

"No wonder. Spending fifty weeks a year on the road on a damn tour bus would be exhausting enough, without the grueling performance schedule Cody's booked her to do this year." She made a sound of disgust. "How much money does any one woman need, anyway?"

"Maybe the plane will help."

"Not if it's just going to force her to spend her free time in discount stores and radio stations. I don't know how she does it. If I was stuck with that controlling, philandering son-of-a-bitch guitar player, I'd have been sent up the river for first-degree murder before our first anniversary," Laurel said.

"His affair with that backup singer was two years ago."

It had made the news when the woman, with a frail, out-of-tune voice, oversized hair, and paid-for boobs, had told reporters that she and Cody Armstrong had been making music off stage as well as on, and that she was having his baby.

Lark had found out about her husband's infidelity when she appeared in the press room after winning the CMA Entertainer of the Year

134

award, and found a hoard of reporters wanting to know if the band would stay intact during the singer's pregnancy.

As it had turned out, the troublemaking bimbo wasn't pregnant and had made the announcement to push Cody into leaving his wife — which hadn't worked since he obviously knew which side his bread was buttered on, and the bimbo couldn't have supported him in the style to which he'd become accustomed.

He made his public repentance on Letterman, Leno, and *Entertainment Tonight*, then wowed the die-hard romantics in the band's fan base with a blatantly emotionally manipulative duet with Lark at the Grammys, about a man who'd done his woman wrong and was begging her forgiveness.

Which, since Lark was an incredibly generous woman, he received, both in the song and in their marriage. Things seemed to have settled down, but it had been a very long time since Lily had heard Lark laugh. And this wasn't the first time she'd sounded suspiciously as if she'd been drinking.

"I suppose, in a way, this wedding could be a good thing," Laurel suggested. "Whether Daddy actually goes through with it or not, it'll give us a chance to convince Lark she ought to dump that guy."

"I'm not interfering in anyone's marriage."

"Fine. You can play the good, supportive sister and I'll play the tough, mean one. Fortunately Congress is going out on break, so I can steal a few days away."

"I know Daddy'll be pleased."

"I'm not doing it for him. Or that child dollmaker he thinks he's going to marry."

"She's twenty-five."

"Lord," Laurel groaned. "What on earth does she see in a man who has daughters older than she is? Don't answer," she snapped. "Despite that bogus prenup offer, it's obvious the girl's a gold digger who took one look at Stewart's Folly and thought she'd struck the mother lode. Dad's always had his little affairs, but I never expected anything like this. I agree with Lark. It's obvious the little bimbo's leading him around by his dick, and if that's the case, there's a chance she's already landed him hook, line, and sinker. At least for now."

She cursed again, one even riper than the first, which certainly would have raised a few eyebrows in Highland Falls. "I just hope she doesn't expect me to call her Mother."

Not bothering to say goodbye — part of Laurel's warp-speed city ways — she hung up.

As Lily replaced the receiver in its cradle, she realized she'd forgotten to tell her sisters about Ian MacKenzie's arrival in Highland Falls.

She returned to Stewart's Folly and found Missy waiting for her in her room.

"Oh, Lily." Her moist eyes threatened tears. "I just can't bear living with Mother anymore.

Could I please come over to Tennessee and be with the rest of the family?"

Lily sighed. Didn't she have enough problems, without dealing with a mother-daughter spat? "Your mother means well."

"She always wants things her own way. That's why Daddy left."

"I suspect the breakup of a marriage is always more complicated than it appears from the outside. But whatever the reason for your parents' divorce, your mother loves you. Surely you wouldn't want to leave her all alone."

Maybe playing the guilt card would smooth this over, so she could get on to putting out one of the other fires that had begun to flare up around her.

"I'll be going off to college in the fall. Besides, it's not as if I'd be on the other side of the planet," the teenage girl mumbled. "I'd just be moving across the great hall."

"My point exactly. It's only for a few more months and you wouldn't be putting enough physical distance between you to make any difference, so why create hurt feelings, and risk your relationship with your mother unnecessarily?" Sometimes it was hard to remember her aunt Melanie wasn't Scots; she certainly was capable of holding a grudge longer than anyone Lily knew. "Can't you find a way to work things out?"

"Not if I have to wear a hoopskirt." Wet eyes hardened; lips firmed. "She is so hardheaded.

She can't understand that not everyone's life's dream is to be a damn debutante."

"And yours is to play the bagpipes?"

"Yes."

"I seem to recall last summer your life's dream was to work for NASA."

"I did. I still do." Missy dragged a hand through her rain-straight blond hair. "There's no reason I can't be a piper and a rocket scientist."

"No, of course there isn't." Lily recalled something her aunt had been complaining about over dinner last week. "But if you want to go to MIT —"

"I do!"

"Then I don't have to tell you that you'll need to keep your grades up. Which apparently you haven't been doing, since you started spending so much time on your piping."

"I only got a B on one crummy test."

"You've always gotten A's in the past. Not that anyone in the family expects you to be perfect, sweetie, but you just don't seem to be yourself lately."

"I'm growing up." She tossed up her chin. "Mother's just going to have to understand that I'm not just a boring little girl who keeps her nose stuck in a book all the time. I have depth. Facets." Missy nodded, obviously pleased with that one. "I'm a Renaissance woman with a wide range of interests."

"It's always good to have interests. But I don't

recall your being bowled over by pipers in previous years' competitions."

"That was before I learned about the history of piping from Brad Campbell at last year's games."

"Ahhh!"

Finally this all made sense. Brad Campbell was the mayor's son, a studious young man who'd won the gold medal in the Highland Falls high school's science fair for the past four years. He was a member of the high school's Fighting Scots drum and piper corps, worked as a box boy at the Tartan Market, was unfailingly polite, and surprisingly, for a geek, was also the town's teenage hunk. Lily figured if she'd been seventeen, she probably would have had a huge crush on him, too.

"So you started piping so Brad would notice you?"

"Well, I needed something to get his attention. It's not like he's going to fall in love with me because of my dazzling beauty."

"I think you're pretty."

"My hair is too straight."

"When I was your age I would have loved straight blond hair."

"You could be bald and it wouldn't matter. You're beautiful."

Lily laughed at that.

"It's true. One day Brad and I were standing in front of the athletic awards display, and he pointed out that picture of you doing splits in the air — the year you won the state cheerleader crown? — and he said you were a hottie."

Teenage boys weren't known for their social skills, and the careless remark had obviously hurt her cousin. "I was a year older than you when that picture was taken." Missy had skipped the fifth grade, making her younger than her classmates.

"Madison Sugarbaker is younger than me, but she has these huge breasts she keeps shoving in his face. It's disgusting."

"I know." She did. Lily's high school breast nemesis had been Patsy Kendall. "You just need to give it time, sweetie."

"And I have these ridiculous railroad-track braces." She pulled back her lips, baring steel-clad teeth.

"I had braces. So did Lark and Laurel."

"Really? Lark had braces? She's the most beautiful person I've ever seen in real life."

"In great part due to those braces."

"Did she hate them?"

"I don't think so." Lark was the least conscious of looks, which was why it was so ironic that she'd grown up to be the one who was constantly getting her picture on the cover of *Country Music Weekly*, *People*, and *Time*.

"Well, I detest wearing braces. There's no way any boy's going to risk kissing me; he'd get his mouth torn to shreds."

"It's possible. Tricky, but possible," Lily remembered.

"Really?" Hope brightened up Missy's face.

"Absolutely."

Missy sighed. "I really, really love him, Lily."

"I know, sweetie."

Remembering her own teenage years, Lily fully understood how her cousin would state that she wanted nothing to do with boys, then mere hours later do a one-hundred-eighty-degree turnaround and declare her undying love.

Lord, she wouldn't want to be that age again for anything. Though even at twenty-nine, her mind kept drifting to Ian MacKenzie all day like a moony high school girl's.

"Mother says it's puppy love, but she's wrong. It's the real thing and I'm going to do whatever it takes to get him."

"Are you talking about having sex?" Oh, damn. She didn't need this.

"Maybe." Missy tossed her hair with defiance.

"Going to bed with a boy may get his attention for a while." Like three minutes. "But it's no way to keep him interested in you for the long term."

"Well, duh. I'm not stupid, Lily. I already figured out that, since there are too many other girls who are panting to climb into the back seat of his car with him, I ought to use my brains and appeal to the one thing he really likes that all the others can't do."

"Like piping."

"Yeah. It's turning out to be a lot harder than I thought, but you know what?"

"What?"

"Today, when Mother started ragging on me about missing the ball, I realized that I'm not piping just for Brad anymore. Oh, I still want to impress him. And I really want to make the finals. But I'm piping for myself."

Lily smiled and hugged her cousin. "That's just the way it should be, and the entire family will be rooting for you."

"Thanks." There was a huge sigh. Missy took off her glasses and swiped at her tears with the back of her hand, looking as heartbreakingly young and vulnerable as she had when her father had deserted the family. "I've got a physics test tomorrow, and I am so behind. I guess I'd better go cram."

"Good idea. Missy?" Lily called as her cousin left the bedroom.

"What?"

"If Brad just doesn't realize how special you are, it's his loss."

"I know that in here." Missy tapped her head. "But in here . . ." She placed a palm against her breast and sighed deeply.

"I know," Lily said. Only too well.

13

An hour later, as she spritzed a cloud of cologne around herself, Lily decided that beneath the skin, women were not that far removed from their teenage years.

"It's not often you get so dressed up," said Zelda, who was sitting on the edge of Lily's bed.

"I just felt like a change." Concentrating on not falling over, Lily turned on the skyscraper heels she'd borrowed from her aunt and eyed her reflection in the tilted cheval mirror.

The black silk dress with thin crystal straps clung to her body like plastic kitchen wrap and ended high on her thighs. It'd been a present from Laurel last Christmas and this was the first time Lily had worn it. It was admittedly overkill for Highland Falls.

"Ian MacKenzie's going to swallow his tongue when he gets a look at you," Zelda predicted.

"I'm going out with Donald." She tugged a bit on the scooped neckline and wished she'd bought the Wonderbra Laurel had recommended to go with the dress.

"Well, that's a damn waste." Her aunt shook her bright head. "Donald Forbes wouldn't begin to know what to do with a woman who looks like you do."

"That's not nice."

"He's dull."

"Studious."

"And egotistic."

"A strong self-image is a good thing."

"He's also as stuffy as an attic in August."

"He can be a bit old-fashioned," Lily allowed, thinking of that plaid bow tie.

"That's putting it mildly. Did you know he was trying to get a petition started to close down your Scots in Kilts photography display?"

"He mentioned being unhappy, but I didn't hear anything about a petition."

"Well, he is. Irma Brown told me he'd asked her to sign it when she stopped into the bank to deposit the check you gave her for those pies she's been baking for the dinner crowd. She refused, of course."

"Why of course?"

"I suspect she doesn't want to risk losing such a healthy addition to her Social Security check every month. But mostly I'd guess that just because she's in her seventies doesn't mean that she can't appreciate a good-looking man in a tartan. She told me she was hoping the rumor's true that Sam Logan, from down at MacScrooge's Hardware, is one of the models."

"You know I can't tell you that." Caroline had been very vocal about building anticipation and speculation regarding the showing.

"Can you at least tell me if it's true that Caroline used local people instead of professional models?"

"I suppose it wouldn't hurt to say yes to that." Lily held up two pairs of earrings, hoping to change the subject. She'd never been very good at subterfuge. "Which ones?"

"Might as well go all out and wear the dangly silver ones, not that the stuffy banker will appreciate them. Are you one of the models?"

"I may be." Lately Lily had been second-guessing her decision to pose, agreed to over a pitcher of margaritas with the photographer.

"You realize that Donald's going to have a cow when he finds that out."

"He doesn't have any say over me or my life."

"Try telling that to him. I've gotten the impression that he seems to think he does."

"Then he's wrong." She picked up a cobalt-blue atomizer and spritzed a bit more perfume. "What do you think of the MacKenzie?"

"I think he's my favorite type. Tall, dark, and dangerous."

"I'm meeting with him tonight after dinner to talk about the film," Lily said.

"That explains the dress." Zelda swept another glance over Lily from the top of her head to her spindly, pointy-toed shoes. "Well, if you're out to bag the MacKenzie, darlin', you're certainly wearing the right ammunition." Her laugh was rich and deep. "The poor sucker doesn't stand a chance."

"Of course the Forbeses accepted the reformed faith," Douglas droned on, as he'd been doing through the entire dinner.

Lily was used to hearing tales of the Forbes clan, but she'd never realized how excruciatingly boring the stories could be.

"Then the eighth Lord Forbes married Lady Margaret Gordon. She was the eldest daughter of the fourth earl of Huntly. The Gordons were the principal enemies of the Forbeses, and, of course, being Catholic, were rebellious by nature."

She glanced up from the dessert menu, where she'd been trying to decide between the chocolate almond cake with raspberry-cassis coulis, or the cream cheese pound cake with chocolate glaze.

"We're Catholic." She wasn't as up on her family history as he was, but she did know that a great many Stewarts had fought wars to retain religious freedom.

"Your family's also rebellious."

She tilted her head, surprised a little at that. "Perhaps my father and aunt. And Laurel can be headstrong at times. But Lark and I don't have a rebellious bone in our bodies."

He shook his head and clucked his tongue in a way she'd grown so used to, she'd stopped noticing. She noticed tonight. "You're the most rebellious of the three of you."

"Do you really think so?" She was suddenly interested in the conversation. "How so?"

"You ran off to Europe."

Lily laughed. "Lots of people go to Europe."

"You had a fling with a married Italian."

She frowned, wishing she'd never made the mistake of telling him about that. "I didn't know he was married. And it wasn't a fling; I thought I might be falling in love with him."

"You only told yourself that to give yourself permission to have sex with him."

That was surprisingly perceptive for a man who spent most of his life in the past.

"I don't really want to discuss my sex life."

"Neither do I," he agreed. "It's in the past. But the ill-fated affair with your Italian makes my point, and is merely one of a dozen examples I could cite of times when you've jumped in over your head without first testing the waters."

"Let's get back to those rebellious Gordons," she said sweetly. Perhaps she'd get the chocolate almond cake for here, and order the pound cake to go. Then there was always the chocolate mousse fudge torte.

His eyes lit up in a way she'd never seen them do when looking at her. Even tonight, when she'd been dressed to kill, he'd taken one look at her high heels and reminded her that there were ten stone steps up to the front door of the restaurant.

"When their son turned Catholic and entered a religious order, Forbes naturally disowned his wife."

"Naturally?" Lily went from bored to piqued on the wife's behalf. "Are you sure you want to put this ancestor in your family tree?"

"Clan loyalty was all-important."

"What about loyalty to a spouse?"

"Marriage was about clan alliances and land. And wives were expected to respect their husbands."

"I think that should go both ways. And respect should be earned, not granted automatically."

"You can't change history, Lily."

"More's the pity. So, what happened next in the saga of the feisty Forbes?"

"As it turns out, Forbes's treatment of his wife led to a clan battle."

"See, I'm not alone in thinking his behavior was wrong."

"They were rebels," he reminded her with satisfaction, as if she'd just proven his point. "It was at Clatt in Aberdeenshire. Unfortunately, the Gordons had the better of the day."

"Good for them."

"They killed Lord Forbes's brother."

"Well, I am sorry for that. But they could have avoided the entire problem if they'd been more tolerant."

Her point made, Lily decided on the chocolate torte. It wasn't that she didn't appreciate history, because she did. You couldn't live in this part of the country and not be surrounded by it, and Italy had opened her eyes to a past that at times had seemed so immediate that she wouldn't have been surprised if Botticelli or Leonardo da Vinci had strolled beneath her apartment balcony.

"I plan to be finished with the book by Christmas," Donald said.

"How wonderful."

Lily cast a surreptitious look at her watch. Nine o'clock. Still another hour before her meeting with Ian. Was he thinking about her? Was he reliving those kisses in vivid detail, as she'd been doing all evening?

"So I thought we'd get married on New Year's Eve. That way we can file a joint tax return next year."

"New Year's is my favorite time of year," she said absently. "Fresh start, new opportunities, all that sort of thing."

Was Ian wondering if she was kissing Donald? Was it hopefully driving him a little insane with jealousy?

"Then it's settled. In a way, it's good that you're doing your father's wedding. It can serve as a dress rehearsal for ours." He frowned and took a sip of coffee. "Of course, ours will be more tasteful and discreet than the medieval carnival Jennifer wants, and we'll want a strictly A guest list, but —"

"Guest list?" Lily dragged her reluctant attention back to their conversation.

"For our wedding."

"Wedding? As in yours and mine?"

"Of course. Whom did you think I was talking about?"

"I don't recall ever saying I was going to marry you, Donald." Okay, so her life had been a bit hectic lately, but she was certain she would have remembered a detail that important.

"Of course you are," he replied with serene confidence. "We both agreed long ago that as soon as I finished the Forbes family history, we'd become man and wife."

"I never made any such agreement."

"You slept with me."

"That was three years ago. Once."

At the time she'd been horribly upset about her father's accident, which, if he'd hit that tree a little differently while racing down that steep ski slope in the Rockies, could easily have been fatal. She'd also been devastated by watching Dante die in that racing accident, and furious at the man she'd thought she might be falling in love with for forgetting to mention that he had a wife and two children stashed away in a cozy little house in Naples.

Donald had met her plane at the Asheville airport and driven her to the hospital. After she'd visited her father, he'd taken her to his house for a drink — okay, several drinks — held her while she'd wept (who would have suspected she'd be a sappy drunk?), and one thing had led to another, and they'd landed in bed. The sex, while

150

underwhelming, had at least gotten her mind off her problems. If only until the next morning.

"I like you, Donald." She covered his hand with hers. "But not in the way that leads to love. Didn't you think, if I were in love with you, we would have ended up in bed again?"

"We both have demanding schedules," he said vaguely. "And we've been a bit preoccupied, me with my book, and you getting your little shop started and handling your father."

"No one handles my father." Though irked at the way he'd referred to her gallery as a "little shop," she refused to get sidetracked into a public argument. "Besides, it's more than that." She looked into his eyes, which revealed honest confusion, and wondered how in the world she'd missed seeing this coming. "We don't have any chemistry."

"There are more important things than chemistry," he argued. "Like shared values, friendship, respect. As for the chemistry, it could still come. With time."

"I'm sorry." She shook her head. "Perhaps it works that way for some people, but I need the zing."

"Give the idea time to sink in," he suggested. "We'd be a good team. You're a bit impulsive, which we'll have to work on, but —"

"Work on?" It took a great deal to make Lily angry, but he'd managed to hit one of her hot buttons.

"We can all use some improvement." As he

waved his hand, she couldn't help contrasting his narrow palm and short, manicured fingers with Ian's broad, rugged hand. "You're a charming girl, Lily. Smart, funny, beautiful in a down-to-earth way."

"Thank you." Not that "down-to-earth" was much of a compliment.

"Did I tell you I liked that dress?"

"It didn't come up." From his lack of response when she'd glided down the stairs to the great hall, she could have been wearing her raggedy old orange UT sweats from college days.

"It's quite nice."

"Thank you."

"Albeit a little tight, especially to wear out in public."

"It's a cocktail dress, Donald. It's made to be worn in public."

"True. But once we're married, I think it might be better if you dressed more discreetly."

"I always dress discreetly. This just happens to be a gift from Laurel."

"Well, that explains it. Laurel has always been too brash, for my thinking."

"That's my sister you're talking about," she warned quietly.

"And thank goodness you're nothing alike. Being the branch manager of a bank doesn't just come with a great deal of prestige; it requires a lot of responsibility. A banker's wife has to stay above reproach so she creates a positive image in town, worthy of respect."

Lily couldn't help it. She began to laugh.

"I don't know what's so humorous," he said stiffly.

"I'm sorry." She pressed her fingers against her lips, trying to hold the giggles in. "It's just that if there's one thing the Stewarts are terrible at, it's remembering their position in town."

"Zelda and your father are definitely over the top, and Lark certainly hasn't chosen a career that draws automatic respect."

"I disagree. Winning two CMA awards and a Grammy signifies an enormous amount of respect."

"By the music industry, perhaps. Populated, for the most part, by nonmonogamous substance abusers."

"Don't be so stuffy."

"Excuse me if I believe in striving to be the best I can be."

Dammit, she couldn't keep the laughter from bubbling out of her. She pressed her fingertips against her lips again. "I'm not laughing at you, Donald."

He appeared surprised by the suggestion she might be. "I didn't think you were."

Well, at least she hadn't terminally wounded his self-confidence; it still surrounded him like a Teflon shield. "I'd make a terrible banker's wife."

"I'm thirty-five years old, Lily. As Mother keeps pointing out, it's time I settled down and ensured the Forbes dynasty will continue."

"So you're looking for a breeder?" It said a great deal about the man that he didn't even seem to realize that statement was no way to get a woman to marry you.

"Of course not." He huffed out a breath. "I'm not looking for a litter, for heaven's sake. One son would be efficient." His brow furrowed in concentration. "Perhaps two."

"An heir and a spare," she murmured.

"I didn't quite get that?"

She shrugged her bare shoulders. "I was just thinking about the royal family." Her gaze skimmed around the room, settling briefly on a brunette in the far corner. "What about Sandra Fraser?"

He frowned at the apparent leap in topic. "What about her?"

"She'd make a perfect banker's wife." The tax attorney was also the most boring woman Lily had ever met. "And I think she likes you."

"Really?" He followed her gaze.

"I saw her sneaking looks at you during a Tartan Ball planning-committee meeting."

"I didn't notice." But he was interested; Lily could tell by the way he was absently straightening his Forbes tartan bow tie.

"We got to talking in the ladies' room during the break, and she was wondering why you hadn't gone into politics, since you're obviously such a born leader."

A gleam she'd certainly never seen directed toward her appeared in his pale blue eyes.

"That's an interesting coincidence, since I've been considering making a bid for mayor."

"I think that's a grand idea."

With his penchant for details and need to control the entire world around him, at least the trash would get picked up on time. The flip side was that he'd undoubtedly be the closest thing to a dictator the town council would ever know.

"Would you vote for me?"

"You know I would." It was only a little white lie. Besides, this was America, land of the secret ballot. "Did you realize Sandra majored in poly sci at the University of Virginia?"

"Really?" His sudden alertness reminded her of Robbie, her father's old Gordon setter, pointing out quail. "Did she ever work in politics?"

"I believe she mentioned doing some work on a past governor's race. Her candidate won by a landslide." Fifty-two percent wasn't bad these days, when voters were so divided on so many issues.

"Well." He sat back in his chair, folded his white damask napkin — which, she noticed, had remained spotless — and put it on the table. "That's very interesting."

"Isn't it?"

She smiled, pleased that she'd solved three people's problems with one clever stroke. She'd dodged the matrimonial bullet with no hurt feelings, Donald needed a respectable wife, and along with stating her admiration for the banker, Sandra had also mentioned that she wanted to begin having her family before she was thirty-one, which was only a year away.

Lily smiled up at the waiter, who'd arrived with the dessert tray. "I'll take the chocolate mousse cake, to go."

That way she could keep her appointment with Ian, having her mousse and eating it, too. Life was definitely grand.

14

Ian knew Lily had been annoyed when he hadn't leaped in to help her out of her dinner date with that prig of a banker. But even if he hadn't been eager to distance himself from temptation, he'd been telling the truth about needing to make some calls.

Not having planned to actually make the film, he hadn't lined up any funding beforehand.

Duncan would be willing to spring for production fees, just to keep Ian at the castle long enough to find the damn brooch, but while there'd been many times when he'd been as lean and hungry as Cassius, Ian had never sacrificed his creative freedom for money. And he wasn't about to start now. Fortunately, since he'd never acquired a lot of possessions, most of the money he'd made over the years was safely stashed away.

Technology had done away with the truck-loads of equipment and engineers, so he wouldn't need a large crew. Although he preferred directing another cameraperson — which allowed him to concentrate on the big picture and what was happening beyond the range of the lens — in the early days he'd shot his own video. And could again.

He planned to use mostly natural lighting — except for the wedding in the castle chapel, which he could also handle himself — which would eliminate the need for a gaffer to manage the electrical. An assistant would be nice, but he could do without that. One person to handle sound should do it. The film would undoubtedly end up on television, rather than as a theatrical release, which gave him more leeway since television was a more forgiving medium.

It took him a while, but he finally tracked down in Tibet a soundperson he worked with whenever their separate schedules allowed. Like so many soundmen, Brady O'Neill was easygoing, outwardly cheerful, and low-key. But he shared Ian's tendency to gravitate toward serious issues, which was why Ian didn't expect him to be overly enthusiastic about a puff piece.

"So, what gives?" he asked after Ian had finished explaining the project.

"What do you mean?"

"This is a really different subject matter for you."

"John Stewart's been after me for years to come take a look. And I think the idea of all these Americans having this need to connect to their roots could be interesting. If that doesn't work out, we can always switch gears and concentrate on the guy himself, since he's rich, famous, and an eccentric artist."

"It's not like you to start filming without a working hypothesis."

"True." But then, nothing about this trip to Highland Falls had gone as planned. "I figured we'd just take a chance and wing it. The worst that'll happen is we end up with a bunch of videotape we end up pitching out at editing time."

"Hey, you're the visionary. I just take care of the sound."

"We both know that's a vast understatement." Sound could make or break a film, and it was nearly impossible to fix after the wrap. Fortunately, Brady also shared Ian's perfectionism when it came to his work.

"When would you need me?"

"Yesterday."

"Since when do you decide on something at the last minute?"

"The opportunity sort of dropped into my lap."

"There's just one little problem."

"Oh?"

"Lukasz Zacharczuk has offered me credit above the title and half a point to work with him on a look back at the Solidarity movement after two decades."

The Polish filmmaker was brilliant and probably Ian's only real competition these days. While they managed to remain friends whenever they ran into each other, they were warriors in the field. Just the thought of losing Brady to this man's project irked Ian.

"Is that half a point net or gross?"

"Net, of course."

Of course. They both knew it was just something to sweeten the offer, since by the time the financial wizards were through juggling the books, there wouldn't be any profits.

"Have you signed a contract yet?"

"His lawyers are still working on it."

"I'll bet they are." Zacharczuk was also infamous for his draconian contracts, while Ian and Brady had always worked on a handshake arrangement. "Look, I'll up that with an assistant producer role, your name above the title, and a full point of the gross."

"That's damn tempting. But I also happen to have a potential time-crunch problem: if the interviews we just managed to shoot with some pro-separatist Buddhist monks don't get safely smuggled out of the country, the entire damn sequence is going to have to be rearranged in editing. Which could mean another week in London."

"Tell you what," Ian suggested, not yet willing to throw in the towel. "I'll do some preliminary scouting, get a lay of the land, and take some video so you can see what I've got in mind. We can get together to talk about the project next week in New York."

"This Highland Games thing sure doesn't sound like you," Brady said. "But hey, it also sounds like fun, which would be a huge change for both of us."

After finishing up his conversation with Brady, Ian located the library. The room was paneled in bird's-eye maple, with soaring beamed ceilings and bookcases two stories high. The collection of first editions was extraordinary; Ian wondered if the brooch could be stashed away inside one of the leather-bound books, but decided that would be too obvious. Then again, sometimes, the most obvious turned out to be the correct choice.

But it'd take the rest of his lifetime to check out every damn book.

A familiar title caught his eye. *Flemington*, a novel dealing with loyalty and betrayal during the Jacobite rebellion by early-twentieth-century Scots writer Violet Jacob, had become one of his mother's favorite books after she'd played the role of the author in a small local theater in Arbroath, where the Declaration of Scottish Independence had been signed in 1320. Surprised to find a copy, Ian was skimming through the pages when Lily breezed in, bringing with her the scent of night rain.

"You're early." Forty-two minutes. Not that he'd been counting.

"Service was fast tonight; it's not often the case." She put a white foam box onto a Hepplewhite table, shrugged out of a short black jacket, and tossed it onto the back of a wine-red leather wing chair.

"Nice dress," he said mildly as he struggled not to swallow his tongue. He replaced the novel on the shelf.

"Thanks." She crossed the room, took the glass out of his hand as if it were the most natural thing in the world to do, and took a sip. "It's the first time I've worn it, and I feel as if I've been shrink-wrapped."

"That's not such a bad look."

Dynamite, actually. A woman in a dress like that would inspire lust in any man. Lust was a good thing; it kept the species going and was damn enjoyable. But the feeling stirring inside him, which seemed stronger and more complex than mere lust, was decidedly discomfiting. It made him wish he'd turned Duncan down flat, gone to Monaco, and gotten laid.

"I'm surprised Forbes let you get away tonight." Ian damn well wouldn't have. If he'd been the one having dinner with her, they wouldn't be wasting time in the library. They'd be upstairs in his bed.

"He didn't have much of a choice." She handed the glass — which now bore a rosy lipstick crescent on the rim — back to him, perched on the edge of the desk, and crossed bare legs that looked as smooth as silk. "I go where I want to go. Do what I want to do." When she lifted her hands to comb them through her rain-sparkled curls, the provocative gesture did intriguing things to her breasts.

"If that's the case, why are you hanging out here in Highwater Falls?" He could more easily picture her on Ipanema Beach wearing nothing but suntan oil, a string bikini bottom, and a smile.

"If you're going to do the film, you might want to remember the name of the town is Highland Falls. Not Highwater," she said mildly. "As for why I'm here, I sometimes ask myself the same question."

"And?"

"I suppose because it's home. I'm comfortable here."

"Comfort can be overrated if it leads to stagnation." And roots could wrap around your ankles and hold you so close to the ground, you never got a chance to soar.

"Good point. And coincidentally, one I've been thinking about a great deal lately . . . So, what do you want me to do?"

Lie back on the desk so I can peel that dress off, for starters.

"I was hoping you could give me a tour of this place — both the castle and the town — and fill me in on the logistics of the games, any interesting characters, that sort of thing, so I can get an idea of what shots I'm going to want to set up."

"Didn't you know?" When she switched her crossed legs, he had to clench his jaw to keep from biting that smooth, golden thigh. "Everyone in Highland Falls is fascinating."

"From what I've seen so far, I'd almost have to agree with that."

"Almost?"

"Your banker's a bit low on the sizzle scale."

"He's not *my* banker. Well, to be perfectly accurate, he is, but nothing else. Would you like to begin tonight, or will in the morning be soon enough?"

"Morning's fine." He ran a finger along the shadow beneath her eyes. It gave her a faintly fragile look that contrasted with her sex-siren look. Ian had always been drawn to — and fascinated by — contrasts. "You look as if you could use some sleep."

"Good idea," she said dryly. "Why don't I go on up to bed and let you plan my father's medieval wedding?"

"Your father's getting married?"

"During the games. To a very much younger woman who wants to celebrate his heritage with a medieval Scots heritage ceremony."

"Isn't it usual for the bride to plan her own nuptials?"

"It is. Unfortunately, she feels it's over her head."

"One could argue that if she can't handle something as simple as a wedding ceremony, she's not mature enough to get married."

"As you'll discover, nothing to do with my father is ever simple. I can understand how she'd be overwhelmed."

"And when your father's fiancée feels overwhelmed, it's up to you to come to the rescue." Ian was definitely getting a handle on how things worked around Stewart's Folly. "Did anyone ever explain to you that the word *no* can be a declarative sentence?"

Her answering laughter was rich and warm and flowed over him like the warm honey he'd been fantasizing spreading all over her body. Then licking off.

"Spend a few days with my father and see if you still believe that. Besides, it's one of those family loyalty responsibilities; if I did manage to duck it, I'd just end up feeling guilty."

Ian wouldn't have thought he and Lily had anything in common, but he could definitely identify. "I suppose the up side is that it'll be a dry run for your own wedding."

"That's assuming I ever get married."

"Forbes can't work on that ancestral tome forever."

"I wouldn't bet the farm — or the castle — on that, although he does seem to believe he'll be wrapping it up by Christmas. But why would you think Donald's book has anything to do with my getting married?"

"As a rule, engagements tend to lead to marriage."

She frowned in thought, then her remarkable eyes narrowed dangerously, giving him a window into her thoughts. "Did Donald tell you we were engaged?"

"He claimed he was going to marry you, and

that the two of you had an understanding."

Color stained her cheeks, revealing an unexpected flash of anger he found inordinately intriguing.

"Perhaps Donald had an understanding." There was an edge to her voice he hadn't heard before. "But as I explained over dinner, I certainly don't have any plans to get married."

"Ah." He turned the glass in his hand and, with his gaze on hers, took a sip, his lips on that lipstick crescent. "That explains why the evening was cut short. Well, he'll get over it."

Lily's little flare of anger was over as swiftly as it had arisen, and her lips curved in a half-smile. "I'm hoping he'll fall in love with a woman more suitable for him."

"You mean stuffy."

"Sandra Fraser isn't stuffy; she's just a little subdued."

"Don't tell me." He shook his head in disbelief. "Are you actually planning to fix him up to prevent him from a broken heart?"

"I think his pride was more injured than his heart. And what's wrong with wanting people to be happy?"

"Not a thing." He wondered how far she'd go to see her father happy. Would she steal The Bruce's brooch? "What are you going to do for a grand finale to the games? Organize all the clans into holding hands atop Stewart's Mountain and singing the Coca-Cola song?"

She tilted her head and studied him. "I sup-

166

pose it's not surprising, given all you've seen and the tragedy in your personal life, but you really are the most cynical man I've ever known."

"Known a lot of men, have you?" Something stirred deep in his gut, and this time it was decidedly green.

"Scads." She waved an airy hand. "I'm surprised your research didn't discover I finally had to put one of those little machines, like at the bakery, in my bedroom, so all my lovers could take a number."

"Having never been known for my patience, I guess I'll just jump to the front of that line."

15

He gathered up her hair in a fist at the back of her neck. It was like holding flame-colored silk. With his eyes holding hers, he took her mouth.

Ian had thought that this time he was prepared for the jolt. This time he was the one initiating the kiss; *he* was the one in control.

He'd thought wrong.

His mind was swept clear the moment his lips brushed hers. Her scent, both fresh and seductive, surrounded him, ribboned through him. She lifted her arms around his neck and clung. Her lips parted avidly beneath his.

She felt so soft. So warm. So willing. Ian had always gotten an adrenaline kick from danger, but never had he experienced anything like the chain reaction rioting through him. And certainly never from a mere kiss.

As his mouth blazed its way down her throat, she moaned and tilted her head back, inviting more. His lips returned to hers, drinking deeper, longer; when he skimmed his fingertips over her silk-clad breasts, her nipples pebbled to diamond hardness.

Not wanting to take his hands off the body

that was so eagerly arching against him, he caught one of the crystal straps in his teeth and dragged it off a pearlescent shoulder.

"Ian." She gasped out his name as he nipped at the cord at the base of her slender throat. He pressed his open mouth against the hollow where her pulse was beating hard and fast, and tasted desire flowing from her pores. "I don't think —"

"Good idea." A flick of his fingers sent the other strap sliding down, as well. "Don't think."

Her voice was ragged with need. She was trembling from it. Ian knew that he could have her, here. Now.

He lifted his head and took in the powerfully erotic sight of her. Without the straps to hold it up, the silk dress was clinging to the tips of her breasts, revealing an enticing bit of barely-there black lace. When he'd coaxed her legs apart, the better to fit between them, the tight skirt had risen dangerously high on her thighs. One stiletto heel had fallen off onto the faded Persian carpet; the other was barely hanging on.

Her face, surrounded by those wild strawberry curls, was flushed, her eyes wide and unfocused, her lips parted. Gone was the fresh-faced forest nymph. The friendly, briskly efficient shop owner who looked sweet as sherbet had disappeared. This woman was stunningly sexy. Wonderfully wanton.

Never had Ian wanted a woman more than he wanted this woman at this moment. Never had he needed a woman as badly as he needed Lily Stewart.

Which was why he forced himself to back away.

"You'd best be getting upstairs to bed." With a powerful pang of regret, he replaced one strap. Then the other. "We don't have much prep time, so I'll want to get an early start in the morning."

She blinked slowly. "I don't understand."

"A good documentary takes planning. It's not like a home video of Dollywood. There are storyboards to plan, scenes to block, decisions to be made —"

"I'm not talking about the film." She ran her fingertips over her swollen lips, drawing his attention back to that luscious mouth he could still taste and wanted to taste again. "I'm referring to what just happened here."

He dragged his gaze from her mouth and looked her straight in the eye. "Nothing."

That was the biggest lie he'd told her yet. Ian feared there'd be many more lies before he left Highland Falls. And the longer he was around her, the more that idea pricked at a conscience he hadn't been aware of possessing.

"No." Red-gold curls kissed her cheeks as she shook her head. "It *was* something. Something we need to talk about."

"I kissed you. You kissed me back. End of discussion."

Bloody hell. He'd no sooner said the words

than he wished he could take them back. He'd sounded exactly like the Duncan he'd met over his parents' open graves. The cold, unfeeling bastard who'd put all his emotions in deep freeze.

But once again, Lily surprised him. She didn't look wounded. In fact, she looked determined to put things on the table in her forthright way and sort them out.

"You kissed me like you wanted me."

"Darling, there's probably not a man on this planet who wouldn't want you at first glance."

The air in the library had turned as steamy as a Swedish sauna. It no longer mattered that she wasn't dark and sultry, or classically blond, or worldly. He ached for her in every atom of his body.

The problem was, he had the uneasy feeling that if he took her, it wouldn't be that easy to walk away. Whether she was a thief or not, he had a niggling feeling she might be able to hold him. And there was no way he was ready for that.

"But you're not the kind of woman for quick, hot sex on your father's library desk."

"I haven't been in the past. Perhaps I've been missing something."

"You want to try it out and see, it's your call."

"Is that all it would be? Just sex?"

"If you want orange blossoms and happily-ever-afters in some nice suburban tract house, baking cookies and changing nappies, go back to your boring banker." Better she be hurt now, than later. "If you're looking for a guy who'll take you up on what you keep dangling in front of him, then walk away without worrying about any emotional rubble left behind, then I'm your man."

"Well." She blew out a breath and studied him a bit warily. "That certainly sounds tempting." Her dry tone said just the opposite.

"It isn't supposed to be. It's supposed to be a warning. I want you and I'll probably have you before I leave town. But I believe you should know the score going in."

"I appreciate your honesty. I've always believed in facing facts, even when they're not terribly appealing."

"Now that we've laid our cards on the table, why don't you do something about those shadows under your eyes." His fingers ached. Glancing down, Ian realized he'd curled his hands into tight fists to keep them out of trouble. "Go to bed, Lily."

"That's probably a good idea. I think I will. Alone."

"Your choice." His tone was curt as he tugged her dress top up the rest of the way, putting bloody damn temptation out of reach.

"You were the one who stopped things from getting out of hand," she reminded him. "So you shouldn't sulk just because I decided to take your warning to heart."

"I'm bloody well not sulking." He'd been

called demanding, impatient, even temperamental, but no one had ever dared accuse him of sulking.

"You certainly are." Her smile was soft, her eyes warm. She was obviously pleased with that idea. "Which is even more flattering, since I have the feeling you don't do it very often." She slid off the desk and picked up the sandals that had fallen off her feet during that heated kiss. Then she pressed a button on the desk and a sliding wall panel opened, revealing a hidden bookcase.

"Clever." It made him wonder how many other little secret hiding places had been built into Stewart's Folly.

"Daddy had it installed because while he loves to read, he believed the bright dust jackets on contemporary books detract from the ambiance." She plucked a book from one of the shelves; the background was a glossy black and scarlet blood dripped from a lethal-looking dagger.

"I never would have taken you for a thriller reader."

"Which just goes to show how deceptive appearances can be. Behind this disgustingly perky exterior, which I unfortunately can't do anything about, I am a woman of eclectic tastes and hidden depths."

"I'll keep that in mind." He took the book from her.

With a casual, easy gesture, she linked her fingers with those of his free hand as they left the library. "Your carrying my book and walking me home reminds me a bit of high school," she murmured as the gilded elevator creaked its way up to the top.

Thinking back on a particularly hot London afternoon with Nora the summer of his sixteenth year, Ian suspected they'd had very different high school experiences.

They exited the elevator and walked a few doors down a hall lined with marble busts of ancestral Stewarts. Lily stopped in front of an arched oak door. "I'll meet you in the breakfast room at nine," she suggested. "We can begin with a tour of the grounds."

"Make it eight." Now that he'd committed to doing the film, his perfectionism had kicked in. "And I'd rather begin with the interior." The better to case the joint. Being a thief wasn't turning out to be nearly as glamorous as Cary Grant or Pierce Brosnan had made it seem in American movies.

"Fine. Good night, Ian."

He touched her hair because, dammit, he couldn't help himself. Then he framed her uplifted face between his palms.

Needing to prove to himself that he could kiss her and walk away, he captured her lips again, a quick flare of heat that ended far too soon.

"Eight o'clock," he repeated as he reached past her to open the door.

He got a glimpse of walls covered in heavy

174

antique-gold tapestry. A tester bed, draped in the same fabric, took up most of the small room. As he walked back toward the elevator, he heard the closing of the thick door and tried not to regret an opportunity lost.

With her nerves still jangling from her encounter in the library, Lily couldn't sleep. After an hour of tossing and turning, her mind swirling up all sorts of erotic scenarios starring Ian, she turned on the bedside light and began leafing through one of the books Jenny had given her.

"Where on earth am I going to find parchment scrolls?" she muttered as she took a bite of a dark chocolate Hershey bar. "And a printer at this late date?"

She'd have to improvise on the paper for the invitations. As for the lettering, she seemed to recall her computer at the gallery came with an Old English script.

"I'll just run them off in my spare time." Between selling souvenirs, doing myriad other wedding tasks, and dealing with Ian MacKenzie.

Ian. She closed her eyes and leaned back against the pillows. It took no imagination at all to remember how his lips had felt on hers, how his hands had felt on her body, and how his obvious arousal had sent her own soaring into the stratosphere.

She knew she shouldn't get so rattled by a

mere kiss. Okay, three kisses, but she could hardly count that one just outside her door. It hadn't lasted more than a couple seconds — though her entire world had narrowed to the taste and pressure of his mouth on hers, and it had seemed as if the earth had ceased spinning, suspending time.

She was not a love-crazed teenager like Missy. She'd eagerly ditched her virginity ten years ago on a sun-gilded Labor Day, down by the old mill. She'd known Jimmy Duggan — who was returning to Duke for his junior year of college the next day — was not the man with whom she was destined to spend the rest of her life.

Since Jimmy had a reputation for chasing everything in skirts, Lily had seriously doubted they'd still be together by Christmas vacation. That afternoon picnic had been the first time she'd drunk champagne. The first time she'd gone skinny-dipping alone with a boy, and the first time she'd had sex.

She'd had other lovers over the past decade. Men who were more skillful in bed, more adept at the pretty words women wanted to hear. But there'd been no one who'd seriously tempted her heart. Until Ian.

Unfortunately, Ian MacKenzie was the proverbial rolling stone. Any woman foolish enough to hope that he'd settle down in an ivy-covered house with two-point-five children who'd crayon murals on the family room wall, and a dog that would track mud onto the carpet and bury bones in the garden, would be setting herself up for a huge disappointment.

"It's just sex," she assured herself. That was all she would allow it to be.

16

According to an old Gaelic legend, when God finished making Britain, some earth and stone were left over in his ample apron. He flicked them out, sending them tumbling into the western sea to form Argyll and Brute. Another of those bits landed in the bay of Oban to become the island of Kerrera.

At the southern end of Kerrera, Gylen Castle jutted pugnaciously into the sea atop a jagged cliff. The looming gray stone L-shaped structure, known as the castle of the fountains, had been built more than a hundred years ago by a MacDougall, sworn enemy to Clan Campbell.

And under a blue banner proclaiming FOR CHRIST'S CROWN AND COVENANT, Andrew Campbell was part of an army of Covenanters come to sack Gylen Castle. Ignoring the screams of the MacDougalls being murdered, he made his way through the flames and smoke to the bedchamber. There, just as foretold by the seer, was a heavy wooden box carved with the MacDougall motto: "To conquer or die."

He stuck the box beneath his arm and ran out of the room just as the heavy draperies exploded in fire. *Your days of conquering are gone, MacDougall.*

It was chaos. A woman ran past him, her hair aflame; the central courtyard was littered with bodies, some with spears imbedded in their chests. Others writhed on the stone floor, pleading the soldiers or God to put them out of their misery. As blood flowed like a dark red burn to the sea, Andrew could not imagine eternal damnation in hell being any worse than this.

His stomach lurched, but a rigid self-discipline kept him from losing his dinner. That self-discipline also enabled him to wait until he was on the small boat, moving away from the massacre, to break the hasp of the heavy lock with his dirk.

There, lying on a bed of royal-blue silk, just as the old blind crone of Kerrera had promised, was a silver brooch. The Brooch of Lorn, stolen from The Bruce — who was, in the interconnecting way of the Highlands, Campbell kin — had been locked away at Gylen Castle for safekeeping during the civil wars.

"So how will ye feel, ye bluidy MacDougalls," he murmured as he ran his finger over the center crystal surrounded by pearls, "when ye learn that your treasured Brooch of Lorn has been ripped from your royalist hands?"

As the boat made shore, Andrew looked back

over his shoulder at the clouds of black smoke billowing upward from the stone walls, filling the sky. His duty done, he smiled.

17

His second morning in Highland Falls, Ian was sitting at a heavy, hand-carved table in the dining room, when an older woman approached from the kitchen. She was wearing a calf-length skirt and tunic woven in swirled shades of blue, green, and heather, a turquoise pendant strung on a silver chain, and darkly tinted glasses. She was accompanied by a golden retriever guide dog.

"Was everything to your liking?"

"I can't remember ever having better." Ian pushed back the oak chair and stood up. He'd eaten like a man who hadn't had a scrap of bread for months. Opting for the traditional Highland breakfast buffet, he'd started out with juice and oat porridge, then moved on to eggs, bacon, slices of vine-ripened tomatoes, smoked salmon, and finished up with a tattie scone served with blackberry jam and honey that reminded him of his mother, who'd cooked the fried potato pancake every year for his birthday breakfast. "In fact, it was so good I may never eat again."

She smiled at that. " 'Some hae meat and canna eat, some wad eat that want it: But we hae meat and we can eat, sae let the Lord be thankit.' "

"Robert Burns," Ian said.

"You know your poets."

"It'd be hard to be Scots and not know Robbie Burns. I'm Ian MacKenzie."

"I know. My eyesight may be nearly gone, but even if you hadn't been pointed out to me, I would have recognized your voice from that television program. I'm Annie Stewart. We're pleased and honored to have you in our home, Mr. MacKenzie. I'm sorry I wasn't here to greet you, but I was off getting acquainted with Freedom."

She indicated the dog, who was eyeing the plates with decided canine interest.

"He sounds appropriately named."

"Isn't he?" She smoothed a hand over the large head. "He's also a sweetheart who stole my heart the first moment I met him. We've only been together three weeks, but I'm madly in love."

Her hair might be a soft cloud the color of snow over the moors, but her smile was young and warmed by genuine friendliness, and Ian began to understand why Duncan, despite having been married for forty-five years, had continued to carry a torch for more than half a century.

"I'm sure it's mutual on his part," he said. "I've been looking forward to meeting you, Mrs. Stewart."

She lifted a snowy brow. "I'm surprised you've heard of an old woman hidden away in the American highlands."

"I admire your work." He'd gone looking for her paintings after he'd come across a yellowed local-girl-makes-good article Duncan had clipped from *The Northern Scot* newspaper. "It's warm, inviting, and evocative, without crossing the line to sentimental."

"Are you certain you aren't Irish, Mr. Mac-Kenzie? For surely that's one of the more flattering statements I've received from a man lately."

"Then there must be something seriously wrong with the men in Highland Falls."

Her answering laugh was light and musical and eminently appealing.

"You've made an old woman's day." She paused. "Would you mind if I touched you? To feel your features, so I'll have a better sense of who I'm speaking with?"

"Of course not." That wasn't true; Ian was not a toucher by nature. But he wasn't about to refuse this friendly blind woman who, if things had turned out differently, would have been his grandmother.

Since he was a good head taller than she was, Annie had to lift her hands to skim her fingertips over his face. They explored his forehead, his eyes, which closed momentarily beneath her feathery touch, the blade of his nose, his cheekbones, his jaw, before continuing down his neck,

183

along his shoulders and across his chest. He was beginning to wonder exactly how far she was going to take things when she stopped at his belt.

"You're a bonny man, Mr. MacKenzie. I realize, if you decide to make the film my son is so keen on, you'll be quite busy while you're here. But if you could spare an hour or so, I'd love to sculpt you. I took up sculpture after I lost my vision to glaucoma."

"That must have been a difficult time."

"It was, and no less upsetting because it was so gradual. It's partly my fault, of course, since I was a bit of a workaholic in those days and ignored the symptoms for too long." She waved the hand that wasn't holding the cane. "If we're going to be having a little chat, please sit down. You are, after all, a guest."

"I will if you will." He pulled out a chair across from the one he'd abandoned.

"Thank you." Her billowy skirt flowed over the chair seat. "To get back to my tale, at first, when my vision began being blurry, being terribly nearsighted to begin with, I kept chiding myself for not keeping my glasses clean enough. I'm terrible about such things, especially when I'm deep in a creative mind-set, which I was a great deal of the time in those days. It was, ironically, the most prolific period of my life.

"Then I began to lose peripheral vision, but made adjustments, being more careful climbing stairs, becoming more organized so I could find things in my studio or the kitchen, turning on every light in the room, until even John, who's certainly not the least bit thrifty, began complaining about the electricity bills. It was about that time I began seeing bright halos, and stars."

"Like van Gogh."

"Exactly." She nodded, her smile like a gold star a teacher might hand out to a student who'd gotten all the answers correct. "Although my paintings always sold well, and people, if not always the critics, seemed to enjoy them, there were times during my career when I'd despair that I was lacking in van Gogh's or Monet's talent.

"I found it ironic that after years of devoting so much of my time to becoming a better painter, I finally had something in common with the genius who painted *Thatched Cottages at Cordeville* and all those glorious sunflowers. That's when I finally went to the doctor, and was diagnosed with glaucoma."

"I'm no expert, but I thought glaucoma was treatable." Ian seemed to recall Duncan's housekeeper talking about her husband recovering from eye surgery.

"It is, as a rule. But unfortunately I waited too long, and the eyedrops the doctor prescribed caused other side effects. After some time feeling horribly sorry for myself, I decided that since the diagnosis wasn't fatal, I'd just have to consider my impending blindness an opportunity to take a new direction in my life. Which has turned out quite well, actually. Not only have I discovered that insight can be stronger than sight, I doubt I'd ever have turned to sculpting if I hadn't gone blind."

"I believe you Yanks call that making lemonade out of lemons."

"Exactly."

"I'm impressed."

"Oh, please don't be. Since I've been so much more fortunate than many people, it's only fair that I receive a bit of rain with my sunshine." Her grin was quick and bright and reminded him of Lily. "I have to admit that the past year of tap-tap-tapping with a cane, and running into light poles and flower boxes on the street had begun to make me cross. That's when I finally decided it might be nice to have a dog that would steer me around things."

When she stroked the golden's head again, it wagged its tail in a wide sweep. "I'm already discovering that his companionship is even more special than his guide skills."

"Still, I doubt everyone would have your positive attitude." Duncan, for instance. "And if I do decide to stay on and make the film, I'll try to fit in time for a session. It'd be an honor to pose for you and I'm flattered you'd consider me model material."

"Dear boy, your face tells a world of stories. As for your body, well, surely you've been told it's magnificent." She sighed. "Since you've been so sweet and obliging, I must make a wee confession."

"What's that?"

"An excuse to go feeling up handsome men has turned out to be one of the up sides of losing my sight."

His surprised laugh drew the attention of guests seated at a nearby table. "It's always pleasing when someone lives up to their reputation."

"Oh, dear. So they're still telling the old stories back home, are they?"

"Most Scots, even those raised outside the Highlands, have heard tales of the quarrels between the MacDougalls and the Stewarts. The story of your elopement particularly intrigued me."

"The *scandal* of my elopement, you mean. That was a strange time," she murmured. She'd lived in America more than half a century, but Ian could still hear the heather and the moors in her voice. "Strange, and exciting. And, I've always felt, inevitable . . . Do you believe in fate, Mr. MacKenzie? Destiny?"

"I believe we all make our own fate and control our own destiny."

"Still, paths taken and not taken can often lead to that one place or decision when you no longer have a choice."

"Is that what happened to you?" he asked, curious.

"I believe fate played a huge hand in my

choosing my husband. I also accept your premise that I was a willing participant."

"Do you miss your home?"

"My home is here. I made that decision when I chose to marry an American."

The American she'd run off with just before her wedding to Duncan MacDougall. The thief who showed up hours before she exchanged vows, and convinced her to go to the States with him.

"Have you ever been back to Scotland?" Ian asked.

"No. I'd like to. I thought, after my dear James passed away, that I might. But although times change . . ." Her voice drifted off for a moment. "I'm not sure people do."

So she suspected, or knew, that the man she'd jilted would still be holding a grudge. And that reason alone, Ian considered, was evidence that she'd made the right decision.

Having made the decision not to let her heart get entangled with Ian's closely guarded one, Lily was still a bit disappointed when he directed every bit of his attention toward his work the following day.

There were times when she felt almost invisible, when every atom of his mind was working out the logistics of a potential shot. Doing all this intensive research and checking out the lighting and acoustics in seemingly every room of Stewart's Folly seemed like a great deal of trouble.

"So, what exactly do these Highland Games consist of?" he asked as she showed him around the meadow where most of the activity would be taking place.

"I'm surprised you don't know, being from the Highlands yourself."

"I told you, I didn't grow up there. Besides, just because I'm of Scots descent doesn't mean I'm an expert on all things Scottish."

"You know, I'm beginning to think I might have been wrong about not wanting you to film the games."

"How so?"

"Making this documentary could be a way to get in touch with your roots. To discover your feelings about being a Highland Scot in a civilized world, where raiding and hand-to-hand combat has given way to high-tech weapons."

"You've just managed to make the olden days sound far more civilized by comparison. The flaw in your idea is that I don't make documentaries to explore my views of the world."

Unlike many men in the arts community she'd met over the years, Ian had proven surprisingly reticent when it came to his life or work, which gave her the impression he was a man who cared little for fame or fortune.

"That's right. You're only interested in shining a spotlight on the world's inequalities." She remembered what he'd told her his first night at Stewart's Folly. "There's an anonymous quote we use to open the games," she said. " 'If

189

we dwell too much on the past, we neglect the present; if we ignore the past, we rob the future.' I suppose that could apply to what you do, as well."

"Those who forget the past are bound to repeat it," he agreed, thinking of how his grandfather had twisted the saying to continue the MacDougall–Stewart feud.

Ian was growing increasingly uneasy about lying to Lily. "Tell me about some of the events you've scheduled," he said.

She angled her head and gave him a look that suggested she knew he was dodging the topic, but wasn't quite sure why. "Well, when people think of the games, the tossing of the caber is usually the first thing that comes into their minds. But most Highland Games also have six other heavy events: the stone throw, the twenty-eight-pound weight throw, the fifty-six-pound weight throw and toss, the Scottish hammer toss, and the sheaf toss."

"What's the difference between a throw and a toss?"

"A throw's for distance and a toss is for heights. In Scotland the sheaf toss is considered a farming event rather than a heavy sport, and there's a movement among the professional athletes to remove it entirely from the competition. But spectators enjoy it, so it's going to remain in our Highland Games."

"This is looking more promising by the day," Ian said. "So far we've got a teenage girl who'd rather be a piper than a debutante, and stone throwers up in arms about burlap bags of wheat. Next you'll be telling me that the dancing judging is rigged."

"Oh, I don't even want to get into the dancing." She shook her head. "It's definitely the most controversial part of the games, and there've been times when people have argued for years about the outcome. But it draws the most attendance, so we wouldn't dare take it out."

"Scandal, conflict, controversy, and history. Sounds right up my alley."

"Now you're making fun of us."

"You're not exactly a peasant uprising, darling, but I'm beginning to find certain aspects of my visit to your burg more than a little appealing."

That was to be the only marginally personal thing he said to her all day.

He seemed interested, yet Lily was still having trouble understanding why he'd chosen to film the games. Highland Falls was nothing like any of the war-torn places he usually traveled and she seriously doubted that this project would earn him the same critical acclaim. Yet he was approaching it with the single-minded focus of the Joint Chiefs planning a military invasion.

"It's just as well," she told Annie later that night, as she watched her grandmother smooth fragrant cream into skin nearly as unlined as it had been when Lily was a little girl. "Getting involved with anyone right now is one more complication I don't need. It's best to keep things on a professional basis."

Annie arched a perfectly shaped white brow and lifted her head, as if to meet her gaze in the dressing-table mirror. Sometimes, even with Freedom lying at her feet, it was hard to remember her grandmother was blind. Especially now that he was officially "off duty" and wasn't wearing his harness, switching roles from guide dog to pet. "It's been my experience that we often regret the things we don't do, more than the things we do."

"Perhaps." From what she remembered of her grandparents' marriage, Lily was sure Annie had never regretted her elopement. She dipped her finger into the pink jar, lifted it to her nose, and inhaled a slight hint of mint. "This is new."

"Zelda added a bit of pennyroyal to the comfrey and witch hazel. You should try it. It's wonderful for your complexion and incredibly soothing. You've been sounding as if your nerves are a wee bit on edge lately." Her grandmother closed the lid and tucked the jar into Lily's hand. "And you changed the subject."

"There's nothing to discuss."

"Pity," Annie said.

To which Lily couldn't honestly disagree.

18

By the fifth day of Ian's stay, Lily doubted there was a corner in the castle she hadn't shown him, from his room in the tower to the wine cellar. And his questions about her family, the games, and the town seemed never-ending.

There were also those times when she'd felt him looking at her with the unsettling intensity of a predator. There was something building between them, something more complex than mere sexual attraction.

Lily sensed he was harboring secrets. But stranger still, she kept picking up on the feeling that he knew something about her. Something she didn't even know herself.

"I'm glad you're staying," she said with that openness he was becoming accustomed to.

He framed the tidy town, adorned with bright tartan banners and backdropped by rolling purple mountains, in his mind, shifted his gaze to the even more appealing sight of Lily's face, then skimmed the back of his fingers up her cheek, touching her for the first time in three very long and frustrating days.

"So you say now. If you knew what's good for you, you'd probably tell me to get lost."

"And explain to my family that I chased you away?"

"Sounds as if you're caught between a rock and a hard place." He looped his arms around her waist and drew her close enough that she could feel the hard place in question.

Her laugh was bright and pleased. "You're disgraceful."

"And you're lovely." He pulled back just enough to focus on her face. "Perhaps I'll switch gears and make a video about you."

"I can't imagine anyone being interested in me."

"I'm the expert. And I find you fascinating." It was one of the few truths he'd told her since arriving in the mountain town.

"And how would your film end? On a happy note, I hope?"

"That's the thing about documentaries. They tend to be open-ended. How would you like it to end? With the girl living happily ever after in her hometown, surrounded by the loving husband she's grown old with, passel of loving children, grandchildren, and great-grandchildren?"

"That's close, though I'm not certain how many children make up a passel. But I suspect most women picture themselves with a husband and family."

"And you have." It was not a question. She

194

was the most naturally nurturing woman he'd ever met.

"Of course I have. But wouldn't you need something more exciting to jazz up your film?"

"Such as?"

"How about the girl learning how to spin straw into gold? She then uses her newfound wealth to travel the world, doing good deeds for the less fortunate, then finally, when she's an old lady, she settles down back here in her homeplace — surrounded by those grandchildren and great-grandchildren you mentioned — where, in the final frame, she gazes out over the mountains and looks back on the world she's changed."

"That's a pretty hefty goal for one woman."

"And an impossible one, but everyone's entitled to a dream."

"Absolutely. Want to hear a few of my more recent ones?"

The glint in his eyes was sexy as hell, as tempting as the devil himself. It had been sprinkling rain on and off all morning and he was standing close enough to her that Lily could see the droplets of water sparkling like diamonds in his jet-black lashes.

"I think I'll pass." *Coward.* She took hold of his hand in a casual, friendly way meant to lighten the mood that was threatening to turn the misty air to steam. "There's something else I want to show you. Something special."

He laced his fingers with hers. "Lead on, MacDuff."

The waterfall was within a few minutes' walk of Stewart's Folly, but hidden so deeply in the woods that if Lily hadn't taken him to it, Ian doubted he would have ever found it.

The sight of the water rushing over moss-green rocks flowing into a clear blue pool, water reflecting from bank to bank, would have been arresting enough. The rhododendrons surrounding the pool gave the place the look of a secret garden.

"Not many people know about this spot," she said. "Zelda and Annie believe fairies live here."

"Now, why doesn't that surprise me? I suppose you believe in them, as well?"

"Of course." She smiled. "I've never seen any, but when I was younger, I'd sit here for hours, hoping to catch sight of them."

"Younger being . . . ?"

"Last year."

They both laughed, and for that fleeting moment, Ian felt the strain of the past few days ease.

"There really is magic here, though only a handful of people outside the family know of it. For a few nights the magic lights up the sky, like Brigadoon." She squeezed his hand. "It may just turn out to be the highlight of your visit."

"I don't suppose you're going to tell me what it is?"

"It's magic," she repeated. "And a surprise."

Like the woman herself, Ian thought.

They fell silent, comfortable in each other's

presence, content to merely sit on the bank of the blue pool while water skippers darted back and forth, the bugs' feet dimpling the surface tension of the water while silvery minnows darted beneath.

The misty air was what they'd call a soft day in Scotland; the mountainside was quiet, save for the birdsong threading through the trees. Ian looked out over the apple orchard they'd passed on the way up here, and beyond that, the dark evergreen smudges she'd said were a Christmas tree farm.

There was a grandeur in the shimmering green blanket stretching out as far as the eye could see, a patchwork quilt of green fields, rushing rivers, small towns, and unique family stories. Ian figured if those Hollywood types and international jet-setters who were always looking for a new in place to vacation were to stumble across Highland Falls, they'd abandon Wyoming's wide skies and France's Alps in droves.

He was surprised to feel an odd emotional connection to these hills. Having grown up in hotel rooms, he'd never thought much about roots. And the past fifteen years of roaming the world had added to his ability to remain disconnected. When you spent your life viewing human brutality through your viewfinder, it was wise to try to remain emotionally uninvolved.

"I suppose I can see why so many Scots settled here," he said.

"Scotland has always reminded me of home," she agreed. "Which isn't surprising, since during Mesozoic times, Scotland's Caledonide mountains were split by the formation of the Atlantic Ocean and became the Appalachians."

"Is that true?"

"I learned it in Mr. Parker's eighth-grade geology class," she confirmed. "The same serpentine in these mountains can be found in the west of Ireland today, then it extends back up through the Scottish Highlands." She leaned back on her elbows, savoring the dappled sunshine and the thought of the link between continents. "Just think how it must have been for the early settlers. They left a land they loved, traveled all the way across the sea, then continued searching for a place to settle, ultimately ending up in the same mountains they began in."

"I suppose you think it must have been like coming home." A feeling he'd never experienced.

"Exactly." She smiled her approval that he understood. "I also love that they're so old. The fact that my home is built on a two-hundred-million-year-old mountain doesn't just point to a long past, it suggests a long future. Which reminds me of something you might want to use in your film."

"What would that be?" he asked absently, his mind on the way her cotton T-shirt had pulled snugly over her breasts. Although he still hadn't gotten a glimpse of that photography display that had some of the citizens up in arms, Ian had been fantasizing about filming Lily in bed, clad — for a very brief time — in nothing but a smile and the royal Stewart tartan.

"A long time ago, before I was born, TVA — that's the government power agency around here — was going to buy Highland Falls."

"The entire town?"

"Lock, stock, and castle. They wanted to build a dam to provide cheap electricity for the expanding populations of the cities in both states. Needless to say, people were upset, but they tried to calm everyone's complaints with a fancy film about how flooding the town would create this wonderful lake for fishing and waterskiing."

"Which is just what all those people whose homes would be under water needed," he said dryly. "Obviously they failed."

"They did, indeed. But they hadn't counted on my aunt."

"That'd be Zelda," he guessed.

"You're partly right. Zelda got everyone riled up in the beginning, but Aunt Melanie went to Washington and turned on her charm — which you haven't seen yet, but believe me, no one can charm like a belle — on one of the best environmental lawyers in the country, and got him to take the case pro bono. Not only did he genuinely care about the issue and succumbed to my aunt Melanie's persuasion, but he also turned out to be a fan of Zelda's. I've always thought that was another reason he never charged any fee.

"Both aunts and my grandmother circulated petitions throughout three counties, and even my father left his studio long enough to collect signatures down at the Gothic Dragon pub."

"I thought everyone around here was of Scottish descent. Dragons tend to be Welsh."

"So are John and Hannah Rhys, who immigrated from Gwynedd. He's a former musicologist who came searching for a lost ballad. He never did find it, but they fell madly in love with the town, and stayed. It's an interesting story. You might want to put them in your film."

"Does it have anything to do with the games?"

"Everything in Highland Falls has to do with the games this time of year. Anyway, the plan was nipped in the bud and the dam was built farther downstream, where it wouldn't flood out any communities."

"Bravo for community involvement." There was no sarcasm in his tone.

"My aunts and my grandmother are like West Highland terriers with a bone. Once they get their teeth into something, they just won't let go." She picked up a leaf from the ground and began absently shredding it. "I love all three of them dearly, but it's Zelda who's been most like a mother to me. I honestly don't know what I would have done without her. She may not look it, but she's the most responsible person I've ever known and as steady as a rock.

200

"My father was devastated when my mother died after giving birth to me. I was born early, during a blizzard, which stranded them in the castle and kept the doctor from getting here. Since he could barely take care of himself on a good day, there was no way my father could handle a premature newborn and two toddlers. And my grandmother's career was demanding back then, so Zelda left Lexington, where she'd moved after she got married to her second husband, and came to live with us.

"Not trusting any of the Stewarts to rear us like proper ladies, Aunt Melanie showed up when I was three. She can be a challenge to get along with from time to time, but none of us have ever doubted that she loves us."

"You're fortunate to have family." Having been a loner for so many years, he'd forgotten what it felt like to receive unconditional love and support.

"I know." The warmth returned to light her eyes and banish the uncharacteristic sadness. "Growing up, I had two unwavering constants in my life: the mountains in the background and my family in the forefront."

He felt himself being pulled into those mermaid-green eyes, and even as he fought against it, felt himself becoming more and more drawn to her. And not just sexually. Oh, he still wanted to take her; even while she'd been telling the tale of her family saving Highland Falls, he'd been thinking about lowering her to the wildflower-sprinkled ground and losing himself deep inside her.

He wanted oblivion. He wanted to take her hard and fast until they were both damp, exhausted, and satiated. Then he wanted to do it all again, but slower this time, exploring every curve and hollow of her soft, feminine body with his hands, his mouth, his teeth, until she'd never be able to be with any other man without imaging his touch, his taste, his body claiming her for all time.

Now there was a dangerous, fanciful thought.

"We should probably be getting back."

"I suppose so." She didn't sound any more eager to leave this secret green spot than he was.

Dammit, he didn't need this. Not now. Not ever. He didn't need those big, soft-focused eyes looking up at him with such trust. Didn't need that soft, warm smile that seemed to light her up from the inside out. He didn't need to have his concentration constantly interrupted by her scent.

He didn't need to be constantly imagining tumbling her in the meadows he viewed every morning from his tower window, didn't need the continual pricks of conscience when he thought about his real reason for coming to Highland Falls.

And he damn well didn't need her.

Liar. The truth was that somehow, during the past five days, even as he'd been working overtime to ignore all the appealing things about

Lily Stewart, he'd somehow let his guard down. He felt as if he were standing on a rocky cliff, where a single misstep could send him over the edge.

Having never considered himself an emotional coward, Ian didn't like the feeling.

It was only lust, Lily reminded herself as she stared up into those mesmerizing eyes, which had warmed to a soft pewter. Unadulterated lust. The MacKenzie wasn't her destiny, as she'd so foolishly wished from time to time over the past days, he wasn't even a good candidate for any type of future.

She hadn't needed that sketchy *Biography* program to know that the man was unable or unwilling to settle anywhere for very long. He'd created a life which gave him the luxury of only taking on work that interested him, only going where he wanted to go.

Her first thought was that she and Ian might as well have come from different galaxies. The second, and far more surprising, was that she didn't just want Ian. She envied him.

"This could be a bad idea," he said, his words at odds with his wickedly seductive voice.

She didn't have to ask what he was talking about. "I know."

"But that doesn't stop me from wanting you."

"I want you, too." She trailed her hand down his face, feeling a sudden need to experience the scratchy roughness of his late-afternoon beard against her bare flesh.

"It would complicate things."

"And you're not a man who likes complications."

His harsh laugh lacked any humor. "Darling, if you only knew." He shook his head and closed his eyes.

When he finally looked at her again, in that hard, deep way he had that made her feel as if he were focusing on her through a close-up lens, his mood was typically unreadable. "I've got to leave."

Her stomach plummeted like a stone from the top of the waterfall into the blue pool, sending waves spreading throughout her body.

"Does that mean you've decided against making the film, after all?" she asked with a calm she was a very long way from feeling. She also knew she wasn't fooling him for a moment.

"No. I'll be making the film, but first I have a meeting with someone in New York."

"Oh." Lily knew she was in deep, deep trouble when the sudden mental photograph of Ian on the town with a sleek blond socialite, who possessed more sophistication in her French-manicured fingertip than Lily could summon up in a lifetime, caused something frighteningly like jealousy to stir deep inside her.

"Brady O'Neill is a soundman I've worked with a lot in the past. I need to convince him to sign on to this project, and I'll rent my camera and equipment while I'm there."

"You already have a camera." He'd shot at

least a mile of tape while she'd been playing tour guide.

"This is just a small one I carry around to decide on what I'm going to shoot. Buying a professional-quality one for the actual shoot isn't cost-effective. Technology's improving every day, so it makes more sense to rent what I need."

He'd never considered himself a romantic, but looking down at her, her hair misted with droplets that shone like diamonds on red silk, her eyes as soft and alluring as the mountain meadows, he was determined, whatever happened between them, to remember her like this forever.

"Damn."

"What's wrong?"

"I've been dreaming of you," he heard himself admit. "From that first night." Dreaming of tumbling her beside a waterfall just like this, dreaming of all the wicked, wonderful things he'd do to her. And all the things she'd do to him.

"Have you, now?" She obviously loved that idea; her face could have lit up the entire valley for a month of Sundays. "It's a sad imagination ye must have, Mr. MacKenzie," she said on a pretty fair Scots burr, "that you'd be dreaming of anything in me small life."

"Your life is far from small, Lily. In fact, I'm starting to wonder how anyone around here exists without you."

"I'm sure they'd do splendidly."

"Why don't you give it a try? Come away with me." He hadn't planned to invite her to New York, but now that he had, the suggestion sounded eminently logical.

Take Lily Stewart out of this stunning environment, plunk her down on the streets of Manhattan, and she'd be just another pretty woman in a city overrun with beautiful, sophisticated females. A weekend together would put not only Lily, but their entire relationship in perspective. Then, when they went to bed — and he had no doubt they would — there'd be no chance of confusing sex with anything more complicated.

"You can go shopping while I meet with Brady; afterward we'll have a ridiculously expensive dinner, take in a Broadway show, make mad passionate love in a feather bed —"

"If it's a feather bed you're wanting, we needn't go farther than the one in my apartment above the gallery."

"That's very appealing." The idea kicked his already rampant hormones into overdrive. "But I'll bet yours doesn't have a view of the Chrysler Building at night."

"No. But it does have a skylight and a view of the stars."

"You win." He couldn't think of anything more enjoyable than lying beside this woman in a soft down-filled bed, enjoying the cooling aftermath of passion while watching the glitter of stars wheeling in a midnight-black sky. "That's definitely something we'll have to try out when we get back." He skimmed the back of his hand down her throat in a slow, sensual sweep of a promise. "I've another thought."

"About me?"

"About you," he agreed. "During these past days you've demonstrated a great sense of how to tell a story, and you know so many of the games' participants. Perhaps we'll pick up a second camera while we're in New York, and you can shoot some video yourself."

"Lily Stewart, moviemaker." She laughed at that. It was also so, so tempting. "Don't they say that the devil comes tempting with a pretty face?"

"If a pretty face is one of the prerequisites, you should feel safe enough around me."

He didn't see it, Lily thought. The strength and raw beauty of his bones, the intensity of his gunmetal-gray eyes, the sensuality of his mouth, which could have appeared feminine in a face not so lived-in as his.

The man who'd been described as the Dark Prince of Documentaries was not cruel or uncaring; his sensitivity toward his subjects told her that. But feminine intuition told her that he could well end up hurting her before this was over.

Should she protect her heart? Or experience what could possibly be the most exciting few days of her life? If she had only herself to think of, she would have taken off with him in a New York minute. "I'd love to go with you, Ian."

His satisfied smile suggested he'd never expected any other outcome.

"But I can't," she added with very real regret.

The only sign of his irritation was a faint narrowing of those flinty eyes. "Your choice."

Lily blew out a frustrated breath. "There you go, getting all huffy again. I've already taken so much time to show you around, not that I'm complaining, but there's no way I can possibly leave now, just when people are starting to arrive." The two-lane road leading into Highland Falls had been clogged with traffic all day, and workmen were beginning to set up the clan tents around the edges of the meadow. "Then there's the damn wedding."

As if on cue, her cell phone rang. "It's my father's fiancée," she said as she looked down at the caller ID screen. "Again." Annoyed at the interruption, she punched Talk. "What is it now, Jenny?"

Ian stood up, making her all too aware of his height as he towered over her.

"No, I don't think it'd be a good idea for the guests to eat the wedding supper with their fingers," Lily said, praying for patience.

"I'll be leaving you to plan the nuptials," Ian said.

She covered the mouthpiece with her hand, feeling as frustrated as he looked. "Have a good trip."

"It'd be a helluva better one with you along." He looked down at her in that silent, brooding way that could melt her bones, then walked away.

"Yes, I know that's the way they did it in medieval times," Lily snapped into the phone. "You said you wanted a theme wedding, not a precise reenactment. You surely wouldn't want to prevent the guests from using indoor bathrooms, would you?

"Of course not," she echoed Jenny's response. "So believe me, they'll be grateful that you're providing silverware."

As Ian went around a corner, out of sight, a very strong part of Lily wanted to run after him.

19

Ian was taking a shortcut across a meadow when he heard the unmistakable sound of pipes. A moment later he came around a corner and there, in a wildflower-studded clearing, he saw the teenager who'd stormed into the gallery after that fight with her mother.

Today's T-shirt read BAGPIPES — HOW SWEET THE SOUND, and she was playing with an almost otherworldly concentration that kept her from noticing him.

She was a long way from being the best piper he'd ever heard. Which wasn't that surprising, since conventional wisdom said it took seven years and seven generations to master the instrument. She hit a particularly strident grace note, and broke into tears.

"Surely it's not as bad as all that."

She spun around, looking like a startled doe. "I didn't know anyone was out here."

"I was just getting the lay of the land for the film."

"Then you heard how ghastly I am."

"On the contrary, I thought you did rather well for a beginner." More lies.

"I'll never get that damn grace note right," she muttered. "Do you know how pipes work?"

"Not really. Other than knowing that a piper has to have strong lungs."

"You don't force the air in by blowing hard. You inflate the bag, then keep the air in it by breathing normally and play by applying pressure to the bag while breathing."

"Sounds a bit like walking and chewing gum."

"You're laughing at me." Her eyes filled up again.

"I wouldn't do that." He might be on the brink of becoming a thief, not to mention breaking a very special woman's heart, but even he had limits. "You still must have pretty good breathing control."

"I take a breath about every two seconds. A really good piper can take nearly sixty a minute. After a while you kind of get the hang of it, but it's the embellishments that are tricky." She frowned down at the instrument. "One of the hardest things is that once you get the air flowing, there's no way to stop it. It makes music even when all the chanter holes are closed, so you have to stick all these grace notes between the melody notes."

"It sounds extremely difficult."

"It is." She heaved a huge sigh. "If you were a boy, would you like a girl who could pipe?"

"That's never been a criterion in choosing a woman, and it probably wouldn't be enough by itself, even if I was a huge bagpipe afficionado," he answered honestly, suspecting she was hoping for a far different answer. "But admiration and liking go hand in hand, at least in my book, and I've always admired anyone who works hard to achieve something."

"I hadn't thought of it that way." She sounded encouraged by that idea. "My mother doesn't understand."

"There's probably always a difference in viewpoints between the generations, even more so, I've heard, between mothers and daughters. From what I could tell, she wants you to continue your family tradition, which is important to her."

She stuck out her lower lip. "It's not to me."

Ian wasn't about to put himself between a steel magnolia and an emotional teenage girl. "My grandfather plays the pipes," he said. "I believe he's competed as well, in games back in Scotland."

"Really? In a band? Or solo?"

"Solo."

"Ceol Beag? Or Ceol Mor?"

Ian could hear both Stewart and Duncan scoffing at his lack of knowledge. "I don't know. What's the difference?"

"Ceol Beag is what I play. What piping bands play. It's light music, marches, reels, hornpipes, jigs, that sort of thing. Ceol Mor is like classical music. It's also called *piobaireached*."

"That's it." He remembered hearing his mother mentioning the term on one of the rare

212

occasions she'd been reminiscing about her home.

"Wow." She looked at him as if he'd just turned into some sort of rock idol. "That's so cool. Ceol Beag can be played by other instruments, like fiddles, which is how the music stayed alive during the time the pipes were banned in Scotland. But there's no other instrument made that can play Ceol Mor." Her tears were gone now, her small, freckled face intense with interest.

"I didn't know that."

"Oh, it's true. Piobaireached goes back to the sixteen hundreds on the Isle of Skye," she said, warming to her subject. "The MacCrimmons had been pipers to the MacLeods since the fifteen hundreds and founded a school at Borreraig, which any piper who wanted to know how to play piobaireached had to attend. They had to learn to chant the melodies before they ever even picked up a pipe, because of course they didn't know anything about reading music in those days. There's a cairn there, to mark the very spot the school was on." She sighed and looked wistful. "I'd love to see it."

"Maybe someday you will," Ian said encouragingly.

"I intend to," she said with determination, and Ian suspected Melanie Lancaster's daughter could well match her in a battle of wills. "Does your grandfather still compete?"

"I don't know." He was starting to sound like

a broken record, making him uncomfortably aware of how little he knew of his roots.

"It'd be neat if he was coming to the games. Then you could introduce us."

If there was one thing Ian was sure of, it was that Duncan MacDougall would never set foot on Stewart ground. "Well, I'd best let you get back to your practice."

"I don't have much time. Jenny asked me this morning if I'd play for her wedding to my uncle John. I thought I'd pipe him in with 'Cock of the North.' "

"Sounds like a good choice."

"It's very masculine, which I thought he'd like. When you came by, I was working on 'Flower of Scotland.' Brad, he's this piper I know, said it'd be perfect for Jenny's processional. And I'm playing 'Scotland the Brave' for the recessional. Fortunately, I already have that one memorized."

"That's always a favorite." And probably the one Celtic tune most identified with the pipes, since even he knew it.

She smiled up at him and in that fleeting moment he saw a touch of Lily in her, which gave a hint of the appealing woman she'd become. "Thank you for making me feel better and for telling me about your grandfather. He must be a very impressive man."

"I suppose that's one way of putting it," Ian said dryly. "Good luck."

"Thanks. I'm going to need it."

The sad sound of the pipes drifted over the hilltops, following him as he went back to the house, the grace notes floating on the air. He might not be able to teach the girl how to pipe well enough to win the competition, but there was one little problem he thought he might be able to help with.

"What makes you think you have any right to interfere between a mother and daughter?" Melanie Lancaster demanded after he'd sought her out and suggested she rethink her insistence about dragging her daughter away from the games.

"I don't mean to interfere. I just know from experience that you could be risking a schism you'll regret later."

She put her fists on her hips. "I hadn't realized you had a teenage child."

"I don't. But I *was* a teenage boy who grew up without knowing his grandfather because of a rift between my mother and her father. My grandfather's a stubborn man, who always had to be in the right. Unfortunately, she died before they had time to overcome their problems. I hate to see anyone else risking such regret."

"I'm sorry about your mother. But neither Missy nor I are going to die anytime soon."

"That's undoubtedly what my mother thought."

She paled a bit at that.

"It's only a dance," he said. "Perhaps more

important to your family because of your long family tradition, but with all the dangers in the world that kids can get involved with these days, I'd say wanting to play the bagpipes is a fairly small offense."

"I don't know." Somehow she managed to frown without wrinkling her smooth brow. "I'll have to think about it."

"Why don't you do that?" he suggested agreeably.

Duncan, unsurprisingly, did not prove as amenable to suggestion as Melanie Lancaster.

"What do you mean, you're going to New York?" he demanded when Ian called him to tell him about the trip.

"Exactly that. There's no way I can continue to stay here without the Stewarts beginning to get suspicious, if I don't make the bloody film. In order to do that, I'll need a crew."

"Do you intend to be making me pay for this trip?"

"Don't be such a bloody cheapskate. This was your damn idea," Ian reminded him.

"I sent ye to find the brooch and bring it back home, where it belongs. Which is going to be difficult to do when ye're off traipsing around New York City."

"I'm not going to be traipsing, I'll be working. Besides, as I keep pointing out, you don't have a shred of proof the brooch is even here."

"It's got to be there. The Stewart lass stole it."

It was getting to be an old tune, one Ian was damn tired of. "No." About this, he'd become sure. "She's no thief." She was also the only person he'd ever met in his life who didn't appear to have some personal ulterior agenda.

"Women have wily ways."

"Not Lily Stewart. With her, what you see is what you get."

"And what you see is bonny?"

"Very. But it's been a long time since I did my thinking with my glands. I'm not about to be distracted by a pretty face and long legs." He *was* distracted, though. By a lot more than Lily's legs and face.

"There's no' a man with blood stirring in his loins who isn't attracted to a pretty face and long legs. Have you bedded the lass yet?"

"That's none of your bloody business."

There was a pause on the other end of the line. "You haven't," Duncan decided, "or you wouldn't be so out of sorts. Make love to the girl, laddie. Bring up the brooch while you're sharing a little pillow talk. See what she says once you've gotten her guard down with some good sex."

"Since I can't punch you out for that suggestion, I'm going to hang up now. I'll be back in a couple days. Just maybe, if I've cooled down by then, I'll call and fill you in on the trip."

He pressed the End button on the cell phone with more force than necessary, missing the satisfaction of slamming down a receiver in the old bastard's ear.

Deciding that it would do him good to get back to the real world, Ian began packing and had just finished when someone knocked. He didn't need that insight Annie had mentioned, or the second sight Zelda claimed to possess, to know that it was Lily.

"I was talking with Missy earlier," she said when he opened the door. "She told me you were very encouraging about her piping, which was very nice of you."

"You obviously weren't paying attention during that *Biography* show or you'd realize that the Dark Prince is never nice."

"I think that's a ridiculous description, probably made up by people who are jealous of your talent or angry at the work you do."

"Did you come here to talk about your cousin?"

"No. Well, in a way. I wanted to thank you, but mostly I wanted to say goodbye and wish you a good trip, in private."

She stepped across the threshold.

Ian kicked the door shut, cupped a hand on the nape of her neck, then, prepared for the punch this time, he lowered his mouth to hers.

Her sigh feathered against his lips. She wrapped her arms around his waist and leaned into the kiss, inviting him to deepen it. Which he did. Which only had him wanting more.

What was a man to do when response was so sweet? So open? So utterly giving?

To keep his hands — and the rest of his body

— out of trouble, he framed her face between his palms and felt her skin heat to the touch. As she sank willingly, eagerly, deeper into the kiss, Ian could feel himself sinking into quicksand.

He could have her. Here, now, naked and bucking beneath him on that high bed. So what if he missed the plane? There'd be others. And he could handle his business with Brady over the phone; the only reason for going to New York was to distance himself from this increasingly sticky situation.

"Amazing," she murmured as she went up on her toes and twined her bare arms around his neck.

"What's amazing?" When he slipped his tongue between her lips, her breath caught. She released it in a soft, ragged moan that nearly stripped away the last of his tautly held restraint.

"Every time I almost convince myself that I've exaggerated the way you made me feel, you kiss me again." If she got any closer against him, she'd be inside his shirt. "It's as if you set off fireworks inside me." Her head fell back, inviting more.

Which he hungrily took. But even as his mouth roamed down her throat, conflicts raged within Ian. Part of him wanted to just pull her to the faded needlepoint rug and quench the fires burning inside him, consequences be damned. But another, stronger part, tugged at the conscience that was growing more vexing by the day.

When his lips returned to hers, his mouth crushing hers in a burst of hunger, she trembled. Or perhaps he did. And because he couldn't be sure, he forced himself to back away yet again.

"Just give me a moment." He rested his forehead against hers, waiting for his blood to cool and his heartbeat to return to something resembling normal. "I keep thinking I'm ready for this." He took a deep breath. "But, dammit, I'm not."

"Don't worry about it." Her voice caught as she pressed her hands against his chest to sever the still close contact between them. "I understand; you don't have to explain. After all, a man has the right to change his mind —"

"Is that what you're thinking?" Christ, could he screw things up any worse?

He snagged her slender wrist and pressed her hand against the front of his jeans, realizing he'd made another tactical error when his erection strained even more painfully against the zipper. "Does this feel as if I've changed my mind about wanting you?"

"Not really."

He had to grit his teeth when her fingers stroked him in erotic exploration.

"Of course I want you, with every fiber of my being. So much that I can't stand it. But the timing's wrong. And not because of my trip, which I'd just as soon cancel to spend the time in bed with you. But there's something that needs to be said first."

There was no way he could sleep with Lily without telling her the truth about his reason for being here. She'd probably be furious with him at first, but because of her warm and generous heart, she'd undoubtedly forgive him. Then he could set about driving them both crazy in that feather bed he'd spent too much of the afternoon fantasizing about.

"I don't need the pretty words, Ian. I understand this would just be a brief Highland fling while you're here in Highland Falls." He wouldn't have thought he could feel any lower, until she managed a brave smile obviously meant to reassure him.

"It's more than a fling. I don't know what the hell it's going to turn out to be, but I've had enough affairs to know this is different. Which is another thing we're going to have to talk about. When I get back."

"All right."

"I've got to get going, if I'm going to make it down the mountain in time to catch my flight." Needing one last taste, he kissed her again, long and deep. "Keep that thought."

20

Major Campbell of Bragleen was dead. He'd been piped to his heavenly reward only hours earlier during a drenching rain, and now stories of his exploits — many true, equally as many exaggerated — were being exchanged by clan members in the drawing room. Wanting a bit of privacy to read the letter the major's solicitor had given him, General Duncan Campbell of Lochnell, trustee of the major's estate, escaped to the library.

The letter was brief and to the point, directing the general to a locked chest that had been sitting in the corner of the room beside the statue of The Bruce for as long as the general had been visiting Bragleen House.

Unfortunately, the note didn't mention where he would find the key. Fortunately, all the moist sea air and rain had rusted the lock, making it relatively easy to pry open with a letter opener.

"Bloody hell." The general didn't need to read the papers in the chest to know what he was looking at. The silver Brooch of Lorn, with its crystal center surrounded by pearls, was not just a vivid part of Scottish history, taught in every classroom across the country. It was part of his own Campbell clan's history as well, having supposedly disappeared after it had been taken in a raid on Gylen Castle two centuries ago.

The general's knees were shaking and his hands trembling as he poured a glass of the major's single malt Oban whisky. The whisky warmed his mouth and burned his throat, leaving behind a hint of peat and the taste of the sea from the salt water used in the distilling.

After tossing back the first glass, he poured a second, and sat down in the big leather chair behind the desk. Whisky in one hand, the brooch, which seemed to be warming his palm, in the other, he pondered his options beneath the unblinking marble eyes of the stag heads hung on the walls by previous Campbells. The gale blowing in from the icy Atlantic moaned down the chimney like a funeral dirge by a chorus of lost souls, and turned the rain to sleet that slashed wickedly at the tall leaded windows.

A pale white moon had risen high in the night sky and the whisky was a great deal lower in the decanter by the time the general made his decision. There was only one honorable thing to do and the general was, indeed, an honorable man. He'd return the treasure to its rightful owner: clan chief of the MacDougalls.

21

Zelda and Melanie were harvesting herbs when Ian drove the rental car past the raised beds and down the long driveway away from Stewart's Folly.

"So, what do you think?" Zelda asked as she cut some southernwood. The bark would provide just the right color dye she needed for the bridesmaids' dresses, and the feathery leaves always added a soothing fragrance to a bath.

"About what?"

"Lily and her Highland hunk, of course. Snip a few of those lemon balm leaves, and I'll make you some tea to calm your nerves."

"What I need is a magic potion that will turn my daughter back into the sweet, agreeable little girl she used to be," Melanie muttered, but did as instructed. "And I think Lily's asking for trouble."

"Probably." Zelda grinned wickedly as she moved on to the balsam-scented clary she planned to include in the potpourri she placed in all the guest rooms. "But life with the man certainly wouldn't be boring." She added the light blue flowers to her basket.

"Life?" Melanie shook her head. "The longest a woman could count on a man like Ian Mac-Kenzie staying around would be a few days. The fact that he's chosen a career that takes him all over the world proves that he's got wanderlust in his veins."

"Perhaps he's ready to settle down."

Melanie scoffed at that idea. "Surely you don't believe that?"

"No." Zelda didn't often see eye to eye with Lily's other aunt, but about this, she had to agree. "But perhaps that's not such a bad thing," she mused. "After all, Lily's a young woman. She should be spreading her wings."

Like her mother, Zelda certainly had explored life to the fullest when she'd been Lily's age and didn't regret a single moment. Her experiences, both good and bad, were what had made her the strong, independent woman she was.

"She already spread her wings by going to Europe."

"And might still be there, if John Angus hadn't skied into that damn tree. But it's been three years. He's producing well, fell in love, and is about to get married. It's time Lily got back to living her own life."

"She has her business. She's made her little shop quite successful."

"It's a lovely gallery, which could hold its own with those in much larger cities. But she needs more excitement in her life. And I think Ian MacKenzie exactly fits the bill."

"He'd be a problem," Melanie warned as she bent to trim some flower stalks emerging from the curly green leaves of a border of parsley. "The man has trouble written all over him."

"You're just angry because you think Missy's refusing to make her debut to be in the film."

"I think he's a very large part of my problem." Melanie wasn't prepared to discuss her conversation with the filmmaker. Especially since she was beginning to fear he might be right. "But putting Missy aside, Lily would be better off, and safer, with Donald."

"Safer perhaps," Zelda allowed. "But better off? I'm not so certain. Forget you're her aunt who wants to protect her, for a moment. Which man would you pick, if given a choice? The MacKenzie, or that obsessive, uptight banker who only cares about his damn Forbes family history?"

"Donald isn't uptight. Merely serious."

"Seriously obsessive," Zelda shot back. "So are you saying you'd actually choose him over that Scots hunk?"

"No. There's no question." Melanie sighed. "Since we're merely talking rhetorically, I'd choose the Scot, of course. *If* I were merely looking for a hot brief affair. If I were seeking a long-term commitment and reliability, not to mention a family, I'd choose the banker."

"There's nothing to prevent her from having a family with the MacKenzie. He has the looks of a strong breeder."

"Zelda Stewart!" Melanie glanced around the herb garden, as if afraid someone might have overheard. "You're talking about him as if he's a bull."

"From the package he's carrying in those tight jeans, I'll bet dollars to Krispy Kremes that he's built like one."

Melanie tsk-tsked, but from the color that touched her high cheekbones, Zelda knew that while she'd noticed the MacKenzie's attributes, she'd probably throw herself off the mountain before admitting it.

"Oh, to get that delicious Scotsman in a kilt," Zelda said on a long sigh.

"I think you've been writing those books too long. You have sex on the brain."

"It's been too long since you've had a man in your bed if you've forgotten that sex *is* mostly in the brain. However" — Zelda's grin was quick and wicked as sin — "it's always a helluva lot better when the other parts are involved, as well."

"He'd look terrific in a kilt," Melanie allowed. Her eyes took on a faraway look. "He definitely has the look of a warrior. He'd probably be an exciting lover, but I still can't see him being monogamous."

"Just because that weasel you made the mistake of marrying dumped you, you shouldn't paint every male with the same broad brush." The lavender, which would soon be made into pretty bars of guest soap, was beginning to bloom. "The MacKenzie's a Scot, which means he's stubborn. Which suggests he's a sticker."

"Then why isn't he married?"

"Perhaps because he hasn't found the right girl."

"What makes you think our Lily is the right girl?"

"They have chemistry together. If she ends up with Donald, Lily will die of boredom before they reach their first-week anniversary."

"She could have her heart broken if she chooses the other one."

"Perhaps." It was Zelda's turn to frown as she considered the possibilities. "But she'll have had an experience most women could only dream about."

Like everything else, the trip to New York didn't go as planned. Oh, it hadn't taken much talking to convince Brady to come to Tennessee and film the Highland Games. They'd shaken hands over that deal before the bartender, at a Celtic restaurant frequented by CNN news-people, had built the second round of Guinness. While the place was more upscale than your usual Irish pub, the Gothic chandeliers, stained glass, rich wood paneling, and exposed brick all came together to create a comfortable, friendly atmosphere to do business or have a drink at the end of the workday.

"Throw some dirt over me, boys," Brady all but moaned around a thick, juicy burger covered in melted Ballycashel Irish cheddar cheese, "and bury me a happy man, because I've died and gone to heaven. After two weeks in Tibet, I began craving a cheeseburger. Another week, and I was having hot dreams about them instead of women. How pitiful is that?"

"Pitiful, indeed," Ian agreed, thinking of the woman who'd been infiltrating his own dreams.

If he'd thought putting some distance between them would ease the ache, he'd been wrong. When a blond woman foreign correspondent he vaguely recognized slanted him a come-hither smile from the long wood bar, he could only compare her smile to Lily's, and find it wanting in wattage. And when the comely Irish waitress delivered their dinners, all Ian could think about was that her dark auburn hair lacked the bright lights that made Lily's strawberry-blond hair look like flames shot with gold.

"So what's this Highland Falls like?" Brady asked.

"I suppose it's your usual provincial small town, where everyone minds everyone else's business, but the people are friendly and the setting is spectacular. And I have to admit, the castle is impressive."

"A real castle?" Brady rolled his eyes in pleasure as he finished off the final French fry dripping ketchup.

"Oh, it's real enough, down to the arrow slits. Lily Stewart, who's been giving me a tour of the place, says it was mostly modeled after Stirling Castle."

"Where William Wallace defeated the British at the battle of Stirling Bridge, which brought Edward back from France to eventually bring Scotland under British rule."

"It seems everyone but me is an expert on Scottish history lately," Ian muttered.

"Hey, I've seen *Braveheart*. So are these Stewarts descended from the royal Scots Stuarts?"

"So they claim." If Duncan was correct about the brooch, there was a good chance the heritage part was true, too. "Along with probably every Scot American in this bloody country."

The sharp edge of his tone had Brady cocking his head. "Sounds as if this film of yours isn't going to be all fun and games."

"The Scots diaspora has been made into a thing of myth that still has people believing they're fighting for 'the cause.' In many ways, partly because of these games, these mountain communities have become more Scottish than Scotland — while completely ignoring the role those clan chiefs played as landlords, removing clansfolk from their lands. Men who were described as petty tyrants at the time have been raised to honored stature."

"They're just games, Ian," Brady said mildly. "A chance for people to come together, feel a sense of connection to something larger than themselves, sing some old songs, wisely eat barbecue instead of haggis, and have fun."

"What about the truth?" Ian demanded. "Are we drawing moral lines here? Is it your point that it's wrong to rewrite history after you've terrorized your own people and won a war, which we both know continues to happen all around the world every day, but it's okay to twist reality in the name of fun and games?"

"No. It's my point that you might, perhaps, be taking this all too seriously. Granted, there are those who might consider you the George Washington of the documentary business —"

"What the hell do you mean by that?"

"While I'm all for truth and justice, there are times when it's crossed my mind — and others' — that anyone who insists on the truth, the whole truth, and nothing but the truth all the time, can be a pain in the ass. You know, there's an old saying I heard from a gaffer I worked with in Glasgow — that it takes a surgical operation to get jokes into a Scotsman's understanding. The same might be said for fun."

Ian let out a long breath. "Shit. You're right." He *had* gotten carried away. Because that insistence on clinging to the past had put him in the middle of a bloody clan feud he'd wanted no part of. One that had turned him into not only a liar, but worse, a hypocrite.

"Well, that may be a first, you backing down from an argument so fast." Brady's deep baritone laugh rolled over the wood-paneled room.

"What do you say we revisit a little personal history of our own? Remember the first time we were in this city together?"

They'd just come off a month documenting a civil war in Rwanda. The four weeks of witnessing the brutality humans could do to one another — and worse, to innocent children — had been the worst period of his life. Even darker and more depressing than when his parents had died.

"Sure. We drank our way through the town, and I got so guttered, the next morning my head felt like a ripe melon that had been dropped off the top of the Empire State Building." The rest of him hadn't felt much better.

"We'll take it slower this time," Brady said, pushing his chair back from the table. "Pace ourselves."

"You're on," Ian said, willing to try anything to block his growing belief that he'd now gotten himself in so deep, there was no way to keep the problem from blowing up in his face.

22

Pacing themselves hadn't prevented the inevitable, of course. All it did was stretch out the length of time it took to get as drunk as a piper. The bitch of it was, Ian thought as he gingerly leaned his aching head against the back of the first class seat of the southbound Delta jet, trying to drown thoughts of Lily in whisky hadn't worked.

She had followed him from pub to pub across the island of Manhattan; then, sultry as a siren, she'd slipped into his sleep, teasing, tantalizing, tormenting him so badly that when the automatic wake-up call shattered a particularly hot dream where he'd been making love to her in that sparkling pool beneath Firefly Falls, his head hadn't been the only part of his body throbbing.

He was going to have to tell her the truth, he'd decided around two in the morning. By two in the afternoon, as he was sitting in the Atlanta terminal, waiting for a connecting flight to Asheville, the continual flight announcements pounding in his brain like a hammer against stone, he still hadn't been able to find a way out of it.

He wanted her. More than he wanted to take his next breath. But while he'd never thought of himself as a particularly considerate man, neither was he the kind of person who'd purposely hurt someone. Which is what would happen if he took advantage of her trusting nature and took her to bed without telling her the truth.

Later that afternoon, as he drove through the green mountains to Highland Falls, he was forced to consider there was always the chance that once he told her, she'd want nothing more to do with him.

It was a chance he'd just have to take.

So much for out of sight, out of mind. Lily hadn't been able to stop thinking of Ian. Not while she'd been planning the wedding dinner menu with Jenny, not while she'd been waiting on the seemingly endless stream of tourists in clan plaids who'd descended on the gallery. And especially not that night, as she'd tossed and turned in a bed that was unbearably lonely.

She was folding a display of Jacobite shirts at the end of the day when the gallery door bells jangled. She didn't have to turn around to know who it was; there was only one person who could make the air around her crackle with electricity, like before a summer mountain thunderstorm.

She turned slowly and knew that she wasn't alone in sensing the charged atmosphere.

"Welcome back." Her breath quickened. It was all she could do not to run across the room and throw herself into his arms. "I hadn't expected you back so soon."

"It didn't take long to take care of business."

"Did you get your soundman and your cameras? I was thinking last night that you might call, but —"

She shut her runaway mouth. Even Missy, at her most teenage-girl-in-love fretful, could not have sounded more pitiful.

"I was out getting drunk."

"Oh." He seemed angry, which she supposed made sense, since he was undoubtedly suffering a hangover. But she wasn't the one who'd poured the alcohol down his throat.

"Sometime during Brady's and my pub crawl, we decided it'd be a good idea to get laid."

That's what she got for wanting a man who'd be honest with her. "Well, I hope you had a lovely time, not that there's any need to be sharing the details with me."

Having never experienced this level of jealousy, Lily was surprised to discover it had sharp and painful claws. She smoothed the stack of white cotton shirts and, with unsteady hands, began rearranging a display of Caithness glass paperweights.

"There's no details to share, since I couldn't do it."

"I've heard alcohol causes problems in that

regard." She resisted the urge to throw a green paperweight at his head, which she hoped was pounding to beat the band.

"It wasn't that. It was you."

"You're blaming me for your inability to have sex with some strange woman?"

"No. I'm blaming myself for getting so hung up on you that I can't even imagine wanting to be with anyone else. You've been haunting my mind since I walked into Stewart's bloody Folly. Day in, day out, there you are, front and center, crowding out whatever I'm trying to think about. And I don't even want to talk about my wicked nighttime thoughts.

"You've been like a ghost, following me every-where, so in the midst of an alcohol fog, I de-cided the best way to exorcise you would be to take some other woman to bed. But even that didn't work."

His voice was rough, harsh. It made her shiver, fear twisting with excitement. "Should I be sorry you couldn't perform?"

He looked shocked by that suggestion. Shocked and furious. And dangerous.

"I've never, ever had a problem in that re-gard." He raked a wide hand through his jet-black hair. Heat flashed in his eyes; a whip of barely leashed temper snapped in his voice. "It didn't work because though there are millions of women in New York City, I didn't want to take a single one of them to bed. Because the only woman who'd satisfy this deep and abiding hunger I've been suffering, in every bloody damn atom of my body, is you."

"Well." It was difficult to speak when your heart was in your throat. "Perhaps we should do something about that."

"What a coincidence." His eyes stayed on hers as he turned the sign with its Celtic border from Open to Closed. "Since that's exactly what I've been thinking all the way back here." He twisted the lock.

"There's still five minutes to go before closing."

"Too bad." He crossed the small room, his steps long and determined, and braceleted her wrists with his long fingers. "If anyone shows up wanting something, they'll just have to come by again tomorrow. If you're even out of bed to open the store by then."

"Goodness." Emotions were battling at her, causing her blood to hum hot and thick in her veins. "And don't you have a high opinion of yourself, Mr. MacKenzie?"

"No." His hands moved up her bare arms, leaving a trail of sparks. "It's confidence." She drew in a sharp breath of anticipation as his thumbs brushed against the sides of her breasts. "In myself." He moved in closer, his body brushing hers. "In you." He lowered his head, so close his features blurred. Lily's heart took an expectant hitch. "In how the two of us will be together."

He paused for a heartbeat. Not in hesitation,

Lily knew, but to give her the chance to change her mind.

"Show me," she dared.

She'd no sooner gotten the words out than he lifted her up onto her toes, pulled her against him, then took her mouth, dragging her into the storm.

It was exactly as she'd dreamed about. Hot, hungry, almost heathen. One hand tangled in her hair, dragging her head back, the other jerked her T-shirt up and closed roughly over her breast.

When he caught the lobe of her ear between his teeth, Lily gasped, the need jolting through her so fast it burned, causing her to drop one of the paperweights.

Somewhere through her roaring senses she heard the sound of a horn, merely a friendly beep to another passing car, but enough to remind her where they were.

"The windows," she managed to say as his possessive, clever hands yanked her shirt over her head. "Anyone walking by . . . Oh, God," she moaned as his lips scorched across the white cotton bra, which had to be the least sexy piece of clothing she owned.

He swung her into his arms. "Where are the stairs to your room?" he asked against her mouth.

"Back there." She waved vaguely toward the back of the gallery.

One more bloody thing that wasn't going to

plan. Ian had planned to seduce her slowly, sensually. He'd intended to take his time, to do things right, to be the kind of tender lover she'd remember decades from now. When she was a little old lady, looking back on her life, he wanted to be a highlight. Hell, he admitted as he reached the landing, he wanted to be the star, the man who'd ruin her for any other man.

Frustration and pent-up hunger made his mouth devour hers rather than sip gently. Passion raked at him, claws vicious, digging deep and hard, making him feel that if he didn't finally take her, here and now, he'd shatter like that piece of glass she'd dropped on the gallery floor.

"Dammit, I don't want to wait another minute. I want you." He bit at her bottom lip and felt her shudder. "Here." Because the second set of stairs looked like Mount Everest and his need was so great, he dragged her down onto the plush carpet runner abloom with sunflowers, and made short work of her bra. "Now."

"Oh, yes." Her hands were on his chest, her fingers fumbling with the buttons. "Ian. I want . . . I need . . . to touch you, like you're touching me, but I can't —"

"Rip it." He yanked at the snap at the waist of her jeans, his own fingers as impatient as hers as he dragged the denim down her legs.

"Yes." She tugged the edges of the white linen shirt he'd picked up on a trip to Dublin, sending buttons flying.

His flesh burned as she pressed her open mouth against his chest. When her roving hands went to his waist, he knew if he let her touch him now, he'd explode like the horny teenager he'd been before Nora had taught him the art of control. A control he never seemed to be able to grasp when he was with this woman.

"No." He caught both her wrists in one hand as he ripped away her panties — white cotton that matched that tidy, practical little bra — with the other. "First I'll have you, Lily Stewart, like I've wanted you from the beginning."

She was hot, wet, and his. Ian watched her eyes go opaque as he plunged his fingers into her. He swallowed her cry as she came quickly, with a shudder that ripped through her.

"More." Still holding her captive, he slid his mouth down her body, fastened onto the hot heart of her, and ruthlessly drove her up again. He felt her pause for a fleeting instant on the brink; her smooth-as-silk thighs rigid, every atom in her body poised for release. Then he gently closed his teeth down, making her scream as she went plummeting over the edge.

Her body went lax and she felt like warm honey in his hands as he shaped the slender curves with his palms, tasted fiery flesh, savored the musky scent of sex that filled the stairwell.

He'd released her wrists after her second climax, and now her impatient hands stroked across his shoulders, down his slick heated back, her fingers dipping beneath the waistband of his jeans. Together they yanked them down his legs, where they got tangled up in the damn cowboy boots he'd thought were such a frigging good idea when he'd bought them in Texas last year.

Lily was frantic, greedy, near weeping as she struggled to pull them the rest of the way down, but Ian was beyond caring. Beyond waiting.

"Forget about them. Put your legs around me."

She didn't hesitate and wrapped her long legs around his hips in a vise grip.

There was no thought of control now as he thrust into her, hot and hard and as ready as he'd ever been. Her back bowed as she arched upward, meeting him in a frenzy of speed, stroke for stroke, hot flesh slapping against hot flesh.

His vision hazed; it was like looking at her through a fog lens, but not so blurry that he couldn't see the way passion had darkened her mermaid eyes to a blazing emerald green. "Look at me."

"As if I'd want to look anywhere else," she said, as breathless as he.

Although it took every ounce of his self-control, he began to slowly pull out. A sound somewhere between a sob and a whimper escaped her; her legs gripped his hips harder as her inner muscles tightened around him greedily.

Gritting his teeth, he paused, holding them both at the precipice. Then, with something akin to pain ripping through him, he thrust back into her, hard and deep, all the way to the hilt. It was like plunging into the heart of the sun. She cried out his name and clung to him as the explosion ripped through them, surrounding them in a blinding blaze of heat and light.

"Are we still alive?" she asked sometime later.

"I don't know." He dragged his mouth from the hollow of her throat and laid his cheek against her breast. "Your heart's still beating." He touched his lips to her silky smooth skin.

"Well, that's a relief. Do you think the town survived the blast?"

"I have no idea." Nor did he care. All he could think about was that he wanted her again. And again. All night long. "It might be lying in rubble."

"I wouldn't be surprised." She stroked his back with a touch as light as thistledown. "Perhaps we should check for survivors."

"I'd rather take you the rest of the way upstairs and do this again. In a proper bed."

She threaded her fingers through his hair, lifted his head, and touched her lips to his. "We'll check later."

He drank deeply, feeling the desire rise again inside her, inside him. "Much, much later," he agreed.

As they struggled to extricate him from the jeans and boots, Ian tried to think of the last time he'd laughed after making love, and came up blank. Perhaps Brady was right about him taking things too seriously.

"Do you find me grim?" he asked as he carried her over the threshold into a room painted the deep color of a Tuscan sunset. The richly romantic shade suited her, he decided, although only an hour ago he would have assumed she would have chosen a sunshine yellow or apricot.

"No," she said quickly. Too quickly, he thought, as he pulled back a ruby and gold satin comforter and laid her on the bed. "You can be serious, which only makes sense, given your work. And you're intense. But there are times when intense can be good." She lifted a hand to his face when he sat down beside her. "Like a few minutes ago."

In a gesture totally unlike him, he caught hold of that slender hand and pressed a kiss against each fingertip, then into her palm. "We need to talk."

He'd come to the gallery planning to invite her out to dinner. It would be their first date, and it had dawned on him that perhaps he ought to do a bit of wining and dining before he told her the truth about why he'd come to Highland Falls. He earned his living telling stories, and had been practicing his lines all the way up the mountain, clever words that would show her the humor in an old man using emotional blackmail to send his grandson on a quest to America.

They'd laugh over the fact that he could have ever thought her to be a thief. He wouldn't ask about the coincidence of the brooch disappearing from Scotland the same time she was visiting the country, because he honestly didn't care what had happened to it. If he could have thrown the bloody damn thing in Lake Ness to be swallowed by the monster, he would have done it in a heartbeat. Then, his confession over, his conscience cleansed, he'd planned to make love to her. All night long.

"All we've been doing for days is talking," she said. She twined her arms around his neck, pulled him down beside her, then rolled over so she was lying on top of him. "We can talk tomorrow. Right now I just want your body."

He might be a liar, but he wasn't an idiot. As she began to trail stinging hot kisses across his chest, Ian decided there was nothing to gain by ruining the moment.

That decided, he surrendered to the moment. To her.

23

"Oh, my God!"

Ian was jerked from sleep by the sudden feminine cry. He first thought that Lily had cried out, but she was still curled up beside him.

"Lark?" Lily blinked into the bright light that had been turned on. When they'd drifted off, the bedroom had been filled with the soft lavender light of dusk.

"I'm sorry." Color rose in Lark Stewart's cheeks. "When you weren't in the shop I figured you'd gone home, so I decided to come up here and unpack and take a bath, then call you to get together for dinner." She slid a quick glance toward Ian, who managed a forced smile while he hoped the sheet was higher than it felt. "I'm so sorry."

"You've nothing to apologize for," Lily reassured her as she tugged the sheet up and held it against her breasts. "I'm the one who invited you to stay here, after all. I just wasn't expecting you for a couple more days."

"It was a spur-of-the-moment thing." Ian, who'd learned to listen to nuances, suspected she was holding something back. No doubt something personal and sisterly she didn't want to share with a stranger. "I suppose that's one of the few good things about not having to make reservations."

"Lark just bought her own corporate plane," Lily said proudly.

"Nice," Ian said.

"I suppose so — although I prefer the bus. I've always been a white-knuckle flyer, and this ten-seater reminds me of something Fergus Graham would have built in his garage."

"Fergus is a local inventor," Lily explained. "He invented a car engine that ran on moonshine. He sold his patent to General Motors a few years ago, and last I heard, he was working on something that allows NASCAR cars to lift into the air and fly over crashes."

"Now there's a concept," Ian murmured. He seemed to be the only one who was uncomfortable with the fact that he was buck naked beneath the thin sheet.

"He's very clever. You may want to put him in your film," Lily said.

If he included everyone she'd suggested so far, the damn documentary would last hours. "I'll keep that in mind."

"Fergus would definitely add color," Lark said. "Though it's difficult to shut him up once he gets wound up. I'm Lark Stewart, by the way."

"I know. I have your CDs."

"Well." Lark seemed to relax a bit. "Isn't that nice?"

"I didn't know you were a fan," Lily said to him.

"There's a lot you don't know about me." That was definitely the truth. "I especially liked the new one," he said to Lark. "The Scots ballads."

"That's a favorite of mine, as well." Her smile barely touched eyes that seemed a bit sad. Everything about her seemed far more subdued than her sister, which surprised him, given the fact that she'd chosen a career in entertainment.

"Ian's Scots," Lily volunteered cheerfully. "He makes documentaries."

"I figured that out when you brought up Fergus." Lark gave him a closer study. "I saw that show they did about you on *Biography*."

"That was unauthorized," Lily said. "Ian says a lot was exaggerated."

"I've been there," Lark said sympathetically. "Why is it when you have a job that puts you in the public eye, people think they have a right to know every little detail about your life?"

It might have been the result of glare from the overhead light, but Ian thought he saw a flash of fire in those whiskey-hued depths. "Well, as lovely as this has been, I'd best be leaving you two to . . . whatever you were doing."

"We'd dozed off." Lily dragged a hand through her tousled curls. "What time is it?"

"A little after nine."

"That late." She dimpled and looked a tad smug. "Well, it's definitely true about time flying when you're having fun. But I don't want you running off, not when you just got here. Tell you what, if you'll just give us a couple minutes, we'll get dressed and we can all go out to dinner together, and you and Ian can get properly acquainted."

"I've got some work to take care of," Ian said. "And I still have to go by Stewart's Folly and unpack. Why don't you visit with your sister, and I'll see you later." He smiled his most winning smile, the one he used to get past uncooperative border guards. "I'm sure you and Lark have a lot to talk about, and she's probably tired from her trip."

"Wrung out is a closer description," Lark said. "Thank you, Mr. MacKenzie. It was lovely meeting you, and now I'll just wait downstairs."

They watched her leave, then Lily sighed. "She didn't look real happy, did she?"

"It's probably just what she said." Ian reluctantly climbed out of the warm bed and began gathering up his clothes. "Small planes have their advantages, but you do end up feeling every bump in the sky."

"I suppose so." Lily looked at her ripped panties they'd scooped up from the stairs earlier, sighed, and tossed them into a woven wastebasket.

"I owe you a new pair," he said.

"That's okay." She shrugged. "I just wish I'd been wearing something sexier."

"You're sexy whatever you're wearing. Or not wearing." He flashed a wicked grin. "Besides, men aren't nearly as interested in bras and panties as they are in what's underneath them."

"Well, then, I guess I'll just have to return the teddy I bought at Susi's Satin and Spice lingerie shop yesterday."

He was sitting on the bed and stopped putting on his boots. "What color?"

"Black. With pretty lace flowers right here." She splayed her fingers over her breasts. "And a thong back."

Ian didn't have to look down to see how his body had responded to that mental image. "I wouldn't want you to be too hasty. Perhaps you could show it to me first, and I could help you decide."

Her quick smile was decidedly inviting. "Are you suggesting I put on a fashion show?"

"Works for me."

"As it happens, the teddy wasn't the only thing I bought." Her eyes sparkled merrily. "It might take a very long time to go through the entire shopping bag."

"It'll be a sacrifice," he said, pulling her down onto his lap and lowering his mouth to her breasts, which were back in that white cotton bra he found surprisingly sexy. "But I'll try to rise to the occasion."

Lily laughed and wiggled against him. "It seems you already have."

Lark had changed. Always reed slender, she'd lost so much weight that her eyes appeared huge in the face that only wore makeup when she went onstage. She was wearing a body-skimming, boat-necked black T-shirt that stopped at her midriff, and flared jeans that hung low on her hips.

"It's good to have you home." Lily hugged her sister after Ian had left, and felt more bones than flesh.

"God, it seems like several lifetimes since I've been here."

"To me, too. You've lost weight."

"There's not that much to do on the bus, other than watch videos or read or listen to the guys tell dirty jokes, so I've been spending a lot of time in our room on the stair stepper." The T-shirt slid off one thin shoulder when she shrugged. "It's either that or balloon up to the size of the Fuji blimp."

"You've a long way to go before you have to worry about looking fat." When Lark had professed to be too tired to go out for dinner, Lily had scrambled some eggs and toasted two English muffins. So far, her sister had ignored the muffin and only pushed the eggs around on her plate. But she'd refilled her wineglass twice.

"I just finished taping that television special, and since the camera puts on fifteen pounds I dumped some weight ahead of time. Besides, as Cody keeps saying, in the music business image is everything, and this fits the Smoky Mountain waif image he's building for me."

When Lark had first taken off to Nashville,

hoping to make it in the music business, more than one producer had recommended she bleach her long chestnut hair blond. Comfortable with who and what she was, Lark had stuck to her guns.

Then she'd met Cody. Lily still couldn't understand what Lark saw in the former rodeo bronc rider from Houston, but he certainly seemed to have been calling the shots the past four years. Unlike so many other singers determined to cross over to the pop charts, Lark had stayed true to her roots, singing ballads, some of which had come to these mountains from the British Isles centuries ago, others which she'd written herself. The songs, usually of a grand love gone tragically wrong, suited Lark's high pure soprano, but Lily wondered about the waif aspect of Cody's marketing plan.

Actually, everything about Lark's husband made Lily uncomfortable. From the day she'd met him, when Lark had been a warm-up act on a country music festival European tour and Lily had taken the train to Rome to see her sister perform, she'd found him too brash, too loud, and too controlling.

She was also pretty certain that the man her sister intended to marry had hit on her during dinner. His hand had brushed her knee beneath the tablecloth just a little too often to be accidental. And when he hugged her after the concert, he'd pressed her breasts a bit harder against his chest than a casual farewell would warrant.

Lily had agonized over whether to tell Lark about her feelings and had reluctantly decided against it. She had not a single iota of proof and the man had certainly oozed charm toward Lark, loudly declaring her sexier than Shania, with a purer voice than Trisha Yearwood, all in a package more appealing than Martina McBride.

"Do you remember," Lark asked, "back when I'd dream of becoming the next Reba McEntire?"

"Of course. Now I imagine an entire generation of little girls dreaming of becoming the next Lark Stewart." Lily also recalled Cody, over several bottles of ruby-red Chianti, suggesting that Lark change her name to Lark Langtree, because he believed the alliteration sounded more like a star. Since she'd always had a strong sense of roots, that had been one of the few things Lark had refused him.

"It's been a strange four years since that night in Rome," Lark murmured, topping off her wine yet again.

"That was an amazing night." The audience was less than happy when the first singer of the night drunkenly mumbled his lyrics, then gave the crowd the finger when they'd booed him. Things had quickly deteriorated into a shouting match, the singer refusing to leave the stage until he received the applause the audience refused to give him.

When the security guards stormed the stage

to carry him off, like a SWAT team quelling a riot, the place went wild.

And then, in the midst of the chaos, a slender young woman with warm brown hair that fell to her waist walked out onto the stage, carrying the Mossman Tennessee Flat Top acoustic guitar she'd received from Annie on her thirteenth birthday.

The noise in the auditorium was close to a roar when she began "John Anderson, My Jo," an old Scots ballad about growing old with your true love. Gradually, the people in the first few rows fell under her spell. The silence spread, seat by seat, row by row. Some in the middle of the huge outdoor arena began to sense that something extraordinary was happening on stage and started loudly shushing those behind them. It had taken less than two minutes for the hush to descend over the entire arena.

"My knees were shaking so hard that night, I was certain the microphone was going to pick up the sound," Lark revealed.

"You sure didn't show it."

Indeed, she'd sounded serenely confident as she segued into "The Lady of Kenmure," then "False Lover Won Back," followed by the achingly soulful "Gin I Were a Baron's Heir" from the Robert Burns poem.

Lily had never heard such silence; the arena was as hushed as a cathedral. There was only the amplified sound of Lark's guitar and the pure soprano notes ringing out over the audience like morning birdsong over the misty mountaintops back home.

When she'd stopped the silence lingered for a few seconds, as if the audience had been so mesmerized, they'd forgotten how to respond. Then, like sleepwalkers awakening from a powerful dream, they began to clap, slowly, seemingly one person at a time, then more and more, until the applause thundered over the coliseum while Lark stood alone on the stage like a princess regally accepting the allegiance of her subjects.

In a cover story that was more love letter than journalism, *Country Music Weekly* proclaimed that no female singer since the late, great Patsy Cline could play an audience like the lovely Tennessee songbird. The buzz that had accompanied her when she'd returned from Europe had sent her career streaming like a comet into the stratosphere, and from what Lily had been able to tell, she'd been on a grueling schedule ever since.

"Cody thinks we ought to add more special effects to the show," she told Lily now.

"That's ridiculous." Lily might not be an expert on the music business, and she might not be as bossy as Laurel, but she did know her sister's abilities. "What does he want you to do, ride a flaming wire down to the stage through a fireworks display?"

Lark's lips, the only thing still full about her, curved in a faint smile. "Nothing quite that dramatic."

"You don't need flash. You have talent."

"The two aren't necessarily mutually exclusive."

"I didn't say they were. But even if I thought it suited your songs, which I don't, wouldn't that counter Cody's waif strategy?"

This time, Lark's smile lit her tired brown eyes. She looked exhausted and frail, and Lily was terribly worried about her. "That's the same thing I told him."

"And?"

"We left it up in the air."

There was something Lark wasn't saying. "Sounds as if you might have left more than performance plans up in the air," Lily probed.

"You know me so well."

"I should. We shared a room for the first sixteen years of my life, until you went off to seek fame and fortune in Music City."

"Be careful what you wish for," Lark murmured to herself, and her gentle mouth hardened. Then she shook off the obviously unpleasant thought. "And now that we've exhausted the conversation about me, why don't we get to the subject that we've both been avoiding? What's going on between you and your Scots hunk? Other than the obvious."

"I wasn't aware that we had exhausted the conversation about you. And he's not my Scot. Exactly."

"I see. He's just your personal Highland fling."

"I suppose so."

"But you'd like more?"

"I don't know."

She was afraid of the way he made her feel, Lily realized. A single smile from him was worth dozens from an easier man. She'd more than miss him when he was gone; she'd hate it when he left.

"Yes." She took a deep breath. Although she'd always been open about her feelings, it was difficult stating these surprising ones out loud. "I think I'm falling in love with him, Lark."

She and Lark had shared more than just a room growing up. They'd shared an Easy-Bake oven they'd use to make the cakes for tea parties, Barbie dolls, New Kids on the Block and Donny Osmond albums, and endless confidences. Lark had been the one Lily had gone to when she'd gotten her first period, and her sister had always listened to every little detail about Lily's weekly crushes.

Lily, in turn, had known when Lark got her first kiss and the night she'd lost her virginity to her high school love, a coal-miner's son from the poor side of town, after the Robbie Burns Birthday Bash. She'd also provided the audience for her sister's pretend performances and had assured her someday she'd be a superstar. Even bigger than Linda Ronstadt or Stevie Nicks.

"Is that love with a big *L* or little *l?*"

"I'm not sure, since I've never felt this way before, but I think it might be the big *L*."

Lark took another sip of the pale gold wine, rubbed her eyes wearily, and sighed. "Are we glad about that?"

"I don't know," Lily said honestly as she ran her finger around the rim of her own wineglass. "I keep telling myself that even if it is, it can't last."

"That's not necessarily true." Lark reached across the table and gripped Lily's hand. "You can't use anyone in our family as an example. My own marriage — which I do not want to discuss now while I'm exhausted, or I'll end up getting drunk and sloppy — is certainly no bed of roses, but my drummer's been married for twenty years to my hairdresser. It's downright embarrassing to see them together, the way they're always billing and cooing."

"I've never seriously considered getting married before," Lily said. "I was attracted to Ian from that first moment, like a bolt from the blue."

"I've experienced that a few times myself."

"At first I thought it was just chemistry."

"Nothing wrong with chemistry."

"No." Lily tingled inside at the memory of how she and Ian had spent the past hours. "I've been under a lot of stress lately, what with the wedding and the games, and sex with a skillful lover is a logical way to release some of the pressure."

"Unfortunately, love isn't the least bit logical. So how did you slide from just needing to blow the lid off, to wanting the moon?"

"I don't know. But you can't tell anyone."

"Who would I tell?"

"Cody?"

"Get real. The only thing we talk about anymore is work." She tossed back the rest of the wine. "Not that I want to talk about him."

"Then we won't. It's just that I can't deal with the idea right now, what with Daddy getting married, and the games. Ian's a rolling stone, and is no more likely to stay in Highland Falls than I am to go off to Nashville and become a famous singer."

"Which is highly unlikely, since you've never been able to carry a tune. But there's nothing keeping you here, Lily."

"There's Daddy."

"Who, as you just pointed out, is getting married in a few days. Zelda certainly doesn't need you hanging around here. She has her work, and if she'd take time to look up from her computer, she'd notice that nearly every man in town over the age of fifty walks into a wall whenever she sashays by. Some men half her age do, too, so it's not as if she couldn't have a partner if she wanted one.

"Melanie's got Missy, and there's no reason for her not to be dating other than the fact that she can't get past her resentment about Uncle Charlie. And if you were in any kind of serious relationship that would keep you here in Highland Falls, I doubt you'd have been in bed with your Scots filmmaker when I walked in."

"Of course not. Donald Forbes somehow got the idea we'd be getting married, but I never did anything to give him the impression that we were anything but friends."

"That man's always been as cold as a mackerel, and he's mean-spirited besides."

"He might not be that warm and fuzzy, but he's not mean."

"You just don't see it because you believe the best of people."

That was mostly true. She hadn't seen the best of Cody, though, and now it seemed that she'd been right.

"There's the gallery," she said, still trying to come up with excuses to protect her heart from taking that last fatal plunge. "I couldn't just lock the door and take off."

"Why not?"

"I have responsibilities to all the artists."

"They can find some other place that'll be happy to sell their paintings and pretty glass. Or, better yet, you could sell the gallery. I'll bet there's a lot of people who'd love to buy it."

"I received an offer from a woman in Asheville just last month."

"See? There's nothing stopping you from going off with Ian MacKenzie."

"Actually, there is one little thing: he hasn't asked me to go off with him." And Lily seriously doubted he would.

"Well, then." Lark stabbed her fork into a

fluffy bit of egg and finally took a bite. "If you truly want him, you'll just have to convince him, won't you?"

24

The party inside MacDougall Manor was in full swing. Champagne and whisky flowed, American big band music was pouring out of the windows, and the level of conversation seemed to escalate with every hour the tall box clock chimed. Everyone was having a grand time. And why shouldn't they? Annie MacFie asked herself as a headache threatened behind her temples.

It was, after all, a time for celebration. The war was over, the soldiers were returning home to the Highlands, and tomorrow everyone would be gathering again to celebrate a wedding. Her wedding.

So why did she feel like weeping?

She was being so foolish. Duncan MacDougall was a good man. An honest and thrifty man she'd known all of her life. He'd make a fine husband, and a good, albeit undoubtedly firm, father to their children. And her parents never ceased pointing out that he was also a wealthy man — partly because he'd inherited land and property, but also because he no doubt had the first penny he'd ever made.

He could have played the role of a country gentleman and lived off his inheritance, but that wasn't his way. Even tonight, rather than enjoying his own party, he was locked away in his library with his lawyers, bankers, and land agent, doing business.

Needing a breath of fresh air, Annie stepped through the French doors onto the terrace and breathed in the night air perfumed with the scent of the garden, which was far less cloying than the expensive fragrances worn by the women inside.

The night was uncharacteristically clear. Looking up at the star-spangled sky, she wondered if the old story her mother had told her about souls becoming stars in heaven were true. And if so, could James Stewart be looking down on her at this very moment? Did he know she was getting wed tomorrow? Was he happy for her?

"Quit being such a daftie!"

What was wrong with her? Everyone in the entire country, undoubtedly the entire world, for that matter, was moving on with their lives. To all outward appearances, she was, as well. What no one knew was that there was a part of her mind and heart that had been frozen in time on another star-spangled night in 1943.

She'd first met James Stewart when she'd been a nurse working at hospital in Fort William and he'd been a member of the American Darby's Rangers, training at the British Commando Training Depot at Achnacarry Castle. Like everyone in the region, she'd gone to watch the men go through exercises that appeared as taxing as war might be. They'd begin with an eighteen-mile run to Ben Nevis, climb to the summit, then back down again, then move on to carrying huge logs on their shoulders, hand-to-hand combat, and practicing assault landings on the deep, dark lochs and the river Arkaig.

The first time she'd witnessed one of their infamous "death slides," which required the soldiers to climb a forty-foot-tall tree, then slide down a rope that was suspended over the raging river, all while under live fire, she'd found the idea that the bullets were real terrifyingly fascinating. After she'd fallen in love with her dashing ranger, she'd merely found it terrifying.

They'd met one day when the tire on her bicycle had gone flat while she was riding home from work. She'd been pushing it along when a jeep filled with soldiers sped around the corner, then, brakes screeching, came to a sudden stop.

A dark-haired Yank leaped out of the truck with the agility of a young lad. He was tall, vigorous, and the most confident male she'd ever seen. He was also the brashest, complimenting her on her penny-bright hair, her green eyes, and the shape of her calves, of all things, as he lashed her bicycle to the bonnet of the jeep and insisted on taking her home.

She'd scandalized her entire street when she'd shown up at the flat she shared with two other nurses, squeezed like a sardine into an open jeep with a crowd of boisterous Yank rangers. She'd thanked him politely, but assured him that she wasn't interested in seeing him again.

Which was a lie, but she knew that a man like this would be more than a handful, and if the rumors circulating around the Highlands were true, he'd be leaving the depot to fight in the war before the summer was over.

A man like James Stewart, she'd thought as he'd insisted on wheeling the disabled bicycle into the entryway hall, could easily steal your heart when you weren't looking. But through no fault of his own, since he seemed genuinely kind, he'd break it.

His pride hadn't seemed a bit dented by her refusal, and apparently her words had rolled off him like rain off a mallard's back, because the following day an enormous bouquet of flowers had arrived at the flat. The blossoms were huge and perfumed the rooms for a week. When they finally dried out, she pressed the petals between the pages of the thick book of Gauguin's South Pacific works, a rare indulgence she'd allowed herself because the bright, sunny paintings were such an antidote to the Highland's gray, wet days.

Oh, the man definitely knew how to plan an assault. The day after the flowers, the delivery boy brought chocolate. And not just the Hershey bars the Americans seemed to have an endless supply of, but an entire chocolate cake!

She'd shared the sweet with her flatmates and neighbors as well, who immediately stopped being scandalized long enough to ponder whether or not Annie's Yank might be sending beef the following day.

Not beef, but perfume. An enormous bottle of Shalimar, in a Baccarat crystal bottle! By now her flatmates were telling her that if she didn't grab him up and marry James Stewart before he shipped out, they would.

She was already teetering on the edge of giving in, when the fourth day's gift sent her heart tumbling over the edge. She never did know how on earth he'd found them in wartime Great Britain, when everything was in such short supply, but when she untied the ribbon on the box and stared down at the colored art pencils she hadn't been able to afford for a year, she surrendered.

It wasn't so much the pencils themselves but the fact that as a photographer, he understood her deep, visceral need to leave something of herself behind, like the stones carved by the Picts found all over the Highlands.

The next ten days had been the most glorious and romantic of her life, and if she lived to be a hundred, she'd never regret them. Whenever he could get away from the depot, they made love. And plans. Then made love again, as if there'd be no tomorrow. Which they both knew there could well not be.

He'd shipped out in early July. Darby's

Rangers led the assault on Sicily, and although Annie had never considered herself a religious person, she'd prayed day and night. When a week went by without a word, then two, she began to seriously worry. After the third week she rang up a friend who worked in the war department in London, who made some telephone calls and discovered that Lieutenant James Stewart had been declared MIA. Later, that designation was changed to Killed in Action.

Annie felt the hot moisture stinging at the back of her lids. "Foolish, foolish girl," she scolded herself. Her voice trembled, as did her hands as she tried to open her satin evening bag to retrieve a handkerchief. "Crying on what's supposed to be a happy occasion."

"Could I perhaps be of some assistance?" a deep, all-too-familiar voice asked from the shadows.

No! It couldn't be! She spun toward the man who was walking across the stone terrace toward her.

Unlike the other men at the party, who were dressed in formal Highland attire, he was wearing a black shirt and black slacks. As he entered the light streaming from the full moon overhead, she could see he was holding a handkerchief out to her.

"James?" Hope and disbelief shimmered in his name.

"It's me, doll face. Your bloody daredevil Yank."

266

It was what she'd called him, with both love and frustration, so many times.

"It can't be." But, oh, her foolish, suddenly giddy heart said otherwise. "You were killed in Italy!"

"To quote Mark Twain, reports of my death have been greatly exaggerated."

As he gently wiped away the tears that were streaming down her cheeks, Annie was grateful mascara was still impossible to come by.

"I was taken prisoner in Italy, then spent the rest of the war bouncing around prison camps in Germany and Austria." His grin flashed in the way she'd never been able to forget. "I escaped seven times, but the damn bastards kept capturing me again."

"Oh, James." She couldn't talk. Couldn't think.

As if he'd engaged the help of the gods to make his point, the band inside began playing the popular hit "It's Been a Long, Long Time."

"Too long," he said, his rich velvet voice roughened with the same emotions that were battering her. He tucked the handkerchief back into his pocket and swept her into his arms with a smooth, masculine grace even Cary Grant would have envied.

" 'Kiss me once,' " he sang lightly against her cheek as they began dancing, " 'then kiss me twice.' " His lips skimmed up to her temple. " 'Then kiss me once again.' " His breath feathered her hair. " 'It's been a long, long time.' "

His eyes, which were fierce and tender at the same time, met hers. "You were all I thought about, the entire time. Just you. And how things were going to be after the Germans finally surrendered and I could get back here, marry you, and take you home to America with me."

"Oh, James," she repeated, like a record with a needle stuck in the groove. Traitorous moisture began to well up in her eyes again. "There's something I have to tell you."

How could she possibly tell a man who'd been through God-knew-what terrible horrors, a man who'd nearly died fighting not just for his country, but hers, that she was pledged to be another man's wife?

"There'll be plenty of time for talk later." He brushed a callused thumb against her lips, which parted unconsciously, expectantly, at his touch. "After you welcome me home properly."

"Oh, James." It was half sigh, half cry. She threw her arms around his neck and clung as he kissed her with all the pent-up passion of their forced years apart.

She'd tried to convince herself that she'd merely imagined the power of his kiss, the way his mouth could turn her into melted wax. She'd almost managed to believe that memory had exaggerated how the mere taste of him could make her more tipsy than if she'd drunk an entire magnum of champagne. She'd been wrong. So, so wrong.

"Come home with me," he said, when they finally came up for air. "Now."

"I can't." Her head swimming giddily, she looked over his broad shoulder at the brightly lighted room, amazed Duncan hadn't already come looking for her.

"You're not going to marry the man, Annie, darling."

"What?" She stared up at him. "How did you —"

"It seems Duncan MacDougall is an important man around these parts. The entire town was abuzz about your upcoming nuptials when I arrived last night."

"Last *night?*"

"I didn't want to just crash in on you." He answered her unspoken question as to why he hadn't come to her immediately. "I needed time to prepare properly, to set the stage back at my hotel. I figured we'd open a bottle of champagne, have a little caviar —"

"You have caviar?" Even Duncan hadn't been able to pull that off.

"Russian." He leaned forward and kissed her lightly, his lips coaxing. Persuading. "I brought it home with me, just for our reunion celebration."

"That sounds wonderful."

"There's more." He reached into his pocket again, taking out a small black velvet box.

Annie's heart was pounding wildly in her ears as she opened it. The stone, set in white gold, the largest she'd ever seen, glistened like an iceberg in the moonlight and left her speechless.

"It was my grandmother's," he informed her. "I know it's a little over the top, but my grandfather, like all us Stewarts, was not given to small gestures. I was hoping you'd overlook the ostentatiousness of it and concentrate on the tradition."

"It's stunning." Although it was entirely un-Scots, Annie decided that there was definitely something to be said in favor of ostentation. "But I can't —"

"Of course you can," he said gently, yet firmly, reminding her of that take-charge ranger he'd once been. "I understand honor, Annie. Hell, I've spent the past years of my life in a prison camp because even though my family connections could have gotten me assigned to some cushy desk job in Washington, fighting fascism seemed the honorable thing to do.

"You promised to marry MacDougall under the assumption that I was dead. Which, as you can see" — he held out his arms — "I'm not."

"You're so thin." But, dear heavens, he still looked wonderful to her!

"I know." He flashed another smile that lit up his eyes with humor. "The cooks in those German camps aren't exactly five-star chefs. I figured I could fatten up again on my wife's cooking."

Despite all he must have gone through, he was still the same wonderful man who'd launched an assault on her heart once before, and was obviously prepared to do so again.

"I'm a terrible cook," she reminded him, torn between laughter and tears.

"That's okay." He drew her close again and nuzzled that special place behind her ear that only he had ever been able to find. "We'll live on love. Come to America with me, Annie sweetest. Be my wife. Have my children and live happily ever after with me in Stewart's Folly."

Heaven help her, she desperately wanted to do exactly that.

"I'm sure MacDougall is a fine man," he continued, "or you wouldn't have accepted his proposal." His eyes were grave and seemed shadowed with a vulnerability she never would have expected to see in their whisky-hued depths. "But I strongly doubt if he needs you even half as much as I do."

Annie was a born caretaker. The need to nurture was in her blood, right along with her need to paint. It was the reason she'd become a nurse. But the idea that this man, whom she'd watched running across an icy raging river while soldiers on the bank shot live ammunition at him, might be even the slightest bit needy, was stunning. The idea that it was her, a small-town girl from the Scots Highlands, that he needed, was her undoing.

"Yes." This time her tears were born of joy. "I'll be your wife, James Stewart."

"Thank you, Annie, my love. And thank God."

He kissed her tenderly.

As they slipped away to the car he'd parked down the road, James felt that for the first time in a very long while, all the pieces of his life had fallen back into place.

He'd survived a war, not that he'd ever doubted he would. Not even on those worst of days, when the Germans sought to ensure he'd never try to escape again. Learning that Annie was about to marry another man had been an unpleasant shock, but except for being captured by that Italian tank brigade, he'd always been a lucky man, and the fact that she was not yet married was a stroke of good fortune. Discovering that her fiancé was the current chief of Clan MacDougall was proof, in James's mind, that destiny was definitely in play here.

It had only taken him ten minutes in the Red Lion pub to learn that before the war, MacDougall Manor had been opened one Saturday each year for the clan gathering. After buying a few rounds of pints for the house, he'd also learned that the Brooch of Lorn was kept locked in the same chest General Campbell had discovered it in more than a century earlier. And that the chest itself was kept in the armory, where MacDougall's collection of ancient Highlander weapons was on display.

Slipping into the house had been a piece of cake for a man trained in night maneuvers. He'd quickly reclaimed the brooch for his family, who should have owned it all along, given their direct lineage to The Bruce. And now that that important piece of Stewart history was nestled comfortably in his pocket, he was returning back to Highland Falls with the woman he'd never stopped dreaming about. The only woman he'd ever loved. The only woman he would ever love.

Life was, he thought with a grin as he opened the car passenger door with a flourish, goddamn perfect.

25

Ian was frustrated when he couldn't get Duncan on the phone. He'd called to tell him that all bets were off, that he was dropping the search for the brooch. There was an outside chance Lily might have it stashed somewhere in her pretty little apartment above the gallery, but if she did, Ian didn't want to know about it.

He was a man used to planning ahead, for plotting out every little detail, and preparing for all the unexpected contingencies that always popped up. But that was before fate had drawn him to Highland Falls. For now, he was just going to take things — and his relationship with Lily — one day at a time.

He'd decided to tell Lily as soon as she arrived from the gallery, when there was a light tap on his door. When he opened it and saw her standing there, smelling like a summer garden, he thought about the black teddy she'd promised to wear beneath that scoop-necked black peasant blouse and gauzy flowered skirt, and all his good intentions flew out the window.

"It's about time you showed up." He took her

by the arm, pulled her into the room, and hauled her against him.

"Gracious." She leaned back a bit when the long, deep kiss finally ended. He was so hard and urgent against her, it was difficult to catch her breath. "For a man who went days without so much as touching my hand, you're certainly making up for lost time."

"I don't have that much time before the end of the games." The strong fingers spanning her waist tightened fractionally. "No point in wasting it."

"I never knew time management could be so much fun." She went up on her toes and brushed her lips teasingly against his. This time it was she who deepened the kiss. "Maybe you should write a book on the subject."

"Later." He tugged on the lacy bow between her breasts, and smiled wickedly as the material parted.

"Later," she agreed.

He kissed her again, a slow, long meeting of lips that had her melting against him.

"Lie down," she murmured against his mouth.

"Gladly." He walked her across the room without breaking the kiss. When he would have pulled her down on the bed, she slipped out of his arms. Pressing her palms against his broad chest, she pushed him back against the pillows.

"It takes two to do this right," he pointed out when she remained standing.

"Granted. But sometimes anticipation is half

the fun." She backed a bit away from the bed. "I seem to recall promising you a fashion show."

The blouse had little pearl buttons. With her eyes on his, she slowly, tantalizingly slipped one of the buttons through its loop. "Do you know," she said conversationally, "that I've never done this before?" Another button undone. "I've had my clothes off before, of course."

"I remember it well."

She smiled, a sexy siren's smile that made the air clog in his lungs. "I should certainly hope so." She leaned down and brushed her lips against his. Needs were churning through him when she straightened again. Three more buttons and the blouse was open, revealing a froth of black silk and lace that he couldn't imagine would have looked half as good on a Victoria's Secret catalog model.

"What I mean is, I've never taken off my clothes while a fully dressed man was lying on the bed watching me."

"I can take off my clothes, too, if you're feeling uncomfortable," he said helpfully.

"Actually, that's a funny thing." She slipped the blouse off and let it flutter to the floor. "I thought I would." The skirt had a side zipper. She lowered it, then pushed the skirt over the swell of her hips, allowing it to slide down her body to pool at her feet.

"But I don't." She was standing just a few feet away, wearing nothing but that outrageously sexy teddy and a pair of high-heeled black sandals that made her legs look as if they went all the way up to her neck. "I love the way your eyes go nearly black when you look at me." She stepped free of the skirt, then slipped out of the high-heeled sandals. "It makes me feel sultry and sexy."

"You *are* sultry and sexy."

"With you," she agreed, seeming a bit surprised at that. Which, truthfully, he'd been, as well. He'd found her sexy from the start, but never would have suspected the quintessential girl-next-door had so much pent-up passion lurking inside her.

She climbed onto the tall bed and unbuttoned his shirt. Her lips followed her caressing hands, her mouth rained hot, moist kisses down his chest. "Have I mentioned that I absolutely love your body?" He sucked in his breath as she unfastened his jeans and lowered the zipper. "I've wanted it from the first moment I saw you."

"It's all yours," he said on a rough groan as she released his cock.

"I know." Her hair draped over him and her tongue created a hot, wet swathe from root to tip, causing flames to shoot up his spine. "I'm still amazed about that."

"I need you, dammit." Never had any words sounded so inadequate. "More than I ever thought it possible to need a woman. More than I ever wanted to."

"Be still, my heart." Her cheeks were flushed,

277

her eyes sparkled. "You're such a sweet-talker, Ian MacKenzie."

He tangled his fingers in her fragrant hair and tugged, lifting her head. "I'm serious."

"I know." This time her smile was gentle as she brought her mouth down to his, letting him taste himself on her lips.

It was the last thing either of them said for a very long time.

Lily was cuddling against him, feeling warm and sleepy, when she sensed that familiar tension return. She'd have thought their love-making would have taken it out of him for at least the rest of the night.

"What's wrong?"

He kissed the top of her head. "Who said anything's wrong?"

"I told you that I don't go to bed with men I don't know," she reminded him. "I know you, Ian. Enough to realize when something's bothering you." A thought slammed into her brain. "If it's something I did wrong, something you didn't like —"

"Don't be ridiculous." He nipped her chin. "You're perfect."

He turned onto his side, taking her with him, face to face, chest to chest, thigh to thigh. It was amazing, considering their difference in height, how wonderfully they fit together.

"Better than perfect." He smoothed a hand down her back, the touch meant to soothe rather than arouse, yet she felt as if he'd taken sparklers to her damp flesh. "You were magnificent."

"It was us," she said, meaning it. She couldn't ever have imagined feeling the way she did when Ian was inside her; empowered yet meltingly weak at the same time. "What we have is different. Special."

"Special," he agreed. She would have been encouraged by the admission if it hadn't been stated in such a flat monotone.

"Ian." She framed his unnervingly grim face in her palms. "Please tell me what's wrong. If you're worried about me taking all this too seriously —"

"It is serious."

He certainly didn't look very happy about that idea.

"So, is that the problem?"

He heaved a deep sigh. Cursed.

This was getting worse and worse. Lily braced herself for him to break the news that he was secretly married and had a wife and children stashed somewhere on a Pacific island; or perhaps that he'd enjoyed their little fling, but had already burned out any desire he might feel for her, and hoped they could stay friends.

Perhaps he was a secret agent, using his documentary career as a cover, or — oh, God! — what if he was dying of some incurable disease contracted in one of those terrible Third World places he'd been filming?

"Do you know the story of The Bruce's coronation?" he asked.

"Of course," she said blankly. Of all the wild scenarios her imagination had been churning up, she'd never expected an event seven hundred years in the past could make him look so grim, almost angry.

"Do you know about the time right afterward? The battles he lost?"

"I don't know the details. Only that he was betrayed both times and came out on the losing end."

"*Losing* being the definitive word. Because he lost his brooch at the second battle."

"The Brooch of Lorn. I know; you saw the copy of it in my gallery."

"A copy of the one taken by a MacDougall in battle."

"That's right." She was growing more and more puzzled.

"The one the Stewarts and the MacDougalls have been stealing back and forth between the clans ever since."

"I'd heard it had changed hands, but I've never heard that the Stewarts were involved."

"It appears they were. You know, of course, that one of The Bruce's daughters married a Stewart."

She nodded. "Which was how the royal line continued through the Stewarts. Or the Stuarts, as they started spelling it the French way."

"Did you also know that the brooch was recently taken from MacDougall Manor?"

"Of course not. How would I know that?"

"Because, coincidentally, it happened to disappear on the day of your visit."

Lily knew that it was impossible for a person's blood to actually freeze. But hers felt as if it had turned to ice. She could also feel it draining from her face. Her head was suddenly so light, if she hadn't already been lying down, she probably would have fallen.

"Surely you can't be accusing me."

He didn't immediately answer; but his gunmetal-gray eyes spoke volumes.

"You are!" Not a spy, she thought. But some type of police? "Are you from Scotland Yard?"

"Of course not." He cursed again. "I'm from Duncan MacDougall."

"The MacDougall of MacDougall Manor?"

"One and the same."

"I don't understand." She dragged a trembling hand through her tangled hair. "He hired you to find a stolen brooch, and you came here because you think I stole it?"

"I don't think that. And he didn't hire me."

"Well, that's a relief." She let out a huge breath.

"He blackmailed me."

Dear heavens, this was getting worse and worse! Beginning to wonder if she could be dreaming, Lily pinched herself, hard. But nothing changed. She was still in bed beside

281

him, still ice-cold, and he still looked as if he were a prison inmate on the way to the death chamber. "What could you have possibly done —"

"Not that kind of blackmail. Emotional blackmail." He drew in a harsh breath that was edged with frustration. "Duncan MacDougall is my grandfather."

"But your name's MacKenzie."

"My father was a MacKenzie. My mother was a MacDougall."

"Oh." She fell silent, trying to fit all the pieces of this surprising puzzle into place. When the picture came together, it definitely wasn't pretty.

"You lied to me."

"Not exactly. I just didn't tell you the entire truth." Hell, it sounded even worse than when he'd tried it out on the drive back up the mountain. "I didn't know you when I first came here to get the brooch back, so it seemed plausible that what Duncan was saying was true. But then I got to know you, and realized how sweet and honest you are, and things changed."

"Well, that's encouraging." Her tone was not. "Were you going to politely ask me for it? Or were you going to steal it? Not that we even have it."

"Duncan wanted me to steal it. But as soon as I got here, I realized there was no way I would have, even if I'd been able to find the damn thing." Shit. Why didn't someone just hand him a bloody spade, so he could dig this bloody hole he'd created for himself a little deeper?

"So that's why you had me showing you all around?"

"Yes." He plowed a hand through his hair and wished the old man were here so he could throttle his scrawny neck. "No."

She pulled away from him, sat up, and folded her arms across her bare chest. Ian found it encouraging that she didn't leap out of bed and begin throwing things at his head. At least not yet.

"Which is it?"

"In the beginning, Duncan kept pressuring me to find it. By the second day I already intended to make the film, so I really did need to start scouting out locations. By the afternoon of the second day, I just wanted to be with you. Any way I could."

He watched the unpalatable idea come into her mind, saw it in her eyes a moment before she asked, "Is that why you had sex with me?" She'd scooted so far away from him that another inch would send her onto the floor. "To get me to tell you about the brooch?"

"Hell, no." In one of his few wise moves of the past week, he refrained from admitting that was exactly what Duncan had pushed him to do. "The one place I didn't lie to you was in bed. Besides, it was more than sex. And you know it." Ian wasn't sure when he'd passed the point of not getting involved, but he'd had enough casual sex to know that this was different. Lily was different.

"Yes." Lily frowned. Then reached down, plucked his shirt from the end of the bed, and slipped it on. She took a long time to button it, her expression as wary as he felt. "And I suppose I should be feeling grateful that you didn't prostitute yourself while betraying me."

Since he was the guilty party here, Ian didn't allow himself to be insulted by the suggestion he might have been willing to do such a thing.

"It gets even more complicated." He wasn't certain how she was going to take this part. "Your grandfather stole it from mine."

A flare of crimson color stained her cheeks, which only minutes earlier had been flushed from making love. "If you'd known my grandfather, you'd know what a wonderful man he was. I refuse to believe he was a thief."

"It's true. He took the brooch from MacDougall Manor after he'd returned from the war. And that wasn't the only thing he stole." Ian forced himself to say the rest, braced for her heated denial. "He stole my grandfather's fiancée."

"Your . . ." Baffled, she pushed at her hair, shoving the curls off her face. "Are you saying . . ." She left the bed and began to pace. "My grandmother Annie was —"

"Engaged to my grandfather. James Stewart was one of Brady's Rangers. He'd trained in Scotland, in the Highlands —"

"I know that!" His denim shirt flared around her knees as she spun back toward him. "He led the assault to take Sicily and was captured. My grandmother was told he'd died, but the war department had it wrong. He returned to Scotland at the end of the war and they got married, and ten years later they settled down here."

"He returned to Scotland," Ian agreed. "The night before Annie's wedding to Duncan MacDougall."

Her hand flew to her breast. "I don't believe that." But she was beginning to. He could see the reluctant acceptance in her eyes.

"It's the truth." And past time he'd told it. "There was a party. The way I've been told the story, my grandfather was in his library doing business, which wasn't unusual for him. When he came out, Annie MacFie was gone. So was the brooch."

"That was her name," Lily murmured. "Annie MacFie, but she wouldn't have done such a thing. Not to someone she cared about enough to agree to marry."

"People don't always behave rationally when they're in love," he pointed out. Yet another reason he'd always avoided taking the plunge. "Your grandfather's photographs show they traveled all over the world. Didn't you ever wonder why they never went back to Scotland?"

She shook her head; pressed her lips together as she considered that. "It never occurred to

285

me. But if my grandfather took it from yours all those years ago, why would you think I'd stolen it when I was in Scotland?"

"The MacDougalls apparently got it back sometime after that —"

"Stole it back, you mean."

"Probably. However, it's been locked away in a safe in the manor house until —"

"I came to Scotland. And supposedly stole it, which in turn made you come to Highland Falls, to use whatever sneaky methods necessary to get it back."

"It wasn't that way, dammit! Look, I'll take any punishment you want to dish out, but you have to believe that everything that happened between us, everything I said, was true. Hell, why do you think I kept running so hot and cold? If I'd just wanted to use you, I would have had you in this bed that first night."

"Arrogant," she muttered.

"Confident," he countered. "About us being perfect together."

"This complicates things."

Although his nerves were more on edge than when that dictator general's goons had arrived at his hotel to arrest him, Ian waited her out.

"I understand all about family loyalty," she said finally. "You must love your grandfather a great deal."

"I'm not even sure I like him." He gave her a brief overview of his and Duncan's history.

"That's so sad," she said in a quiet voice. Her

eyes filled, and she moved closer. "My father frustrates me horribly from time to time, and Aunt Melanie can get a bit tedious, but I can't imagine being estranged as long as you and he were."

Never one to indulge in pity parties, Ian braced himself against her sympathy. "If you knew Duncan MacDougall, you might find it easier to imagine."

She sat on the edge of the bed, her eyes eloquent with a compassion he'd been hoping for, but hadn't dared count on. "The fact that you came here in the first place suggests that perhaps your relationship goes a bit deeper than you realize."

Lines furrowed her smooth forehead; Ian instinctively reached out a fingertip to smooth them away and was encouraged when she didn't bat away the light touch.

"Will this cause a new rift?" she asked. "Your grandfather's obviously not going to be happy when you don't return to Scotland with the brooch."

Trust her to worry about that, when she'd just had her own personal rug pulled out from under her. "Being happy isn't really a state of mind the old man is familiar with. As for the damn brooch, he's a canny man. If he's so desperate to have it back, he'll have to bloody well figure out how to get it himself."

"Actually, since the brooch belonged to The Bruce in the first place, it would seem to me that by rights, it belongs to his descendants. Not the people who stole it from him."

"It was considered spoils of war." Shit. That sounded every bit as ridiculous as it always did when Duncan tried it on him. Ian rubbed his hands down his face. "My point, such as it is, is that the brooch has been in MacDougall hands for a very long time, and as they say, possession is nine-tenths of the law."

"Then if it were to be somewhere in Stewart's Folly, that would make it ours, wouldn't it?" she asked sweetly.

Ian swore. "I should have seen that one coming."

"Yes, you should have," she said mildly. "A great many people go to Scotland every year. I imagine thousands just from America. Why didn't Duncan MacDougall zero in on one of them?"

"I have no idea. You'd have to ask him."

"I may just do that. Meanwhile, I'm going to have to decide whether I'm insulted or flattered that anyone actually thought me capable of safecracking."

A longer silence settled over them. Ian was used to waiting out silences, knowing that people often needed to take the time to sort out their thoughts. But having Lily go silent on him tattered his last nerve.

"Dammit, I owe him, Lily." Having already handled things so badly, Ian decided to be absolutely honest about his feelings, throw himself on her mercy, and hope for the best. She was, after all, a very generous person. He took both her soft hands in his. "Even if I could ignore the family ties, which, as you pointed out, I can't, the old bastard saved my life."

"At the moment, I'm not real certain I'm grateful for that." She immediately shook her head. "That's not true. I wouldn't trade what we've shared for anything. As I said, I can understand family loyalty, Ian. God knows I've spent the major part of my life trying to live up to my family's expectations."

"Expectations you may have contributed to, by always being willing to sacrifice your own wants and desires for everyone else's." He cringed and, if possible, would have taken the hasty words back.

But once again she surprised him, not taking offense at the accusation. "You're right. I also realize that in the past few years, I may have overdone the nurturing thing and invited people — especially my father — to take advantage of me. But that's going to change."

"Good for you."

"Meanwhile" — she slanted him a sexy, come-hither-big-boy look from beneath her lashes — "if *you* wanted to take advantage of me, Ian MacKenzie, I wouldn't be saying no."

"I can't think of a man in the world who'd turn down that invitation."

So he did. Then it was her turn again. And together they took advantage of each other, again and again, all night long.

26

Lily was still thinking about Ian's startling revelation the next morning, while she helped Zelda arrange roses in the butler's pantry. Her grandmother sat on a stool at the counter, making Lily even more uneasy, because of what Ian had told her about Annie's having supposedly been with James Stewart when he'd stolen The Bruce's brooch from MacDougall Manor.

"I think I want him." Despite this new unexpected twist in their relationship, there was no point in denying it.

"Of course you do, dear," Annie said. "I may be an old woman and blind to boot, but even I find him appealing. If I were forty years younger, I'd want him, too."

Lily shook her head as she trimmed the stems below the water in the utility sink. "I mean I really want him. I think I might even want to keep him."

"You'll have to walk and feed him," Zelda said.

Lily's laugh eased her tension. "That's the same thing you said when I brought home that puppy when I was six."

"And you took real good care of that mutt, even though he was as dense as a clay brick and peed all over the carpets, bless his little doggie heart."

Hearing the word *doggie,* Freedom, who was lying at Annie's feet, looked up expectantly and thumped his huge tail.

"I'm serious." Lily's smile faded as she put a trio of roses into a crystal vase and added some baby's breath. "The minute I saw him, it was as if this little click went on in my head." And other places she wasn't prepared to discuss. For someone who'd always considered herself forthright, she was certainly harboring a lot of secrets lately.

"You don't have to tell me. If the atmosphere in the room had gotten any steamier, we probably would have had an indoor tornado."

"Oh, I wish I'd been there," Annie said. She took a bone-shaped dog biscuit from the pocket of her skirt and slipped it to the retriever, who swallowed it in one happy gulp.

"You wouldn't have had to see it to know that something was going on," Zelda said, fanning herself dramatically. "Melanie doesn't believe he's an easy man. And while I hate like hell to agree with her, I believe she's right."

Lily laughed. "That may be the first understatement I've ever heard you make."

Zelda had always been able to make her see the humor in things. Even that time her freshman year of high school, when Bobby

Brown had stood her up for the Blast to the Past Scintillating Sixties dance for Patsy Kendall — who'd grown amazing breasts over the summer.

After Bobby subsequently broke his right leg when he fell down while doing the twist, Zelda denied putting a curse on him, quoting the wiccan rede to do no harm. Lily had laughed, but had always secretly wondered.

"MacKenzie's not the type of man to stay settled down in one spot for long," Zelda said.

"I know. But that's not exactly a bad thing, is it? Maybe some people just need to get some wandering out of their system before they settle down and grow roots."

"Some never do," Zelda warned.

"And some do," Annie said. "James dragged me all around the world the first ten years of our marriage. First we went to all the places he'd been to as a soldier: North Africa, Italy, even the places in Germany and Austria where he'd been kept prisoner. I would have thought he'd never want to see them again, but he said it was important to know not just where you'd come from, but where you'd been, so you'd know where you were going. Those were very important years in his life, and I could understand his need to view them from a different perspective."

"From the outside in, rather than the inside out," Zelda said with a nod.

"He probably needed to understand, deep down inside, that he was really, honestly free."

Lily didn't want to consider the possibility that perhaps her grandfather had stayed on the run to keep Duncan MacDougall from catching up with him.

"You may be right," her grandmother agreed. "Well, you'd think after we'd finished that tour down a not-so-pleasant memory lane, James would have wanted to do what most of the other GIs did and settle down, buy a house —"

"You already had one helluva house," Zelda, who'd heard the story innumerable times as a child, pointed out.

"True. But as large as Stewart's Folly is, it was still, in James's mind at the time, his father's home. And he and his father didn't really have much in common. Oh, they came to accept each other at the end of James senior's life, after he had turned the company around, but only being interested in business in those early years, he never could understand how any son of his could believe it possible to earn a living taking pictures."

"Until those pictures starting selling so well," said Lily, who also knew her family history. Even as she hated to admit it, even to herself, a part of her suspected that Ian was telling the truth. At least as much of it as he knew. But she wasn't going to let him take away all the good memories of her grandfather.

"That did seem to raise James up a few notches on his father's scale," Annie agreed. "Even before we came back to Highland Falls.

For the longest time, I thought he had no intention of ever landing anywhere. We were like Gypsies, traveling to all corners of the world. One night — on the night your father was conceived, Lily," she said with a soft, reminiscent smile — "James explained that having learned firsthand that we can die at any moment, he wanted to see all the places he'd dreamed of going while he'd been a boy here in Highland Falls, devouring *National Geographic* magazines.

"After that, I understood him better. By then, I'd already given up oil painting for watercolors — because they dry faster," she said with a quick grin that revealed the risk-taking young girl she'd once been.

"And you never regretted that?"

"There was nothing to regret. I was with the man I loved, doing what I loved, and even having the family I'd always dreamed about. When I learned for certain I was pregnant, James offered to come back to the States, but I could tell that his heart wasn't in the offer. He was only doing it for me, which wasn't necessary because I'd gotten to love our adventures as much as he."

"So you told him travel was supposed to be broadening for children." Lily repeated what she'd been told so many times.

"And it's true. John Angus was born in India on our fourth anniversary, and you, Zelda dear, will always be my Polynesian princess."

Zelda made a scoffing sound, but Lily had always suspected she secretly enjoyed the nick-name.

"Then a few days after our tenth anniversary, James and I were having breakfast on a terrace with the most stunning view of Norway's glaciers, when he looked up from his eggs and said, 'Let's go home.' "

"So you did." A romantic through and through, Lily had always enjoyed the tales of her grandparents' grand love affair. Everyone else's grandparents and parents had always seemed boring. But not James and Annie Stewart.

Had they been such free spirits that they became, at least that one night at the MacDougall mansion, jewel thieves? Knowing her grandmother as she did, loving her as she did, Lily had a difficult time imagining Annie stealing anything from anyone. Especially a man she'd promised to marry. A man she had grown up with, Ian had told her sometime before dawn.

"We booked the next flight out of there, just like that." Annie snapped her fingers. "And never regretted either one — the traveling or the settling down, not even when James put aside a flourishing photography career to take over the day-to-day operation of the distillery.

"I worried at the time that he might begin to feel suffocated or tied down, but he insisted that he didn't mind scaling back to selling the occasional photograph, because his family would always be the most important thing in his life. Too many generations of Stewarts had struggled to make Highlander's successful, and he wasn't about to stand by and let it be gobbled up or run out of business by those huge, impersonal conglomerates that cared more about the bottom line than they did their employees or the product. The people who work at Highlander's have always been like family, and James appreciated that. He always said that roots grow deep in this rocky soil; that they're elastic enough to let you leave, but would pull you back home eventually."

"I love Highland Falls," Lily said; she couldn't imagine settling down anywhere else. "But it'd be nice to see more of the world."

"Nothing stopping you," Zelda pointed out.

"No." There was the gallery, but it wasn't as if she were feeding the hungry or healing the ill there. The town would certainly survive without her to sell her pretty things. "I suppose not."

"We're so much alike, you and I," Annie said. "You've taken wonderful care of all of us these past three years, darling. Now it's time for you to think about what you want for yourself."

"I'm not even sure I know what I want."

"You'll figure it out. I suspect a very strong part of you wants to run off with Ian MacKenzie."

"He's awfully independent." Look up *lone wolf* in the dictionary and there would be a picture of that tragically beautiful face. "He also hasn't given a single sign he wants me to go with him when he leaves."

"Perhaps you could conjure up some sort of love spell to put on the man," Annie suggested to Zelda.

Zelda frowned. "Love spells are always tricky, because the human heart is so unpredictable. Besides, it's unethical to put a spell on someone without their knowledge."

"It's just as well," Lily said, wishing for a spell that would turn the clock back to that lovely moment before Ian had shared his secret with her. "I'd hate wondering if it was me or some wiccan magic that attracted him."

"Gracious, Lily, don't be so hard on yourself. Even a blind woman could see that it's you, darling," her grandmother said with quiet confidence. "Which just goes to show that the MacKenzie has excellent taste."

Laurel arrived early that evening, along with Ian's soundman from New York and a tall, thin elderly woman who'd come all the way from Scotland for the games.

"We were on the flight together from D.C. to Asheville," Laurel explained as she introduced the friendly-looking man with the laughing blue eyes. "When I realized we were all headed up here, it made sense to share a car." She shot Brady O'Neill a look. "Though I hadn't expected him to complain about my driving the entire way up the mountain."

"Hey." Brady lifted both his hands. "I didn't complain."

"It certainly sounded like it to me." Laurel, the family overachiever, had never taken criticism well.

"I merely commented that I didn't realize the Highland Games included Grand Prix racing as a sport."

"Some people enjoy speed." Laurel's tone suggested that anyone who didn't was beyond worth thinking about.

"I like driving fast. So long as it's below the speed of sound and not on twisting, eighteen-percent-grade mountain roads in the dark."

"It was dusk. Besides, I grew up in these mountains. I know every twist of that road and could drive it blindfolded."

"You might as well have been, as tight as some of those curves were. And do you also happen to know every bear that might decide to cross?"

Brady shot a frustrated look toward Ian, who wasn't looking amused by the argument. In fact, Lily thought, he was looking nearly as grim as he had that first night.

"We almost broadsided a huge brown bear twice the size of the car," he told Ian.

"It was a Smoky Mountain black bear, and probably only about four hundred pounds," Laurel informed him huffily.

"It was brown."

Laurel rolled her eyes as if suggesting some people were too stupid to live. "A black bear is what kind of bear it is. They can be cinnamon, brown, blond, or a mix of colors."

"Then they shouldn't call them black bears," he shot back. "And it looked a lot bigger than four hundred pounds, but even if you're right, it was still a friggin' bear, okay? A carnivore who weighs more than the two of us together, with huge, flesh-ripping teeth and curved killer claws, who'd be really pissed off if you ran into him."

"I never would have expected such whining from the man who did the sound for that Sundance-winning film about the Afghani warlords."

"Hey, war zones I can deal with. I grew up in Hell's Kitchen. It's wild animals and women who drive like maniacs I'm not real comfortable with."

"I wasn't driving like a maniac." She turned toward the blue-haired woman dressed in a long pleated plaid skirt and ruffled, high-necked blouse. "You didn't seem nervous."

"Oh, being from the Highlands, I'm well accustomed to mountain roads," the woman, who'd signed the register as Molly Moodie, said on a high but trembling burr as thick as Scots porridge. "As for bears, we haven't had them in Scotland for a thousand years, so I rather enjoyed seeing that one."

"See?" Laurel put her hands on the hips of the exquisitely tailored tobacco-brown slacks she was wearing with a short-sleeve cream silk blouse and pearl earrings. Not a single glossy hair was out of place and her makeup, including

299

a tawny-rose lipstick, looked as if it had just been applied minutes earlier. Lily couldn't remember ever seeing her eldest sister look anything but perfect, which is why she'd always been surprised that Laurel had chosen print journalism over TV, where, with her looks and brains, she could have been a huge star. "Mrs. Moodie enjoyed the trip."

"I'm glad about that." Brady bestowed what appeared to be a sincere smile upon Molly Moodie, who smiled back, then returned his frowning gaze toward Laurel. "But that doesn't take away from the fact that if those brakes hadn't been working so well, we could have all ended up being eaten."

"Well, you needn't worry about being eaten at the Highland Games," Lily said, deciding it was time to break into the conversation. "Granted, bears do sometimes wander away from the park, but we're very careful about making sure that there's no garbage around to lure them here. Also, while they're often thought of as carnivores, the black bear is actually a true omnivore. Vegetable matter comprises over half their diet."

"That's freaking encouraging," Brady muttered. "So I've only got a fifty percent chance of being eaten."

Lily decided to break this up before the argument between her sister and Ian's soundman got entirely out of control. "Why don't we see if we can find you a room, Mrs. Moodie," she suggested. "We're a bit booked at the moment, but —"

"Why don't you put Mrs. Moodie in my room?" Annie surprised Lily by suggesting.

"Oh, ye needn't be bothering with that," the woman said quickly. A ruddy blush, which Lily took as embarrassment for having arrived without a reservation, stained her lined cheeks. "I wouldna want to be putting you out in any way."

"It's no bother," Annie assured her. "I've quite a large suite, and I'd enjoy the company. I'd love a chance to talk about my former home."

"I'd enjoy that, Mrs. Stewart." The way Mrs. Moodie's thin lips were drawn into a tight line didn't exactly match her words. "And it's quite kind of ye."

"It's Annie." She linked her arm with the elderly guest. "Lily will have someone see to your bags. Meanwhile, why don't we get you settled in?"

"Well," Lily said, "now that we've solved that, I'm sure you and Mr. O'Neill have tons to talk about, Ian. And Laurel, I've put you in with me."

She was about to suggest that Laurel would undoubtedly want to unpack and freshen up for dinner, when she glanced over at Ian, who was watching Annie and Molly Moodie leave the room.

His already firm jaw could have been carved from the side of Stewart's Mountain, and his eyes had turned to flint.

27

"What was that all about?" Ian asked once he and Brady were alone.

"I've no idea what you're talking about," Brady lied unconvincingly as he began to unpack the battered duffel bag that had been all over the world and looked it.

"That act you were pulling on Laurel Stewart. I've watched you drive a jeep without brakes down an eighteen-percent grade on an unpaved road riddled with land mines in the Pamir Mountains, without so much as breaking a sweat."

"You know that, and I know that." He winked. "But the lady reporter doesn't know it."

"So?"

"So, I think she likes me." He dumped his underwear into a drawer of a heavy tallboy dresser.

"You could have fooled me," Ian said. "I rather got the impression that she would have loved nothing better than to throw you over a cliff on the drive up here."

"Hell, that's just her way. Although the accent's not New England, she reminds me a lot of Katharine Hepburn. So, since *The African*

Queen is one of my all-time favorite flicks, I decided to pull out my Bogie imitation."

He'd always been a natural impersonator. Once, when they'd been filming in Bangkok, he'd managed to convince a pretty young Singapore Airlines flight attendant that he was Mel Gibson, despite being at least six inches taller and a decade younger than the Aussie actor.

"Excuse me for being a little confused, not being up on all the nuances of American cinema," Ian said, "but I don't see how complaining about killer bears and whining about a beautiful woman driving too fast parallels Bogie's Charlie Allnut. The whole point of that movie was that the guy was a man's man. He wasn't afraid of anything."

"He was afraid of leeches."

"That's different. Who wouldn't be?" Ian had had a nasty encounter with them while filming the vast destruction of the rain forest in the Amazon, and would rather do hard time in prison again than relive the experience.

"Laurel Stewart likes to argue," Brady said patiently. "You can see it turns her on."

"She looked angry to me."

"Some of the hottest sex I've ever had came out of anger," Brady said easily. "You watch, she won't be able to resist tangling with me, now that I've got things started. I figure by the time the last bagpipe has finished squalling, I'll have nailed her."

"You've such a way with words."

He grinned. "That's why I'm just the sound-man." He looked out over the expanse of misty blue meadow. "Nice place."

"Yeah. It is."

"I'll bet it reminds you of Scotland."

"Yeah. It does." Damned if the place hadn't gotten under his skin, just as Lily Stewart had.

"Those Stewart sisters are real babes, too. Lily may not exactly be your type, but from the vibes between the two or you, I'm guessing she's the reason you didn't want to shag that foreign correspondent in New York."

"I realize this may be a radical idea for you to accept, but believe it or not, not every man is led around by his dick," Ian said. "And my type would be?"

"A female who's tall, brunette, and knows the score. This one looks like she should be leading cheers at a homecoming game, though I gotta admit she's damn cute in a wholesome, small-town-America way." He leered wickedly. "I can just picture her jumping around in one of those short little skirts. There's probably not a man alive who wouldn't fantasize playing star quarterback with her beneath the bleachers."

"Knock it off." Ian's cool, even tone warned of a killer temper not many had witnessed. Brady, who knew him better than most, narrowed his eyes and looked at him more closely. "You're either frustrated as hell, or you've already gotten laid and don't want to talk about it."

"She's different, okay?"

Ian wasn't sure how he felt about Lily, and being brutally honest with himself, he suspected he was blocking off the answer rather than deal with it. He did know that sometime between that kiss in the gallery and making love to her after he'd confessed to his reason for having come to Highland Falls, he'd slipped from want to need to something else. Something foreign that had him feeling unnaturally possessive. And protective.

"Holy shit." Brady whistled. "I never thought I'd see the day any woman got her hooks into the slippery Dark Prince."

Brady O'Neill had always been perceptive, which made him one hell of a good partner. The trait was not endearing itself to Ian at the moment.

"Why don't you finish unpacking?" he suggested through gritted teeth. "I've got something to take care of. Then I'll show you around the place so you can take some sound checks."

"Yessir, boss." Brady snapped a salute.

If they hadn't been through so much together, Ian would have been tempted to knock that shit-eating grin off his face. But also, at the moment he had something more important to do. Like murder his grandfather.

Ian tracked Duncan down in the armory. Taking in the wall festooned with instruments of war, he wondered how on earth Lily could have grown up in such surroundings and remained so cheerful and optimistic.

"What the bloody fuck do you think you're doing here?"

"What does it look like I'm doing, laddie? I'm checking on you."

Ian's scowl sent his brows crashing down toward his nose. "So now you don't trust me to follow through?"

"I'm not saying that." Duncan had forgotten that his grandson's temper could be a fearsome hot thing. "I'm just saying that this is a big job and it might be better done by two men."

In truth, he had begun to fear that sending Ian to Highland Falls might not have been the best idea he'd ever had. Then again, there'd been no way he could have known the lad would get himself involved with the Stewart lass.

"Would you look at those claymores," he said in a blatantly unsubtle attempt to shift the topic to the gleaming swords displayed in their glass cases. "I hate to be admitting it, but the damn Stewart may have a better collection than we have at MacDougall Manor.

"They bring to mind an old story me own grandfather once told me about the old days, when the English and Scottish armies used to fight by gathering their armies on the top of the hills. They'd wait until daybreak, then run down the hillsides into the deep gorge below to fight.

"One morning a fog, as thick as pea soup it was, rose up and the two armies were waiting for the day to clear, when a voice with a Scottish burr came echoing across the mountains. 'Any one Scotsman can beat any ten Englishmen,' it called out.

"Well, wouldn't ye know it, but this fool English general sent down ten of his soldiers. There was the sound of steel clashing, and shouting, and no one returned. An hour later, the same voice shouted out, 'Any one Scotsman can beat any fifty Englishmen.'

"When the English general sent down fifty of his soldiers, another terrible fight ensued and again no one returned. An hour later —"

"How long does this go on?" Ian asked impatiently.

"Would ye be ignoring a history lesson from an old man? To be getting on with me tale, an hour later the same voice called out, 'Any one Scotsman can beat any hundred Englishmen.' Now the English general was getting quite angry, so he sent down one hundred of his best solders and not a one returned.

"An hour later, the voice said, 'Any one Scotsman can beat one thousand Englishmen.'

"By this time the English general had had enough, and was about to send down his elite troops when a lone Englishman came crawling up the hill. He was bloodied and battered to a pulp.

" 'Don't send any more troops down,' he warned the general. 'It's a bluidy trap. There's two of them Scots bastards.' " Duncan chuckled; he'd always enjoyed the story.

"Ha ha ha," Ian said, not sounding the least bit amused. "Now that I've had my history lesson for the day, would you mind telling why my grandfather has turned into a transvestite since I last saw him?"

"I'd be no such thing!" Duncan was good and truly shocked at the suggestion.

Ian swept him with a disgusted look. "Are you or are you not wearing a dress?"

"It's nae a dress. It's a disguise. I feared Annie might recognize me and realize a plot was afoot."

"In case you didn't notice, Annie Stewart happens to be blind."

Duncan bristled, because it had been a shock. "How was I to know that? Being how me grandson didn't see fit to mention it."

"You said you didn't care about her anymore, so it didn't seem relevant."

"I'd be deciding what's relevant and what's not." He was still shaken at the sight of his lovely Annie sightless. He'd also never been one to reveal his feelings. It was, he'd often thought, one of the few things he and his only grandson had in common. "That's a fine grouping of thumbscrews," he murmured, moving down the wall.

"Stop trying to change the subject. Blind or not, it's been sixty years. What makes you think she'd possibly recognize you after all that time?"

"Because I recognized her, dammit." He dragged a blue-veined hand down his face, hating the fact that after six decades apart, the woman could still make his heart stop. "It could have been yesterday."

There was a flash of something that could have been sympathy — Duncan refused to accept pity — in his grandson's eyes. "But you knew she'd be here," Ian pointed out. "There's no reason for her to make the connection, because you don't belong at Stewart's Folly."

"I'd have known her anywhere," Duncan said stubbornly. "As she would me. And now that we've established what I'm doing here, let's get down to business. I was thinking that we need to get the brooch back before the bloody wedding takes place. There'll be a party on the eve of the ceremony."

He could still vividly recall when he'd finally come out of the library after buying that building in town, and found Annie missing. "Everyone will be distracted by the celebration. That's when we'll get it back."

Ian shook his head. "Count me out."

"I knew it!" Duncan slammed his right fist into his left palm. "I knew you were about to weasel out on me."

His grandson's stony jaw firmed. "I'd be careful how I threw around that word. Because some might consider stealing something under the cover of a wedding party to be a bit weasellike."

"It won't be the first time someone used such subterfuge," Duncan said.

"Forget it." Ian threw up his hands. "I'd remind you that two wrongs don't make a right, but there's just no talking to you. Do whatever the hell you want. I'm washing my hands of the entire fool scheme."

"You'll not be able to inherit the brooch if I don't get it back."

"I don't want the damn thing."

"It's your birthright."

"It's *your* obsession."

Ian marched out of the room, slamming the thick door behind him. Duncan cursed, but understood his grandson's behavior. Although he might not have been as bold as the damn Yank and admittedly hadn't had as glib a tongue, he'd loved Annie MacFie to distraction and would have done anything to make her happy.

If the pretty red-haired Stewart lass possessed even a tad of the charms of her grandmother, Ian hadn't stood a chance.

28

Norway, 1955

It was Midsummer's Eve, and James had brought the family to Norway to photograph the single biggest reason to party across all Scandinavia, the summer solstice.

Even having grown up in Scotland, with its many lakes and rivers, Annie had been unprepared for the extraordinary beauty. She had no words to describe this magnificent landscape of mirrored lakes, rushing rivers, plunging waterfalls, lush pastures, and always, everywhere, the *fjell* — towering cloud-shrouded mountains that made the Highlands of her homeland look hospitable by comparison. Within mere miles, the land could soar from sea level to some of the highest summits in all of Europe.

Solvorn, set in the hinterlands where fjord gave way to mountains, was a tidy little town of turf-roofed homes on a far inland branch of the mighty Sognefjorden. The fjords were surrounded by high, steep walls of rocks and ice. The color of the water was constantly changing, from green to yellow, to blue, to black, which James had explained was the result of the water reflecting the fascinating light racing by in the milky sky overhead, constantly changing with the weather. Having lived with a photographer for ten years, she suspected it was the challenge all this ice and water presented that had brought so many other camera-carrying visitors to such a small isolated spot.

The men of the village had spent the past three days piling lumber onto the world's largest bonfire. Here in the land of almost perpetual winter darkness, a twenty-four-hour sun was reason to celebrate.

Pretty girls in white dresses searched the narrow inlet meadows, seeking out wildflowers, a different variety from each meadow. Some of the delicate glacier blossoms would end up in garlands worn on their blond heads; some floated in the cloud-shadowed water, others would be slipped beneath pillows, each girl dreaming of the man she'd marry.

"I don't need to gather flowers to put beneath my pillow tonight," Annie murmured.

James glanced up from adjusting his light meter. It was an odd, almost eerie light, too pale to show stars, even at midnight. The ice of the glaciers hovering over everything was tinged pale blue and green, presenting another photographic challenge to a man who appeared to live for challenges.

"Oh?" he asked, his eyes sparkling in a way that told her he'd already predicted her answer.

"Because I'll dream about the same man I've

been dreaming about since the day I met him," she said with a smile.

He leaned over and kissed her, a long, very unmarried type of kiss that drew a few hoots of good-natured laughter from bystanders who enjoyed the romantic display as much as they were enjoying everything else about the Midsummer's Eve festival.

"Later," he promised, with a quick, significant glance toward their children. It was difficult to get children to sleep in a land of so much sun, but Annie and James were motivated. After all, it was their tenth anniversary.

"Later," she agreed, running her fingertips over the brooch he'd given her earlier this evening over dinner.

Consisting of a crystal surrounded by pearls and set in silver, it was far larger than the jewelry she usually wore and too masculine for her taste. But when he'd told her that it was a family heirloom, she could tell how much the brooch meant to him and was moved that he'd marked their anniversary with something so personally special.

"I wonder what people do here," she murmured, watching as a group of young girls danced around the maypole that had been erected near the towering pyramid of logs. "During the long winter."

"I know what I'd do."

"What?"

"Sleep." He skimmed a hand down her cheek.

"Then wake up and spend the two summer months making love to my bride."

"I'm not exactly a bride anymore," she pointed out.

"Nonsense." After a decade together, his ready, rakish smile still had the power to curl her toes. "When we're celebrating our seventieth wedding anniversary, you'll still be the same gorgeous girl I married."

He turned to John Angus. "Your mama," he said, "was the most beautiful girl in all of Scotland."

"I know, Daddy," the six-year-old said with a child's absolute faith that everything his father said was true. The strange thing was that every time he'd said it, from the day they'd first met, Annie almost believed it herself.

"I'm going to grow up to be pretty just like Mama, aren't I, Daddy?"

"You're going to be a heartbreaker all right, Zelda, baby. Just like your doll face of a mama." He laughed and swooped his four-year-old daughter into his arms, bestowing a huge smack of a kiss on her puckered-up lips. The little girl was still giggling as he returned to work.

A trio of men touched lighted torches to the bonfire, which exploded into a burst of flame, sending orange sparks flying upward into the sky. In an echo of pagan times, merrymakers began to dance and sing around it.

"You can almost see the longships plowing up the fjord," Annie murmured. She imagined the scene as she planned to paint it: Viking warriors striding with much fanfare into the great hall of Valhalla, to be welcomed by their pagan gods.

"I rode on one of those ships one time," Zelda said matter-of-factly.

"You did not," John Angus said.

"Did, too." Tiny hands fisted on her hips. "It had a dragon head that scared away our enemies."

Annie exchanged a look with James, who shrugged. It wasn't the first time Zelda had told such a fanciful story. Their daughter had a very vivid imagination, making her parents wonder if she might be the first writer in the family.

As James grinned at her over his daughter's penny-bright hair, Annie wished she could freeze this perfect moment in time.

She had no way of knowing that the moment was actually frozen on film by a photographer from the Oslo *Aftenposten*. The family tableau appeared on the front page, and was picked up by other papers around the North Atlantic. Including *The Northern Scot*.

Five days later, their room at the hotel was broken into and the brooch stolen. Two days after that, they were all on a plane to America.

James Stewart was finally taking his family home.

29

Although Duncan hated to admit it, the Stewart who'd bought the land upon which this monstrous fake castle stood had chosen his location well. His window in the suite he was, amazingly, sharing with Annie possessed a splendid view of a sun-sparkled waterfall, woodlands of hardwood and evergreen, and seemingly unending verdant, mist-draped hills. There was a grandeur in the view that reminded him of home; if a man couldn't live in the Highlands, Duncan admitted these mountains just might be the next best thing.

Nearer to the house, several small bands of pipers were marching on the emerald-green croquet lawn, practicing for their upcoming competition. There were gardens everywhere: rock, herb, and an old-fashioned English country garden, complete with a maze.

A glimpse of yellow caught his eye; looking closer, he saw it was her — his dear Annie — wearing a flowing tunic and skirt as colorful as her garden, and a broad-brimmed straw hat.

She was carrying a wicker basket and a set of gardening shears. He watched her bend down to smell a pink blossom nearly the size of a dinner plate, and was surprised when she snipped off its long stem and placed it in the basket before moving on to the next bush.

When he'd first realized that she was blind behind the dark glasses she wore, the grudge Duncan had been nursing for years had given way to a deep sadness.

But as she'd walked him to this suite, maneuvering the castle's twists and turns that made the garden maze look simple by comparison, she certainly hadn't seemed to feel sorry for herself. Indeed, she'd chattered away like a magpie, but one with a rich, warm inviting voice that seeped beneath his skin and into his blood.

Now, remembering the way she'd wheeled barrows filled with soil all over her parents' rocky land to build her gardens, recalling the way she'd planted those impractical roses into the MacFies' vegetable garden, Duncan realized that she was still capable of surprising him. Which was one of the things that had once vexed him.

Life, he believed, should be carefully planned. And executed with precision, never wavering from your chosen path. So what if he was the pessimist some people — including his wife and daughter — had accused him of being? An optimist was too often disappointed.

There were no wishy-washy pastels in this garden, which didn't surprise him. The explosion of vibrant oranges, reds, purples, magenta, and yellow suited Annie's personality. He caught up with her just as she cut a bloodred rose; it joined the pink in the basket.

"Molly." Sensing him, she turned unerringly with a smile. "You're just in time to help me pick some flowers for the dinner table."

He altered his normally gruff voice to a wavering falsetto that, at least to his ears, sounded like the elderly postmistress back home. "I don't want to be rude," he said carefully, unaccustomed to censoring his words. "But isn't it difficult? Cutting flowers when you're, well . . ." He couldn't say the word out loud.

"Blind?" She smiled. "Not as much as you'd think. I planted every bush in all these gardens, so I tend to recall where they are. And even if I were to forget, their scents speak loudly enough that I can recognize them. Plus I'm not entirely blind yet. I still have some fogginess at the center of my vision, which allows me to see color."

"Your garden's certainly bright." Blindingly bright, he thought but did not say. Which was unusual for him, since he'd never censored his thoughts before, either.

"When I first moved here, it was much more sedate. But I got together with the gardener, who was a lovely man, and told him that I understood he'd been working here a long time and I didn't want to step on his toes, but I

318

wanted lots of nonstop color from spring to frost. And absolutely no white."

"Well, it looks as if you got what ye wanted," Duncan said, looking around at the sweeps of gaily hued flowers that set a mood that was somehow relaxing and stimulating at the same time.

"It's been a labor of love," she said easily. "It's also special because so many things were planted to celebrate an occasion. I started adding these lilies to the border when Lily's mother was pregnant with her, because my son and his wife had already decided if she was a girl, that would be her name."

The lilies were a riot of reds beneath purple globe-shaped flowers that looked like giant lollipops swaying lightly in the evening breeze. Annie traced her fingers down the stem of a trumpet-shaped scarlet blossom, then clipped it with remarkable precision.

She turned, taking him past leafy green topiary llamas and deer, down another garden path. "This rose is called Curiosity. I've always thought it ironic that I first planted it for Laurel's birth, and here she is, an investigative reporter. Damn." She pricked her finger when she went to cut one of the scarlet and yellow flowers.

"You've hurt yeself." He took her hand in his and wiped at the small red dot.

"Oh, I'm always doing that. It'd be easier if I'd use gloves, but then I wouldn't be able to feel where to cut."

"Why don't you let me cut the stems?" he suggested. "And you can pick them out."

"Teamwork," Annie said approvingly. She held out the scissors, handle first. "What a good idea. We'll get done sooner, and have some time to sit and talk. Early evening and early morning are my favorite times in the garden."

They worked well together, as if they'd been doing so for years. By the third cutting, Duncan had begun to figure out which stems she wanted long, which she wanted short. It wasn't that he had any talent for floral design, but they were somehow in tune. More so than he could ever remember being with anyone. Certainly more than he'd been with Annie MacFie back when she'd been a girl.

When the basket was filled to her satisfaction, Annie laced their fingers together in a casual, easy way and led him to a small white gazebo hidden beneath a grove of white blooming dogwood trees, which were canopied by taller maples, tulip trees, and southern pine.

"This is my secret garden," she said. "I used to love to come here and read. Now I bring my books on tape, but it's not quite the same thing because it disturbs the silence, which has always been one of the special things about the spot."

"It's very quiet." The only sound was the soft sough of a faint breeze through the trees, the burble of a crystal brook flowing over mossy rocks, and the throaty warble of songbirds overhead. Every so often the distant sound of pipes would float by, mingling with the bird-song.

"Do you know, when you first arrived, your voice sounded so familiar," she mused. "Even more so since we've had a bit of time to chat. Not the tone, but the cadence. You're obviously from the Highlands."

"Aye." He didn't dare say where, for fear of her wanting to talk about people they might have in common.

"I once knew someone with an accent a great deal like yours," she said.

"Did ye now?" His Adam's apple bobbed furiously as he struggled to keep the tension from his tone. "So would that be in Scotland, or here in America?"

"Scotland. In the Highlands near Fort William. Do you know it?"

"Of course. It'd be near the Ben Nivas and the Commando Monument at Spean Bridge."

"It is."

Watching her as intently as he was, Duncan saw her lips turn down in a faint frown and knew her mind had drifted to one particular commando. *She's allowed to think of the Stewart,* the little voice of conscience in the far murky reaches of his brain insisted. *Just as you're allowed to remember your wife.*

"It's nice to hear the old home accent again after all this time."

He wondered if she realized that her own

voice was still touched with the burr of the Highlands. "Have ye been away from home a long time, then?"

"Sixty years."

"That's a long time not to see your home. Did ye not have family?"

"Not any immediate family. My parents died when I was in my twenties, a month apart. I was traveling in a distant part of the world at the time, and only heard about it after they'd been buried. Since I was an only child, I don't have any nieces or nephews."

"And there were no other people you were close to?"

Her still-lovely face softened a bit. "There was someone. Once upon a time ago."

"A man?"

"Aye." Her accent thickened the more they spoke, as if a very strong part of her mind — and, he wondered, her heart? — was eager to return home. "A childhood friend. I once thought I'd be spending the rest of my life with him, but it didn't work out that way."

"Did he marry someone else?"

"Do you know, I'm not sure." She absently ran a fingertip over the velvety petal of a deep red rose she'd told him was named Othello. "But I imagine he did. He was a very good-looking man. And wealthy, besides."

"Two appealing aspects in the male."

"I suppose so. But I've always felt that inner qualities were more important than appearances. As for wealth, well . . ." She shrugged slender shoulders.

"You're not exactly living in a crofter's cottage," he pointed out, his voice sharpened with a bit of old resentment.

If she noticed his tone, she chose to ignore it. "No, Stewart's Folly, as we fondly refer to it, certainly isn't a cottage. But I would have — and did for a time — followed my husband anywhere, and would have been happy to live with him in a castle, a cottage, or a cave."

He didn't doubt her. Which meant it had been the man, not what he'd been able to offer her, that she'd fallen in love with. That idea did nothing to ease his pique. "So ye never had regrets?"

"Never about marrying James. I was horribly sorry that I hurt a good man, and certainly didn't handle events as well as I should have, but I've given it a lot of thought over the years, and I honestly believe that I would have done more harm by marrying the man I was originally betrothed to."

"Perhaps that's convenient thinking."

"No." About this she was firm. "My marriage never would have lasted."

"Because you wouldn't have been able to be faithful to a man you didn't love?"

"I know it sounds less than the truth, given the fact that I was technically engaged when I accepted James's proposal, but if I had already exchanged vows with Duncan, I never, ever would have cheated on him." Her voice held a bit of the spark that had accompanied her once-red hair.

"What if you'd met this man . . . what was his name, James? . . . after your marriage?" That idea had bedeviled him for over half a century.

"I would not have allowed myself to fall in love with him."

"Hearts tend to have minds of their own."

"Well, that's true enough," she allowed. "But marriage is a sacred trust. I would not have betrayed it."

"Then why wouldn't the marriage have worked? Was the man you were betrothed to cruel?"

"Oh, no," she said quickly. "Duncan was never the slightest bit cruel. But he was . . ." She paused, as if seeking the right words. "Hard. And stubborn."

"Most Scots wouldn't be considering strength and tenacity a fault." He certainly didn't.

"Perhaps that's what was appealing about an American. I'd grown up surrounded by men like Duncan. James was certainly a strong man; he'd been one of Darby's Rangers in the war and had survived being in German prison camps. But he knew when to be soft and caring. And how to laugh. Duncan, on the other hand, was as rigid as the mountains he was raised in."

She sighed again. Then smiled. And in that moment, she claimed his heart just as she had so many years ago.

"Enough about my ancient history," she said briskly. "It's your turn to tell a tale. Tell me about yourself. Do you have a husband? Children? Grandchildren?"

Still bedazzled by her smile, Duncan forgot to watch his words. "I had a wi—" He slammed his mouth shut so hard and so fast, his teeth rattled. "A wonderful spouse. But he passed on more than twenty years ago."

She touched a hand to his sleeve. Annie had always been a toucher; he was not. "I'm so sorry."

"So was I." At the time, he'd been surprised at how much he'd missed the woman who, although he tried never to let her know, he'd always considered second choice. He honestly had loved his wife in his fashion, and had done his best to be a good husband, but there had been those dark nights when he'd lain in his bed beside her and wondered what might have happened if the bluidy American had never come to Scotland. "He was a good spouse. We had a daughter."

"Had?"

"She died, as well. With her husband." It still hurt, one of those dull aches he'd learned to live with, like the way his creaky old bones ached whenever it rained. Which, in the Highlands, was most of the time.

"How terrible!" She pressed a palm against the front of her bright tunic, as if feeling the pain in her own breast. "Was it an accident?"

"It wasn't planned." He tamped down the anger and allowed the soothing scent of roses, emanating from skin he longed to touch, to act as a balm to his anger. She'd always had that effect on him. When she hadn't been churning up his hormones, she'd been calming his mood. It wasn't until this moment that he realized he'd taken her nurturing temperament for granted. "They were killed by a drunken driver."

"How dreadful." She placed her hand over his. "Did they have children?"

"Aye. A son." Who, though he'd never told Ian, was Duncan's pride and joy. "He was nearly a man, eighteen years old, when they died."

"Children never outgrow the need for their parents. I have two children and three darling granddaughters who are the light of my life. It must have been very difficult for both of you." She put her arms around him and pressed her fragrant cheek against his. "I'm so, so sorry."

He wanted to hold her tight against him, as he'd once done so many years ago. Wanted to kiss her as he'd dreamed about for too many decades to count. Not trusting himself, he kept his hands to himself, his fingers curled into fists.

The brief embrace, which shook him throughout, ended far too soon. "At least you had each other," she said. "How did he grow up? The boy."

"He overcame it admirably."

But Duncan was not so remote from human emotions that he could not recognize the dark themes his grandson tended to dwell on. Shame for his behavior went deep, but he'd never been able to get the apology out, so he'd tried to show Ian in deeds, rather than words, the regret he suffered whenever he recalled that fateful day in the cemetery when he'd watched them put his darling lass into the ground. The dark day he'd driven Ian away for so many years.

It was going well, Lily thought three days later. Better than well. Only days ago, she never would have thought that she and Ian could work so easily together. She also hadn't realized how much fun could be had in making a movie, and wondered why she'd never tried photography while searching for a talent.

"The sword dance goes back to the eleventh century," Lily explained as they stood side by side at the edge of the clearing, watching a practice session. "When King Malcolm the Third killed one of MacBeth's chieftains, he crossed his swords over the vanquished man and danced over them to celebrate his victory. Ever after that, the dance was performed on the eve of a battle and victory was predicted if the dancer was able to execute the steps without touching the swords."

"Or cutting anything off," Ian murmured as he focused his camera down the line of dancers, capturing a row of burly, kilt-clad men displaying surprising grace as they seemed to be suspended in air.

"Good point." Lily zeroed in on a giant of a man, patiently watching as his preschool-aged son, brow furrowed in concentration, tried to duplicate his steps. "Since those swords were undoubtedly a lot sharper when they were being used for real." When the boy fell down, the father scooped him up, braced him on a kilted hip, and together, father and son finished the dance.

"A nice personalized touch," he said when he glanced over and took in the sight of the two ruddy smiling faces on her view screen.

"That's Donovan MacPherson and his son Jamie. The MacPherson family's been in the whisky business in these mountains for the past two centuries," she said. "He's the first of his family to work for Highlander's. The rest were independent distillers."

"You mean they were moonshiners."

"They were, indeed, and their product, while not up to Highlander's professional qualities, was quite popular. You might want to talk with him. He has some great stories to tell about making moonshine runs with his grandfather when he was a little boy."

"Is there anyone in this town you don't think we should include?"

She laughed. "Well, Donald might put viewers to sleep if you got him discussing all those generations of Forbeses." She waved to a woman seated at a table beneath a tent painted with Celtic symbols and a bright green and silver dragon breathing flames. The hand-lettered sign offered tarot card readings. "That's Una Gunn. She's Lark's godmother."

"She looks nearly as old as these mountains," Ian said as Una Gunn waved back. Her smiling, weathered face reminded him of the shriveled apple-faced folk dolls he'd seen in Lily's gallery. "Isn't a godmother usually someone closer to the age of a mother?"

"I don't know why that needs to be the case. Una's always been spiritually connected to Lark. In fact, she named her months before she was born, saying that she was going to be the one to keep the old songs alive."

"And your parents actually bought that prediction?"

"It turned out to be true," Lily pointed out mildly. "And I suppose the fact that she's Highland Falls's most powerful witch may have had something to do with their believing it."

"I thought your aunt Zelda was the town witch."

"Oh, these hills are filled with people who practice the old ways," she said. "Their descendants came here to escape persecution, the same as other groups. They brought their traditions with them, and every holler had its witch it could call on for dousing, or healing, or spellcraft. Because we're isolated, the traditions weren't lost or modernized as they were in the rest of the country, and since basic needs like crop fertility and livestock health remained as important to the people of twentieth-century Appalachia as it did in the seventeen hundreds, it makes sense that a religion based on nature stayed a current part of people's faith, rather than fading away into some mythic memory like it did in the cities."

"And here I thought all those cauldrons I keep seeing in people's yards were merely a quaint decoration."

"In most cases, they are. The trend unfortunately became popular after one of those Southern shelter magazines printed a photograph of one outside a house in Johnson City. But when Lark and Laurel and I were growing up, a cauldron in the front yard meant the witch inside was open for business. You know," she said, "I think you ought to consider —"

"Putting Una Gunn in the documentary," Ian guessed on a laugh.

Lily grinned back at him, wishing she could freeze time and wondering if he had any idea just how much his bold laughter had come to mean to her.

They'd just returned from the practice field when her father came striding across the great hall, appearing larger than life as always.

"Lily, dear, I'm glad I caught you. We're having a family dinner tonight and I want you there. In the formal dining room, eight o'clock."

Lily didn't want to waste the precious time she and Ian had; she had the rest of her life to have dinner with her family. Perhaps Lark and

Laurel being home at the same time didn't happen that often, but it also wasn't often a man like Ian MacKenzie showed up in Highland Falls. Never before, actually.

"I'm sorry, Daddy, but —"

"This is important." He overrode her. "Mac-Kenzie, you'll probably want to be there, as well."

"I wouldn't want to intrude." Lily noticed that Ian seemed no more enthralled by that idea than she was.

"Hell, man, you won't be intruding. Haven't you become like family? Besides, you'll be wanting to bring your camera. I'm making an announcement that you'll want to put in the film. It's about the Brooch of Lorn. I imagine you may have heard of it."

"I saw a copy in the gallery," Ian said. "It's quite impressive."

"If you think the copy is something, wait until you see the real one," John Angus predicted. "It'll knock your socks off."

Lily felt her blood go cold. It couldn't be, she thought, unable to look at Ian for fear of her shock being mistaken for guilt. "Surely you're not saying you have the brooch," she said faintly.

John Angus stroked his flaming beard with fingers stained with cerulean-blue paint. "I'm not saying I do. And I'm not saying I don't." He winked at Ian. "I'm just saying MacKenzie will want to get my announcement on film for posterity."

"Tape," Ian murmured.

"Tape, film, what's the difference? It's the message that's important, not the medium." Wondering if he'd behave so cavalierly if someone were to confuse his oversized oil paintings with sidewalk chalk drawings, Lily was grateful when Ian held his tongue. "Eight o'clock," John Angus reminded them, and left.

Lily turned to Ian, afraid of the expression she'd see on his face. She'd never — ever! — imagined having to defend herself against being a criminal. It was ludicrous to suddenly have to proclaim her innocence twice in a single week. "I didn't steal it."

He didn't appear angry, or distrustful; there was something else in his eyes. Because he was so good at guarding his emotions, she couldn't read what he was thinking.

"I know."

"If it really is the brooch, this is going to cause you more problems with your grandfather, isn't it?"

His answer was short and succinct. "Yes."

30

The private dining room was an exercise in Gothic style run amuck. Swarming with heraldic devices on the stone walls draped in velvet panels in the yellow, red, black, and white hues of the Stewart plaid, and hung with gigantic brass chandeliers, it looked to Ian like a place Vlad the Impaler might have chosen to dine. Or where the family might enjoy watching a little bear-baiting over dessert. The table linens were tartan, the flatware gold plated, as were the chandeliers.

The huge ceiling beams had been painted with religious scenes featuring Scottish saints, among them the crucifixion of Saint Andrew; Saint Fillan in his cave, battling the cold and darkness of winter to record the scriptures; the martyrdom of Saint Constantine, showing the attack by pirates cutting off his right arm; and the body of Saint Margaret, beloved queen of Scotland, her deathbed surrounded by the poor she always fed before partaking of her own frugal meals, who appeared to be wailing and lamenting her early death from endless days of toil for the church, nights of prayer, and rigid self-discipline every good Scots was brought up to admire.

"Do you actually eat in here?" he asked Lily, who was seated beside him.

"Only on what my father refers to as ceremonial occasions," she said.

"I wouldn't think one would have to worry about overeating."

She glanced up at the painting he was looking at directly over their head, depicting the beheading of John the Baptist, patron saint of the Scottish town of Perth. "They're not exactly cheery, are they?"

"That's putting it mildly. And they say we Scots Protestants are grim."

"Do you know, I haven't noticed them in ages. But thinking back on it, they did give me nightmares when I was a child."

"And no wonder. I'm surprised no one's painted them over in the past two centuries."

"I don't know about earlier Stewarts, but I suspect my grandparents and father would have been reluctant to destroy other artists' work."

"Good point. But they're certainly not appetizing." He slipped his hand beneath the tablecloth, running his hand up her leg, and watched the naked desire rise in her eyes. "Now that's a much lovelier view," he murmured. "How long do you think we have to stay here?" She was wearing a short plaid skirt that left her legs bare and allowed Ian to trace a figure eight on the silky skin at the inside of her thigh.

"If you keep doing that, I'll scandalize everyone by jumping you before we get to the main course," she warned.

"Taking you on this enormous table would significantly improve any memories I'll have of this room."

Ian had always been a restless sort, needing the stimulation of new places, new people. But he didn't like to think ahead to the day he'd be leaving Highland Falls. And Lily.

"Besides, I doubt any of your family members, with the possible exception of your aunt Melanie, scandalize all that easily."

She laughed at that, drawing the attention of Laurel, who was seated across the table. Her sister's narrow-eyed gaze suggested she didn't exactly trust Ian, but she'd always been the most skeptical of the three Stewart sisters. Lily had often suspected that was what made her such a good investigative reporter: she took nothing at face value.

The chef had outdone himself, serving up a cream of chanterelle soup, the broth cloudy with wild mushrooms, Black Angus beef braised with a red Bordeaux and served with roasted carrots and potatoes.

Dessert was a custard, served with a raspberry-flavored tea.

"You haven't eaten much," Ian murmured to Lily when the kilt-clad waiter, borrowed from the public dining room, took away her plate.

"It's hard to think about eating when I may

have to face the fact that my own father set me up," she murmured back.

The idea had been worrying her ever since Ian had dropped the bombshell about the brooch. She feared she knew exactly what had happened to it. And why the MacDougalls believed she'd been the thief.

"What do you mean?"

Laurel was looking at them hard and deep, making Lily feel like a congressman who was about to be caught taking bribes from polluters.

"I'll tell you later."

At that moment, John Angus pushed himself back from the table. He spread his legs and linked his large fingers behind his back. Lily sighed. "We could be in for a long evening," she said. "Daddy's in speech-giving mode."

When she exchanged a quick glance with Laurel, she could tell they were thinking exactly the same thing.

He began with the story they'd all heard time and time again, about how the first Stewart had come to America in 1739 on the *Thistle*, which was the Scots *Mayflower*. The ship had landed at Cape Fear, North Carolina; then the passengers began to move inland, up the Cape Fear River to settle at Cross Creek, named for two creeks which supposedly intersected without mixing currents.

"Seventeen fifty-four was a year of infamy for the family," the deep voice boomed from the end of the table. "A new county was formed, and needless to say there was no way James Andrew Stewart would allow his family to live in a place named to honor William Augustus, duke of Cumberland; the very same butcher who murdered Bonnie Prince Charlie's army and the Highland cause, that dark day on the wet and boggy Culloden Moor, which was then called Drumossie Moor."

He looked around the table, ensuring he had everyone's attention. "Proud Cumberland pranced, insulting the slain, while their hoof-beaten bosoms were trod to the plain," he intoned.

Ian leaned toward Lily. "How long does this go on?"

"Let's see, the battle of Culloden Moor was in 1746. And this is?"

"You're not saying we're going to work our way through two hundred and fifty years of the Stewarts in America?"

"I'm afraid so."

"So," John Angus continued, "the family was cruelly uprooted yet again, moving higher and higher into the hills, where a man could live without constant reminders of the past."

"Failed there," Laurel murmured loud enough for those around her to hear.

Lark, who hadn't smiled since her arrival home, actually burst out with a short laugh, then covered her mouth apologetically as her father's brows knit together. "Sorry," she said, "I choked on my tea."

Seeming satisfied with this excuse, he continued with his saga.

"You might as well get comfortable," Lily advised. "The Revolutionary War and the building of Stewart's Folly after the war take some time."

"If your father and my grandfather ever get together, they'll be talking until doomsday," Ian said. Leaning back, he poured a glass of Highlander's Pride from one of the decanters that had been placed on the table.

With his stomach pleasantly full, his head a bit buzzed from the whiskey, his fingers idly playing with Lily's beneath the tablecloth, Ian had just about stopped listening. Until he realized the Stewart had just gotten to 1955.

"In an evil scheme perpetuated by the MacDougalls, the bonny Brooch of Lorn, which is rightfully Stewart property due to our direct line to The Bruce himself, was taken from my father while he and my mother were in Norway for the annual solstice fires. It was rumored that Duncan MacDougall had hired the thief who'd broken into their hotel room and done the dastardly deed, but the MacDougall, scoundrel that he is, would admit to nothing. Recently, his guilt has been proven."

Lily exchanged a look with Ian and realized that he was thinking the same thing. This was obviously when and how Duncan had reclaimed the brooch. It also made her wonder if part of the reason her grandfather had been willing to return home and go to work in the distillery was because he'd felt guilty about having risked — and lost — The Bruce's brooch.

"I'm pleased to announce that today the brooch is back in Stewart custody." He picked up a small wooden box, opened it, and dramatically lifted the ancient jewel high for everyone to see. The silver had been polished to a gleaming shine, the crystal glittered, the pearls glowed like small moons. "Just in time for me to be giving it to my bride as a marriage gift, when we're wed at the end of the games."

He beamed down at Jenny, who beamed back up at him.

Annie gasped in obvious surprise, which suggested that whatever had happened when James Stewart had returned to Scotland after the war, at least she hadn't been a party to this latest theft.

"Lord, would you look at that thing," Ian murmured. "It appears Duncan was right all along."

"Dammit, I'm going to have to confront my father about this."

"Want some company?"

"No." She seldom lost her temper, but when she did, it wasn't pretty. Lily didn't want Ian to watch her screech like a fishwife. "Though I appreciate the offer."

"No problem. But after you're finished, I want to be with you. Alone."

"I want to be with you, too, but Lark's in my apartment, Laurel's in my room here, Brady's on that rollaway in yours, and I doubt there's a hotel room available anywhere in town."

Ian leaned closer, his mouth right next to her ear. "I want to be with you, Lily. I want to taste you, to touch you, all over. I want to take your breast in my mouth and I want to take you, deep and slow and long. I want to be inside you. I want to feel your hot, moist body surrounding me. I want to —"

"Stop." She pressed her fingers against his mouth. "Or you'll have me coming right here."

"Sounds good to me." He glanced down at the table and once more imagined her spread out like a particularly succulent treat. "Let's meet here. On the stroke of midnight."

Color flooded into her cheeks and he knew she was imagining the possibilities. "Here," she agreed. "At eleven-thirty."

31

"You used me!" Lily furiously paced the tartan carpeting of the library. "You set me up! Your very own daughter. How could you do such an evil thing?"

"Now, Lily, darling, it wasn't exactly that way," her father protested.

"It was exactly that way!"

Not caring if she broke every piece of crystal in Stewart's Folly, her voice screeched up the scale, rivaling her aunt Melanie's in the gallery. "You knew I was going to Scotland on my annual trip." She stopped so close to him, the toes of her high heels slammed against the heavier ones of his brogues. "You paid someone to break into MacDougall Manor, steal that damn brooch, then bring it to me at the hotel to deliver to you."

Having remembered the package when Ian had first told her about the theft, she'd been worried that had been the case, but hadn't been able to believe her own father would do such a thing to her.

"Do you ever think of anyone but yourself?" she stormed.

"Now, Lily," he cajoled, "it's not as if anyone got hurt."

"Only because of dumb luck!" She shoved her finger against the broad wall of his chest. "What if Duncan MacDougall had called the police and reported the brooch missing? What if they'd come to search my hotel room —"

"Now why would they be doing such a thing?"

"Because I was there, dammit!" Her voice had turned strident enough to put her at risk for bleeding ears. She took a deep breath. "I was there. At the manor."

"So I heard. I hadn't expected that."

"Well, excuse me. I hadn't realized I needed to check my itinerary with you."

"It's not like you to be sarcastic, darling." He looked wounded. Lily didn't care.

"I carried the damn box in my carry-on, because the man who showed up at my hotel stressed how important it was for you to get it, and I wanted to keep it safe." She dragged both hands through her hair in frustration that he still didn't get it. "If I'd been stopped by airport security —"

"That would never happen," he said. "You look nothing like a terrorist."

"You've never heard of random searches?"

He finally cringed. "In all honesty, that hadn't occurred to me. I've been so involved in getting my work finished for the showing, and the wedding —"

"You've done nothing for the damn wedding

but steal a priceless piece of jewelry for your bride-to-be!"

"I didn't steal it; it belongs to us, Lily. The MacDougalls were the ones who stole it in the first place, and Duncan MacDougall, damn his black soul, is the one who stole it from your grandfather in Norway after he'd made the mistake of giving it to your grandmother. A photographer snapped their picture, which ended up in some papers, and five days later, it disappeared from their hotel room."

"Did my grandmother know that her anniversary present was stolen property?"

"Not stolen. Reclaimed," he insisted. "And of course she didn't. How could you accuse your grandmother of being a thief?"

"I didn't call her a thief. I'm just trying to figure out what she knew and when she knew it."

"She only knew that it was a family heirloom that once belonged to The Bruce. The actual history has always been a family secret, kept to the men." He rubbed his bearded chin. "In fact, I'd almost put it out of my mind, until I fell in love with Jenny and started thinking about the Stewart dynasty. That's when I decided I had to get it back."

"So Jenny knows you're a thief?"

"That's a hard thing to call your father, Lily. And I thought it best, under the circumstances, to keep her in the dark about the details."

Clearly wounded by her accusations, he'd risen to his full, impressive height, but Lily refused to be intimidated. "Interesting that you had no problem keeping *me* in the dark."

"We needed to get the brooch back, Lily. You were the obvious choice, since no one would suspect you."

Duncan MacDougall had certainly suspected her.

"Just because someone stole something in a battle in 1306 doesn't mean that we have to steal it centuries later."

"It belongs to the Stewarts." His expression was set. The man was so hardheaded, she might as well have been talking to a stone wall.

Ian was right, Lily thought as she left the library. They ought to just bring Duncan MacDougall over here from Scotland and lock the two men in a room to settle this stupid feud once and for all.

She was only sorry that the Stewart who built this castle hadn't put in a dungeon.

Unaccustomed to introspection as he was, Duncan couldn't define the feeling that was eating away at him after his time in the garden with Annie. But whatever it was had left him unable to sit still. It was a lovely night, with a high moon that spilled light all over the rolling hills, making the landscape nearly as bright as day.

He was walking across the property on a small narrow lane that followed a creek, when he heard something that sounded like a cross between a cat fight and a sick calf mooing for its mother. He came around the bend, and standing in the center of a small clearing was a teenage girl wailing away on a bagpipe. Her red T-shirt asked, GOT PIPES?

"You're out of tune," he said.

She took her mouth from the blowstock pipe. "I just tuned it," she said with obvious frustration.

"Then ye'd be tuning it wrong."

She hit a particularly strident note and stomped her foot. "Damn, damn, damn."

Duncan was not a man to interfere in another's business. But the lass looked on the verge of tears, and if there was one thing he could not abide, it was a female's weeping.

"I might be able to help ye."

"You?" She raked a look over him as if there were nothing an elderly woman could possibly do to assist anyone.

"I've played the pipes before."

"Really?" She looked more interested. "I didn't know women played the pipes in Scotland. Especially not in your day. Not that you're so very old," she said quickly, "but —"

"Of course I'm old. But that doesn't mean I wouldn't be knowing how to play the pipes. You need to begin with your chanter. It's off by a half note, which is why your drones are off, as well."

He reached for the bagpipes, which she surrendered with a deep sigh. She was nearly the age his own lass had been when she'd fallen in love with Gavin MacKenzie and gotten herself pregnant. He'd been hard on Mary. Too hard, Duncan had come to understand. Unfortunately, some lessons came too late to be able to do anything about them.

But he could do something for this lass.

"It should be a clear A." Although his hands were a wee bit gnarled from age there were some things, like tuning a set of pipes, they didn't forget. He tuned the double reeds with a quick, deft touch. "Now, we set the tenor drones an octave below." He raised the drone to flatten it. "And the bass two octaves below your chanter." He didn't need to blow, to know it would be correct.

"Now try," he said, handing it back to her.

Shoulders drooping, her small, downcast face looking as if she were expecting the worst, she put her mouth back on the blow pipe and pressed the bag slightly against her body.

"That's it!" She stared up at him, her face glowing with pleasure. It was such a little thing, Duncan thought. A mere moment's fiddling with some tubes, but she looked as if he'd given her a treasure chest of gold. "Wow. You're really good."

"I suppose I'm fair to middlin'," he agreed with false modesty. He'd never been one to boast, and to do so while wearing women's clothing would be even more unseemly. "The pipes are a wonderful instrument, but they're temperamental. Moisture and temperature can change the pitch, and you'll want to spend at

346

least fifteen and as many as thirty minutes tuning them up before playing."

"I'll try, but it's not easy."

"Wouldn't that be why they invented the word *practice?*"

"I've been practicing, but it's hard, because although I went to piping school last year, my teacher moved to Santa Cruz three months ago, so I've been trying to get ready for the competition by myself."

"Well, while you're getting yourself ready, keep your fingers straight. Curling them up like claws will not only make you play poorly, you'll have points taken off in the competition."

"Okay." She played a few notes. "How's that?"

"Better. What have you chosen to play?"

" 'Abercairney Highlanders,' " she said proudly. "What's wrong with that?" she asked when he responded with a scowl.

"You're overreaching, lass. 'Abercairney Highlanders' is unforgiving, difficult to play well on a good day, and if you relax for so much as a moment, you'll throw away any chance ye might have had for a decent score. What ye need is a nice two-four time march like 'John MacColl.' Would you be knowing it?"

"Some."

"Then learn it more. You'll be scoring better if you play an easy tune well, than if you play a hard tune poorly."

"I suppose that makes sense."

He could see she wanted to rush ahead, but

pipes were not something you picked up one day and began playing at funerals the next.

"There's a story about a time when the lads were marching into battle," he said, "with the piper playing away like mad. Well, the enemy's arrows, swords, and spears were creating bloody slaughter all through the Scottish ranks. Ten men down, and the piper, valiant lad that he is, plays on. Twenty men down, and still the pipes ring out. Finally fifty men have fallen, and the chieftain shouts to the piper, 'For heaven's sake, can ye not play something they like?' "

She laughed a bit at that.

"Aye, it's a joke," Duncan said. "But it's something to keep in mind when you're choosing a good song to play before the judges. You'll also want to rehearse your song over and over again until you can play for ten minutes straight without breaking down."

"But the junior competition event only lasts two minutes."

"That's one of the tricks of piping, you see. You should be able to push it past the point where your lips start to give out and your arm begins to fall off. Stamina is important for a piper. You'll want to be developing it."

She looked at him with renewed interest. "Are you here for the games?"

"Aye." Duncan braced himself for what he feared would be coming next.

"I'm going to be competing. Would you help me?"

"With what?" Bluidy hell, what had he gotten himself into by opening his big mouth? Had to show off, didn't he? And now look what had happened.

"With the pipes. Could you give me some last-minute coaching?"

The moment he saw the girl, he should have turned around and walked back to that monstrosity of a fake castle.

"Would ye happen to be a Stewart?" The idea of helping a member of James Stewart's clan grated.

"Sort of. My aunt was married to John Angus. She died before I was born, but everyone says she was a wonderful woman. They say I look a bit like her."

"Then she must have been bonny." When she blushed, he was once again reminded of his own daughter and opportunities lost.

Ian had been right about one thing; there was no way they were going to locate the brooch's hiding place. They'd have to wait until John Angus brought it out to show it off. Meanwhile, he wouldn't want it to be said that a MacDougall ever backed away from a challenge.

"Well," he said, rubbing his hands together. "If we're going to have you in shape by the games, lass, we'd best get cracking."

Ian was not at all surprised to find his grandfather waiting up for him when he returned to the tower room after midnight.

"Where have ye been?" Duncan asked.

"None of your business."

"It's every bit my business, since the only reason you're here in America is because I sent you."

"You may have been the impetus, but you're no longer the reason."

"It's the lass."

"She's also none of your business."

"She is if she stole my brooch."

"Goddammit, I keep telling you, Lily didn't do it." Ian considered keeping John Angus's announcement to himself, but decided the news of the Brooch of Lorn being in Stewart possession would be sweeping the games. "She was merely a pawn."

"Of the Stewart."

"Yes."

"I knew it." Surprisingly, Duncan didn't look as satisfied as Ian would have suspected.

A moment later, Ian understood why. "You're thinking of Annie Stewart, aren't you? And how she'll feel about your stealing her dead husband's brooch."

" 'Twasn't his." There was not quite as much strength in the denial.

"That's a matter of opinion."

Duncan cursed, then poured two glasses of Highlander's Pride and held one out to Ian. "Women," he said, "are one bluidy complication."

Ian lifted his glass. "I'll drink to that."

32

The Kirking of the Tartan kicked off the Highland Games in fine style.

"You realize," Ian murmured to Lily, as they watched the parade of clans piped into the church behind tartan banners held high, "that nothing like this actually exists in Scotland."

"Don't be such a spoilsport." She focused her video camera on a pink-cheeked toddler with an angelic halo of blond curls, dressed in a Cameron tartan. "It's a lovely legend."

"A legend as unbelievable as some ancient sea creature living in Loch Ness. Does anyone really believe that after Highland dress was banned, people actually carried around scraps of tartan to preserve clan dignity? And brought them to the church every Sabbath to be blessed?"

"It could have happened."

"Not in a month of Sabbaths. In the first place, the tartan sticks used to mark out traditional weaves were destroyed after the Act of Proscription banning Highland dress, so except for some paintings, we don't have the foggiest idea what any pre-1647 tartans looked like.

That being the case, any relics would be invaluable, not just to Scottish history, but in dollars. So where the hell did all those bits and pieces of cloth go?"

"I've no idea," she said sweetly. "Perhaps the MacDougalls stole them."

"Cute," he muttered. Since he'd already decided to layer the sound of bagpipes over this part, they were free to argue without worrying about Brady's microphone picking them up. "And how about the fact that blessing bits of cloth, or anything else inanimate, would have gone against everything the Calvinists preached? Can you imagine the punishment for practicing such a rite?"

"Honestly, Ian." She turned toward him. "You can be so cynical."

"And if you were given a pile of manure for your birthday, you'd spend two hours looking for the pony."

"Absolutely. And I'd find it." She flashed those killer dimples again. "And for the record, I believe in Nessie."

"You would." And he wouldn't have wanted her any other way.

Despite his objection, Ian couldn't deny that the ecumenical ceremony was, in its way, moving. During the roll call, members of each clan honored their heritage by standing. Watching Duncan, who was seated in the front of the church next to Annie, Ian could tell that he was itching to stand when they got to the Mac-

Dougalls. Which served the old bastard right, for having perpetuated such a deception.

Of course, he thought as the minister blessed the tartans, he hadn't told Lily about Duncan's subterfuge. Which was one more lie of omission he was going to have to answer for.

At the *Clan Dia,* all those not of Scots ancestry were also called to rise to honor God and family. Then there was another blessing, after which there was a final song.

" 'The Star-Spangled Banner'?" Ian asked.

"It's not usual," she admitted. "But I added it last year, because I thought while we were celebrating our Scots roots, it was also important to honor the country that took us all in."

Just as her family had taken him in. Sometime since his arrival, he'd gone from being a remote filmmaker to actually caring about not just Lily, but the other members of the family as well. He hoped John Angus — even if he was a thief — had made a wise choice in his young bride-to-be; he hoped whatever was causing the sadness in Lark's eyes would soon be solved, and that Missy, whose piping had sounded surprisingly better during the parade of the clans, had managed to convince her mother to forgo the debutante ball. He wished that a miracle cure could be found to restore Annie's sight, or that she'd at least have more time holding on to the vision she had.

And he definitely hoped that after he was gone, Lily wouldn't make the mistake of mar-

rying that supercilious Donald Forbes on the re-
bound. Not that he had any right to tell her who
she should be spending the rest of her life with,
but he knew the uptight jackass would bore her
silly. And could never come near bringing her to
the levels of passion she was capable of.

It was admittedly selfish, but when she was
Annie's age, sitting in one of those rockers on
the porch of her pretty little gallery, he wanted
her to remember him as the only man who'd
ever been able to make her fly. And, he thought,
remembering this morning's quick, hot cou-
pling in the greenhouse, where he'd found her
cutting chives for the cook's omelets, the only
man who could make her scream.

"What are you thinking?" she asked as they
stood to the side of the meadow, which was
filling up with pipers.

"I don't suppose you'd believe I was contemplating whether these games serve as a founda-
tion of, or escape from, people's seemingly
inauthentic lives."

"Perhaps they're just entertainment. You're
familiar with the word, aren't you, Mr. Mac-
Kenzie? Something engaged in for fun?"

"Okay, you've got me. That's what I was
thinking about."

"The games as fun?"

"Not exactly. I was wondering how long we
have to hang around here before we can take a
break and have a little fun of our own."

His grin flashed, as wicked as his eyes, which

were sending her a message that threatened to melt Lily into a puddle of need. "If we'd had any more fun this morning, I'd have broken every window in my grandmother's greenhouse."

"Good goal. Then I'll have a new one built and we'll all be happy."

She laughed, as he'd meant her to. Then sighed when he brushed his lips against hers.

When the mist lifted, Lily realized this was the first time he'd kissed her in public. Did this mean something? Was he ready for the family, along with most of Highland Falls and several hundred strangers, to view them as a couple?

And dear Lord, could she be any more pitiful? She was starting to feel more and more like Missy, whom she'd last seen hanging out at the music tent, mooning over the guitarist for Seven Nations, a fusion group that blended keyboards, electric guitars, fiddles, pipes, and drums into an eclectic Celtic rock sound.

When she'd seen them playing during the Olympic torch ceremonies, Lily had known she had to book them for this year's games. Watching Missy with the hunky guitar player, she was glad they'd agreed to come. Obviously she'd moved on from Brad, which was natural for a girl her age.

The only problem was, Lily mused, that while her heart might be behaving as if it were seventeen years old, her head kept trying to remind her that Ian would be moving on, as well. Out of Highland Falls, out of her life.

The festival was only going to last today and tomorrow; then he'd be staying to film the wedding. Speaking of which . . . Lily sighed in frustration as she saw Jenny coming toward her across the flower-dotted meadow.

"Lily, you need to get your sisters to try on their dresses. It was hard enough to make them from those vague measurements they gave me. I need to make sure they fit, so everything will be perfect."

"I doubt you need worry about that," Ian said. "You'll be a lovely bride. All the attention will be on you."

"Well." She looked up at him, clearly surprised that the glower had been replaced with such a friendly attitude. "That's very nice of you. I was first thinking of a traditional white dress, but I wanted to be authentic and they didn't wear white in medieval times, so I decided to go for blue. That's also a royal color."

"And should look great with your hair," he said encouragingly.

"Do you think so?" She skimmed a hand down her long waterfall of blond hair.

"Absolutely. Don't you, Lily?"

"Blue's great. I'm not so sure about the yellow bridesmaids' gowns —"

"They're wonderful. Zelda used southernwood — that's an herb — from the garden to dye the material an authentic yellow," Jenny told Ian. "She used woad to get my blue. She told me that it's the same plant the Picts used as a styptic on their wounds, which was why the Roman invaders thought they painted themselves blue."

"That's interesting." And a new one on him.

"Isn't it?" Her plain pale face lit up, making her appear almost pretty. "It's just wonderful, learning so much about John's heritage. I can't wait to join the Stewart clan."

"I've no doubt you'll be a true asset."

"I hope so." Seeds of doubt darkened her pale blue eyes for a moment. Then, as if remembering why she'd searched Lily out, her lips pulled into a frown. "Please, Lily. I know Lark's avoiding me, and as for Laurel, well, I think she'd rather see me drown in the Highland River than marry her father. She's been watching me as if she expects me to take off with the family silver."

"It's her occupation," Lily assured her. "Investigative reporters tend to be suspicious of everything and everyone."

"Well, I, for one, think that's a terrible way to live," Jenny huffed, then turned on a Birkenstock heel and marched back across the field, dodging the marching pipers.

"Wedding nerves," Lily diagnosed.

"And once again, it falls upon you to fix things."

"I appreciate your helping to smooth things over. I realize how important all this is to her, but I also understand why Lark and Lily aren't being cooperative. Lark has some personal problems, so I doubt she feels much like being around people right now."

"She certainly came to the wrong place if she's looking for solitude."

"Tell me about it. Laurel, on the other hand, is probably trying to give poor Jenny fits. Though with these dresses, I understand why she's resisting. When Jenny first asked me to be an attendant, I feared some pink taffeta nightmare. Yellow linen is, amazingly, worse. I'm going to look like a giant lemon. Or, with my hair, a skinny flame."

"You're not skinny." He treated her to a long, slow perusal that assured her she was just right for his tastes. "As for looking like a flame, I think it's totally appropriate that outside appearances will match inside heat." His eyes darkened. "I lied to Jennifer when I said everyone in the church would be looking at the bride." The hot intimacy in his gaze nearly buckled her knees. "Because they won't be able to take their eyes off you."

The amazing thing about it was, when she was with Ian, she believed that. "You do realize that flattery will get you everywhere."

He waggled his brows in a broadly wicked way that made her laugh again. "That's precisely what I was counting on."

As the day passed, Ian decided that the main reason for the Highland Games was so all the clans could get together and argue about the dirty deeds one clan did to the other hundreds of years ago. Fortunately, he considered, watching two armies go at it in a reenactment of Culloden, most were too mellow from partaking from the bottles of Highlander's Pride and casks of Dark Island ale to take out any real revenge.

It was easy to see that the Highland Games was, hands down, the most popular annual festival in Highland Falls.

"Yet another American twist that I find hard to believe is authentic," Ian said as he and Brady took in the "ancient" sport of haggis hurling.

"Can you think of anything better to do with haggis?" asked Brady, who'd surprised Ian by showing up in a Ross tartan with a white cockade on his hat, declaring himself to be a descendant of the '45 rebels by way of his maternal grandmother.

"There's a point to be made for hurling it as far as you can," Ian allowed.

Having still not nailed down the message he wanted to portray with this documentary, he wandered around, taping whatever caught his eye. Which was Lily, more often than not. Even when she wasn't serving as narrator explaining the various games, and chatting with festival-goers who were manning the colorful clan tents filled with all sorts of tartans and heraldry and books with clan history, she was in his personal viewfinder. And, he realized, as he watched her laughing as she was coaxed into judging the bonniest knees" contest, she was in his heart.

They caught up with each other again in the

music tent. The Seven Nations had been replaced by a pretty brunette fiddler whose Scottish snap was so energetic, she seemed to lift the dancing spectators off the ground. They'd arrived near the end of the program, just in time to hear her make the old jig "Grace Hay's Delight" sound new again.

"She's damn good," Brady, who was particular about his sound, said admiringly.

"Clever, too," Ian murmured as she started selling copies of her new CD with an outrageous tale about needing funds to get her mother out of a Turkish prison. It was obvious not a soul in the tent believed a word of her story, but appreciating a good tale and even better fiddling, the crowd began lining up to buy the CD.

"She gets better every year," Lily said, as they left the tent. "At last year's games, she was telling everyone she needed to buy her baby new shoes."

She looked out over the field, which had been taken over by huge men and strong women throwing stones and cabers, the colorful standards flying in the mountain breeze, the gaily decorated clan tents, the food and drink stands, and at the crowds, ranging from seemingly ancient to babes in arms, all laughing, singing, dancing, and, always important to the Scots, continuing to argue ancient history. In an area of self-proclaimed MacRowdies, kilt-wearing men and plaid-clad women were loudly and enthusiastically "sacrificing" a watermelon.

"So far, it's going well," Lily said.

"It's the best I've ever been to," Brady surprised Ian by declaring. "Grandfather Mountain may get more press, being the biggest, but this one has a real nice sense of family."

"That's the idea," Lily replied. "A clan is, after all, just an extended family."

Ian didn't want to think about families. Or clans. And he especially didn't want to think about how well Lily fit into it all. He'd never seen anyone more suited to a place; she reminded him of the old saying: bloom where you're planted.

Lily had not only bloomed; she'd flourished. He couldn't imagine her leaving the small insular community — just as he couldn't imagine himself staying here.

"You did good, Lily Stewart," he said.

She fanned herself in an exaggerated Southern-belle fashion. "Why, fiddle-dee-dee, Mr. MacKenzie, the way you flatter a girl."

"It's not flattery." With Duncan's latest deception never far from his mind, Ian was grateful for a chance to tell her the absolute truth.

"That makes it even better," she said with a smile. "I've got to get over to the piping arena; it's nearly time for Missy to compete. Something I hear she owes to your interceding with her mother."

"I didn't intercede." He wasn't comfortable having that come out. "I merely suggested that with all the trouble she could be getting into, wanting to play the bagpipes didn't seem all that serious."

"Well, we're all grateful. In fact, my father's so relieved not to be constantly hearing the arguments over the dinner table, he's going to hang a MacKenzie tartan in the dining room."

Ian murmured something he hoped sounded like appreciation.

Missy's face was pale beneath the sprinkling of copper freckles, and her lips, as she tuned her pipes, appeared to be trembling.

"Is that Molly Moodie?" Lily asked.

Ian focused on the elderly woman standing on the sidelines by Missy, a tartan tam perched atop her pastel blue curls. "It looks like her." Damn, what was the old bastard up to now?

"I didn't know she and Missy had met."

"It appears they have." Duncan had pulled some lowdown stunts in his eighty-some years, but Ian couldn't believe he'd use an innocent child to get to the brooch. He watched in amazement as his grandfather blew into the mouthpiece, fiddled with the pipes, then handed them back to the girl.

"Did Molly just tune those pipes?" Lily asked.

"If I had to venture a guess, I'd say yes." Ian was even more surprised than Lily looked.

As Missy's name was called, Ian realized that they'd been joined by other Stewarts — Annie, Zelda, John Angus, Lark, Laurel, and Melanie — and Jenny.

"I hate this," Melanie muttered.

"I thought you'd accepted the idea of Missy's piping," Zelda said.

"I have. I just hate the fact that she decided to enter this competition. My heart's beating so fast, I'm about to hyperventilate."

"You'll be fine," Jenny assured her. It was not like her father's fiancée to speak up in a family situation, and all the heads swiveled toward her.

"Well, of course I will," Melanie snapped. "We Lancaster women are survivors, after all."

"Does anyone know what, exactly, she's being judged on?" Laurel asked as the teenager began to walk back and forth in front of the judges, playing a slow march.

"I looked up the rules last night," Lily said. "They're judging on tuning, timing, execution, and expression."

"She certainly seems to be in tune," Annie said.

"How can you tell?" Lily asked.

"She's not sounding like a cat who got its tail caught beneath a rocker today," Zelda said.

"I think she's wonderful. Look how well she's marching. And she's playing with far more expression than usual," Melanie said with maternal pride. "It almost makes me wish her father was here to see her."

"Perhaps we should have invited him," Lily said.

Melanie shot her a quick, sharp look. "I said 'almost.' "

It was only two or three minutes, but it seemed like a lifetime. By the time Missy finished, letting the sound play out to silence, Lily realized how long she'd been holding her breath.

The teenager bowed to the judge. Then she grabbed Molly Moodie by the hand and pulled her over to the family.

"How did I do?" she asked.

"You were bonny," John Angus said.

"Wonderful, darling," Annie decreed, to which Lily, Lark, and Laurel instantly agreed.

"It was a bit of home," Ian said.

"I'm so proud of you, Missy!" This from Melanie.

Missy beamed. "I couldn't have done it without Molly. She's secretly been my coach, and I've learned more from her than I did in piping school."

"Imagine that," Ian murmured. When he met his grandfather's eye, Duncan's hard stare warned him against spilling the beans.

"I just gave the lass a few hints," Duncan/Molly said.

"It was a grand performance. You've come a long way since I heard you practicing," Ian said.

"It was Molly." Missy threw her arms around Duncan and pressed her glowingly smooth young cheek against the older, weathered one. "She made all the difference. I don't know what I would have done without her."

This time, when Ian's and Duncan's eyes met

over the top of Missy's head, Ian could have sworn he saw tears swimming in those usually flinty depths.

33

Rather than go all out in clan attire, Lily had chosen to wear a slender black tube of silk she'd borrowed from her aunt Melanie for the Tartan Ball, held in the ballroom of Stewart's Folly. Her only jewelry was a silver thistle on a narrow silver chain, which had drawn Ian's eyes — and lips — to her neck.

"I've never seen Missy look so happy," she murmured as she swayed in his arms. Across the room, an entire string of young men were vying for a chance to dance with her cousin.

"She's a pretty girl. And that dress shows off the woman she's going to become."

"Isn't it stunning? I've never seen so many seed pearls."

"She's not the only one who's stunning. Not only are you the most efficient person at the Highland Games, darling. You're the most beautiful."

"I swear," Lily said on a sigh as she twined her fingers around his neck, "you must have kissed the Blarney Stone sometime in your life."

She smiled up at him as he smiled down at

her. It was a perfect moment Lily wished she could freeze in time.

She glanced around and saw her father talking expansively to a group of men in the far corner of the room. From the sweeping motions of his hand, she suspected he was discussing his latest paintings. She was surprised to see Laurel dancing with Brady O'Neill, who was surprisingly light on his feet for such a large man. Not far from them, Jenny was dancing with Donald. Who, Lily guessed from the intense look on his face, was probably boring her to death with sagas of the Forbes clan.

"I still can't believe you paid all that money for my photograph," she murmured.

Despite Donald's efforts to the contrary, the cocktail party and silent charity auction prior to the ball had brought in a record amount of money, and all had agreed that the photographs of various Highland Falls citizens were beautifully — and tastefully — done.

"As a souvenir, your photograph, darling, beats the hell out of a KISS MY THISTLE bumper sticker."

Susan had posed Lily standing with her back to the camera, nude, draped in a Royal Stewart tartan that dipped far below her waist.

"Who were you thinking of?"

"When?" she asked absently, wondering how soon they'd be able to escape. They were running out of time, and with the wedding tomorrow, they didn't have much time left together.

"When you were flashing that sexy-as-sin smile over your shoulder at the camera. What man were you thinking of?"

She smiled as she remembered that afternoon. The look wasn't as much sexy as it was a result of being plowed from those margaritas she and Susan had downed. "You, of course."

She waited for him to point out the obvious — that they hadn't yet met when the photograph had been taken — but instead he chuckled in a satisfied way she could feel rumbling deep in his chest. "Good answer."

He nuzzled her neck. Before Ian MacKenzie had shown up in Highland Falls, Lily had never realized that there was a direct connection between that sensitive little spot he'd discovered behind her ear and the hot, needy place between her legs.

Those weren't the only needs battering her. She'd entered into this affair with her eyes wide open, knowing the kind of man he was, knowing that he didn't like complications and avoided commitment to such an extreme that he'd actually lived his entire life in hotels. Lily found that both amazing and a little sad.

She could understand his need for adventure, and to want to know what was around each bend, but surely there was nothing wrong with having someplace to call home. Even mountain climbers established base camps.

That was dangerous thinking. Best to take a step back, to keep her heart from getting battered. The problem with that strategy was that her heart was no longer hers to protect. Because she'd given it to Ian.

"So," she asked with forced casualness, unaccustomed to holding in her thoughts, but not wanting to risk ruining their last night together by changing the rules they'd both agreed upon. "Where are you headed off to after you leave here?"

"Brady and I are going to shoot on this tiny island up in the North Sea, Hapus Marchoges Ynys, off the coast of Wales."

"Which translated into English means 'mouth full of marbles'?"

"Happy horsewoman island. Shaggy ponies, which people think may have come across the land bridge from Asia during the Ice Age, roam wild there."

"Another connection to the past."

"Like your mountain serpentine." He nibbled on her earlobe and enjoyed the way her body melted a bit against his.

"So you're making a film about the horses?"

"No. I'm making a film about NATO deciding to drop bombs on the place."

She stopped dancing and looked up at him, disbelief sketched across her features. "Surely you're not serious. Tell me NATO wouldn't really bomb women and horses."

"It's not quite that blatant. Yet." Ian frowned at what he'd seen when he'd taken a preliminary trip there. "It's not a very large island, no more than thirty square miles, but it's long and skinny and there are mountains and glaciers at the north end. That's the end NATO wants to use as a practice range."

"But on any place that small, mistakes will be made. People could be hurt."

"That's exactly the point of Hapus Marchoges's ruling parliament. The members of which happen to be all women, and always have been."

"It's a matriarchy?" Even more interested, Lily wondered why she'd never heard of it.

"Apparently so. The place was originally settled by women who claim to be descendants of the ladies of the Round Table who, with the goddess Ceridwen, took it upon themselves to hold the island for that day when King Arthur will rise from his golden bed and return from Avalon to claim the throne.

"The Church apparently didn't find the little group worth converting, and all the countries in the area appeared to be afraid of any group claiming to have power over nature, death, fertility, regeneration, inspiration, magic, astrology, herbs, science, poetry, and all knowledge."

"Well, that is quite a handful of talent," she said. "Especially considering I can't even seem to find *one*."

"I took a quick look at your tapes before coming here, and you're wrong about not having any talent."

"Oh?"

"Your stuff is terrific, and adds an up-close and personal touch I've never achieved on my own."

"Perhaps that's because you tend to look at the big message picture," she considered.

"Perhaps, but this documentary will be better because of you."

"Well, thank you. So tell me more about this island!"

"Having been an island to themselves for all these centuries, they don't have any allies to help them stop the bombings. They insist they're going to weave a magic spell to deflect the bombs."

It was like a fever with him. His eyes gleamed with an enthusiasm much the way he looked at her when they made love. She wondered yet again if Ian would ever be able to settle down as her gypsy of a grandfather had eventually done.

"Well, that's certainly ambitious. And of course they have allies; they have you." She went up on her toes and touched her smiling mouth to his. Their lips clung.

"Any reason you need to stay around here any longer?" he asked.

"Nope." She twined her fingers around his neck, loath to let him go. "I'm pretty much free until tomorrow's wedding."

"I want to be with you." He skimmed a hand over her hair. "And not just for a few minutes or a couple of hours. I want to sleep with you all night long."

It was something they'd never done. And it sounded wonderful.

"I have just the place," she murmured. "And if we're lucky, you're in for a dynamite surprise."

As they left the ballroom hand in hand, it occurred to Ian that he'd experienced more surprises in the last few days than he had in the past several years — Lily being the best of them. He still had no idea what he was going to do about her, but for this one night, he'd put his usual need for control aside and just go with the flow.

Annie was seated at a small French desk in the suite she and Duncan were sharing. Her elbows were braced on the surface, her fingers making little circles against her temples. She'd taken her hair out of her usual tidy braid, allowing it to tumble freely over her shoulders. She'd creamed off the makeup she'd worn for the Tartan Ball, and rather than revealing her years, which Duncan knew to be just three years short of his own, her bare, remarkably unlined face reminded him of the bonny young lass he'd first fallen in love with on the playground when he'd been six years old.

Over the years, when he'd thought of Annie, he'd only allowed himself to remember her as the gorgeous, impetuous, red-haired risk taker who'd left him standing at the altar in front of the entire village.

Now, seeing her like this, shedding the lady-of-the-manor composure she wore like a second skin, looking small and vulnerable, Duncan felt something inside him move.

He couldn't quite recognize the feeling.

It wasn't quite lust, though he didn't think he could ever be anywhere near Annie without wanting her. And it certainly wasn't the seething humiliation he was used to feeling these past decades since she'd left Scotland, never to return.

Before he could put a finger on it, as if sensing his inner turmoil, she glanced up. Her eyes were red-rimmed from weeping and veiled from the disease that was so cruelly stealing her sight, but he still found her beautiful.

"I must look a mess," she said with a faint smile that was at odds with the sheen of tears in her eyes.

"Don't be talking such nonsense. You're the bonniest lass in Highland Falls." It was a relief to be able to tell her the truth. Over the past days, he'd come to understand why Ian had been so ill-tempered about lying to the Stewart lass.

She laughed at that. "You're a terrible liar, Molly Moodie."

She rose with a grace he remembered her acquiring during that summer she'd suddenly changed from a girl to a woman, the summer he'd spent walking around with his pecker as stiff as a billy goat's. When she put her arms around him, he drank in the painfully familiar scent that had made him refuse to ever allow roses in his home.

"But it's glad I am to have you for a friend," she said.

He touched a bit of moisture on her cheek with a fingertip. "Friends share troubles."

"It's nothing." He felt a deep loss when she pulled away and turned toward the window.

"Then why would you be crying?" He came up behind her and held her shoulders with his palms. "If ye'd be thinking I'd carry tales, I promise you that I'll keep anything you tell me under me wig. So to speak," he tacked on quickly. All the unrecognizable emotions battering at him had almost caused him to give his secret away.

"No." She sighed and went back over to the desk. "We may not have known each other all that long, but I trust you implicitly, Molly dear." She looked out the window toward the bonfires that were blazing in a campground not far from the castle. "I was thinking about Ian when you came in."

"You're weeping because of the filmmaker? What has he done? If he's hurt you —"

"Of course he hasn't. He's been a perfect gentleman, and Lily's madly in love with him."

"Is that a problem?"

"No, I don't think so. I'm a bit concerned about where their relationship is going, but she's a grown woman and capable of taking care of herself. What I'm mostly concerned about is Ian's film. Do you think it will be a success?"

"The man's famous, isn't he? How could it not be?"

"That's what I keep telling myself." She sighed again. "But the unpalatable fact is that he's our last chance. If the documentary doesn't get good distribution and encourage more people to come to Highland Falls, I'm afraid we'll be put out of our home."

He'd never thought such an idea would prove so painful. "Ye'd be homeless?"

"Well, we wouldn't be destitute. But we certainly couldn't afford to keep Stewart's Folly. It's an exercise in extravagance, but it's been in the Stewart family for more than two hundred years, and I know my son would be devastated to be the one who lost it."

"Isn't John Angus wealthy? I thought his paintings sold well."

"They do, and he's certainly well off. But he got into a little tax problem last year which he's still paying off, and when the economy took a dip, the prices collectors were willing to pay for art declined, while the cost of maintaining this huge building continued to rise."

"You said your husband was well off."

"He was. But it's always been a struggle to keep this place up. The property taxes have become downright draconian. And James's illness the last few years of his life — he died of lung cancer — ate up our savings. Every month it becomes more of a struggle to maintain the house well enough for people to be willing to come, but with fewer people being able to take holidays . . ." She sighed again.

"Your room rentals have fallen."

"Like a rock. Which is why I do so hope that Ian's film will be a success."

"That'll take time." An icy feeling washed over him, and it took Duncan a moment to recognize it as gut-wrenching guilt.

"I know. But he's the last chance we've got."

"No he's not," Duncan heard himself saying. "There's me."

"You?"

"I've acquired a bit of money in my old age that I could contribute to the cause."

"Oh, Molly. You are the dearest, most generous person. And while I'm truly touched, I couldn't borrow money from you, because I couldn't promise to pay it back anytime soon. As you said, it'll take time for the film to come out. Even longer to dig our way out of the pile of debts we find ourselves in."

"It wouldn't be a loan, but a gift." What was the point of having money if you couldn't help the people you cared for?

Her eyes widened. "That's incredibly generous, but I couldn't accept."

"Don't go getting prideful on me, Annie luv. I've more money than I'll spend in one lifetime. It'll bring me pleasure to use a wee bit of it to help a friend in need."

"You're a kind and altruistic person. Because I know the offer comes from the heart, I'll seriously consider it."

"That's the good lass." His lips curved into a smile that was becoming more and more natural.

Her laughter was as clear and sweet as a Highland mountain stream. "Do you know how long it's been since anyone referred to me as a lass?" The tender touch of her hand, when she lifted it to his weathered, rouged and powdered cheek, created a slow, deep pull inside him. "And I know it's horribly selfish of me, but we've become so close so swiftly, that I hate the idea of your returning home to Scotland after the games."

She was too close. Too tempting. Duncan kept his arms stiffly at his sides and hoped that the thick pleats of his Moodie-plaid wool skirt would keep from giving him away.

"It's not as if I have anyone to return home to," he said, his voice strained from desire and the effort of holding it in.

She lifted her gaze; hope blazed in her emerald eyes. "Are you saying —"

"Friends are hard to come by." That was definitely the truth. Hadn't he run off too many of them during his younger years with his flashfire temper, sharp tongue, and caring more about business affairs than friends or family? "I'd like to stay on here in Highland Falls a while longer. If you'd be willing to put up with me."

"Put up with you? Oh, Molly, I can't think of anything that would bring me greater pleasure."

As she hugged him again, Duncan could think of quite a few things more pleasurable. All of which had to do with getting her out of that ivory silk robe that hugged her soft, ripe curves like a lover's caress.

Which was impossible without destroying the budding friendship which had already come to mean more to him than all the tea in Scotland. Even more, he was startled to realize, than The Bruce's brooch.

He'd thought he was so bluidy clever, weaving his web of deception. But that web was becoming stickier by the moment.

34

After raiding the refrigerator, Lily and Ian left Stewart's Folly with a brick of Isle of Mull cheddar cheese, some sliced meat, and a loaf of nutty brown bread to go along with the bottle of champagne Ian had snagged from the party.

"Am I allowed to ask where we're going?" he asked as he carried a pair of tartan blankets and the wicker picnic basket out to her bright orange VW Beetle convertible which, like its owner, was an appealing blend of cheery charm and practicality.

"You're allowed to ask." She kissed him lightly, then laughed. "But that doesn't mean I'll tell you."

The drive through the darkened forest took less than five minutes. "We could have walked," she said as they made their way up the moonlit path, "but it's more difficult to see the trail at night. Besides, this way, if it rains, we can put the top up on the car and make out in the back seat."

"Clever girl."

"That's why my father pays me the big bucks to organize the festival."

"Really? I was under the impression you were doing it for free."

"I am." She patted his cheek. "I was only kidding, Ian."

"Oh." Damn. There were times when Ian thought Brady might be right about the Scots needing a humor transplant.

They entered the clearing where they'd sat together the day he'd left for New York. The day he'd begun to realize that whatever was happening with Lily was different from his past relationships with other women. Because *she* was so very different.

"It's incredible." The moon had turned the waterfall to a sheet of sterling silver; the water in the pool was a deep purple indigo.

"You haven't seen anything yet." She glanced down at her watch. "We've got about five minutes."

"Until what?"

"If I told you, it wouldn't be a surprise, would it?" she asked reasonably.

"Good point." He spread out the blankets. "So what do you suggest we do while we're waiting?"

"We're both intelligent people. I'm sure if we put our heads together, we can think of something."

"Our heads." He skimmed the pad of his thumb against her smiling mouth. "Or our lips."

"I knew ye were a clever laddie, Ian

MacDougall MacKenzie." She leaned forward and touched her mouth to his.

Ian splayed his fingers against the back of her head and held her still as he brushed his lips against hers, left, then right, then left again.

"Nice," she murmured when he tilted his head back and looked down into green eyes deep enough to drown in. "Let's do it again."

This time he took her mouth slowly, wanting to savor the taste. When her lips parted with a soft sound between a sigh and a purr, he changed the angle, slipped his tongue between them, and, denying the need that always flared so quick and hot, he slowly, lazily deepened the kiss.

When he grazed her bottom lip with his teeth, a low, ragged moan caught at the back of her throat. When he dipped his head and nipped at her throat, she shivered.

"Are you cold?" Although the nights could be cool, even in summer, the mountains had held the day's heat.

"No." She slid her fingers into his hair. "Actually, I'm surprised the grass hasn't burst into flames beneath this blanket."

When her other hand moved to stroke the hard length of him, he caught her wrist and put it on his thigh.

"Not yet." He closed his eyes, rubbed his cheek against the flame of her hair, and fought for control. "I want you ready for me."

"Ready?" She managed a strangled laugh. "Ian, I've been beyond ready all day." She drew in a sharp breath as he touched the tip of his index finger to his tongue; when he traced such a hot, damp line along the swell of her breasts, Lily half expected to hear the hiss of steam.

"I've never met a woman so lacking in pretenses," he said as he returned his mouth to hers. This time his kiss went deeper. Darker.

"It would be useless to try to pretend with you." An edgy delight shimmered through her as his wicked, clever mouth took her breast, dampening the silk. How could she even attempt to conceal this trembling? Or the pounding of her pulse beneath his lips? "I've wanted you from the very first moment. I thought once would be enough." She strained against him as his teeth erotically tortured a nipple. "But every time you make love to me only makes me want you more."

He drew her down on the blanket so they were lying face to face. Her eyes were luminous in the moonlight, her lips moist and unbearably delectable. "Good." His hands swept possessively over her, feeling every sensual tremor. "All day long, all I could think about was what I wanted to do to you once I got you alone again."

"Yes." Her eyes echoed her breathless answer. "To everything."

His rough laugh vibrated through him. Through her. "Don't you want to know what I've planned for you?" He slid his knee between her legs, rubbing intimately. "Or shall I surprise you?"

"I've always liked surprises." A sigh escaped her lips as he slid a hand between her parted thighs, slipping beneath the elastic of the lacy scrap of panties she'd bought especially with him in mind, and brushed against the swollen, needy folds. "Oh!"

His fingers, which had been on the verge of slipping inside her, stopped at the sudden exclamation. "Am I hurting you?"

"Of course not." She felt a tug of loss as his broad hand returned to rest on her inner thigh. "It's just that you got me so sidetracked, I forgot I wanted to show you the magic. Look!" She gestured toward the waterfall. "They're starting."

He glanced over and saw a bright green glimmer. "Very nice." Not wanting to hurt her feelings, he didn't tell her that while they might not have fireflies in Great Britain, he had seen them before.

"Just wait."

Realizing that they wouldn't be finishing what they'd begun anytime soon, he rolled over onto his back, settled her against him so her head was on his chest, and waited.

A few — probably a dozen or so — began to twinkle. Then another dozen. Then more still.

"Those are the males," she said. "They glow to attract the females, who are lurking in the grass. They glow, too. But not as brightly, or as long."

The flashes grew more brilliant, splashes of

radiant green light, each seemingly brighter than the next, as if they were trying to outshine each other. Which, given that this was a courting ritual, just might be true.

More and more began to sparkle as the fireflies dipped and soared through the tree branches and around the waterfall and the cliff behind, splashes of light in the darkened forest. But they didn't simply flash off and on as usual. They pulsed in a pattern — six bright, consecutive bursts of light, then a pause, then six more bursts.

"That's truly incredible."

"Wait," Lily said again.

It happened gradually, so Ian didn't catch on right away. First two fireflies began flashing in unison. Then a few more picked up the rhythm. In approximately fifteen minutes, every firefly in the forest was flashing together, as if from some unheard signal. Six quick, bright flashes. Then what seemed an eternal eight second of darkness. Then six more. Then another eight seconds.

"My God." It couldn't be happening. They were now surrounded by hundreds, thousands of fireflies, so many that whenever they lit up, it was impossible to tell what was sky and what was ground.

"There are only a handful of places in the entire world where this happens," Lily said. "One is in Southeast Asia. We just discovered them here last year. The researchers at the park want to keep them a secret until they can study them a little more."

"No wonder. I never would have believed it if I hadn't seen it myself."

Her smile sparkled in the moonlight and her face shone with pleasure at having shared her secret with him.

"You can't see this and not think about fairies," he murmured. "And enchanted forests."

"That's what I always think, although the scientists insist it's merely biology. Apparently human beings are the only other living thing that can pick up a rhythm to synchronize actions.

"And as beautiful as it is, it's also very sad. They'll mate tonight, then lay their eggs, then die. A few short weeks, and their lives are ended."

He trailed his fingers up her cheek, lacing them through her hair. He'd never been one for spontaneous touches or tender caresses, but he was finding it impossible to keep his hands off her. "But think how bright their lives sparkle while they're alive."

"That's the important part," she agreed. "So do you like it?"

"It will stay with me the rest of my life."

"Well, then." She lifted her smiling lips to his and let them cling. "Let's see if we can make it even more memorable."

Perhaps it was because of the magic of the

lights sparkling all around them, perhaps it was the way she had of bewitching him, perhaps it was just being with this very special woman at this extraordinary moment in time, that gave their lovemaking a dreamy, otherworldly feel.

Their kisses were slow, deepening degree by exquisite degree; clothes seemed to float away as if carried off by mystical unseen hands. Her flesh gleamed ivory in the moonlight; he caressed, tasted, savored. His muscles rippled beneath her hands as Lily explored, lingered, reveled.

Surprise, pleasure, and delight shimmered around them; needs, both spoken and unspoken, tangled within. Needing her to know how special this was, how special *she* was, Ian murmured promises he didn't know how he could keep. Needing him to know that she was his, heart, body, and soul, Lily desperately wanted those words to be true.

She opened for him fully. Heart, and body. He said her name as he filled her, then again and again as they moved together in a rhythm as old as the mountains, as fluid as the silvered water. Lily wasn't going to think about tomorrow; wasn't going to worry about what she'd do when he moved on.

Pressing her lips against his throat, she surrendered to the magic of the moment. And this man she'd fallen in love with.

The fireflies gradually twinkled off. The white moon floated over distant mountains; the water continued to tumble over the mossy rocks to pool at the base of the falls, as it had been doing for eons.

Ian lay on his back, Lily in his arms, wrapped in silence. As he gazed up at the brilliant canopy of stars, the realization Ian had been steadfastly holding at bay hit like a meteor falling from the midnight sky.

I love her.

In a way, it was ironic. He had come to Highland Falls with theft on his mind, believing her a thief. Which she'd turned out to be, though it was his heart she'd stolen.

What the bloody hell was he supposed to do now?

He was not the man he'd been just two weeks ago. He'd changed. So therefore his goals should change, as well. Shouldn't they?

If he truly loved Lily Stewart, and he did, then he should want her to be happy. Only a selfish bastard would insist she turn her life upside down so that his own could continue exactly as it always had.

Ian had never thought himself a greedy man, but that didn't stop him from wanting both Lily and the career he'd worked so hard to build. The career that was, right or wrong, as much of an obsession as The Bruce's brooch had always been to Duncan.

Lily turned her head and pressed her lips against his chest, above the heart she'd claimed.

Finding no answers, he rolled over, taking her

with him, taking her mouth with a force that echoed his frustration. This was no slow, moon-silvered lovemaking, but passion at its most elemental. Hunger made a mockery of control; ravenous, they fed from each other as if it had been an eternity, rather than minutes, since they'd come together.

As tongues tangled, and his hands ran over her, kneading, possessing, meeting her urgent demands, it was almost possible to forget that in a few short hours he'd be on a plane to a small speck of land in the North Sea.

The night air had turned cool but their bodies were hot and moist as Ian plunged into Lily, taking them both to a far-off place beyond questions.

The wedding, which Laurel had dubbed Camelot in the Highlands, began promisingly enough.

The bride was piped in by Missy, beneath a gleaming tunnel of swords lofted high by men in formal Prince Charlie jackets, waistcoats, and kilts.

"Aunt Zelda did an amazing job of dyeing Jenny's dress," Lark said. The rich, lavender-blue heather hue was reminiscent of Scottish moors.

"It's gorgeous," Lily agreed. She ran her palms down her own floor-length yellow bridesmaid's gown, which had, thank heavens, turned out more of an antique gold than lemon. "She certainly looks happy."

"Which just goes to show how well she knows Dad," Laurel muttered.

"You haven't been here to see it, but he's mellowed a bit," Lily said. "I think she's had a good influence on him. And it's obvious that he's madly in love with her."

Standing in front of the altar, beside the priest — whom Lily had managed to talk into wearing a monk's brown robes — John Angus was standing tall and straight. His beard, now that the contest event was over and he'd won a red ribbon, had been neatly trimmed. He too was dressed in formal Scots attire and was, as always, an impressive giant of a man. His eyes blazed like blue fire as he watched his bride enter the chapel.

Jenny was wearing a fragrant coronet of flowers — including white heather for good luck — that Annie and Molly had picked just this morning, and Melanie had woven atop her pale blond waist-length hair. With a visible edge of nerves atop her usual wispy fragility, she looked a great deal like Lily imagined a young virgin bride would have looked a thousand years ago.

When she reached the altar, John Angus held out his hand; Jenny's small white one disappeared into it. Lily thought she swayed slightly.

"Dear friends," the tall blond priest began sonorously. "We are gathered here today during these games to take part in the most time-honored celebration of the human family, uniting a woman and a man in marriage. John

Angus and Jennifer have come to witness before us, telling of their love for each other.

"We remind them that they are performing an act of complete faith, each in the other; that the heart of their marriage will be the relationship they create. Just as two very different threads woven in opposite directions can form a beautiful tapestry, so can their lives merge together to form a beautiful marriage. In a world where faith often falls short of expectation, it is a tribute to these two, who now stand before friends and family and join hands and hearts in perfect faith.

"Marriage is a bond to be entered into only after considerable thought and reflection. In the art of marriage, little things are the big things. It is never being too old to hold hands. It is remembering to say 'I love you' at least once a day. It is never going to sleep angry.

"It is at no time taking the other for granted; the courtship should not end with the honeymoon but should continue through all the years. It is having a mutual sense of values and common objectives. It is standing together facing the world. It is forming a circle of love that gathers in the whole family. It is doing things for each other, not in an attitude of duty or sacrifice, but in the spirit of joy."

"How about the spirit of brevity?" Laurel muttered.

"I like it," Lark whispered.

"You were married by an Elvis impersonator in Vegas. Anything would sound good after that."

"Shhh," Lily said. She just wanted this wedding to get over smoothly.

"It is speaking words of appreciation and demonstrating gratitude in thoughtful ways," droned the priest, who was also an actor at the local college and a Highland Games reenactor. "It is not expecting the husband to wear a halo or the wife to have wings of an angel. It is not looking for perfection in each other. It is cultivating flexibility, patience, understanding, and a sense of humor. It is having the capacity to forgive and forget. It is giving each other an atmosphere in which each can grow. It is finding room for the things of the spirit."

"It's knowing when to wrap up a monologue."

This time Laurel's comment drew a faint, rare smile from Lark. Even Freedom, who was usually bright and alert when in harness, let out a huge yawn that earned a smothered giggle from Missy. Melanie grinned like a schoolgirl herself as she reached out and laced their fingers together.

"Like a stone, John, should your love be firm. Like a star, Jennifer, should your love be constant. Let the powers of the mind and of the intellect guide you in your marriage, let the strength of your wills bind you together, let the power of love and desire make you happy, and the strength of your dedication make you inseparable. Be close, but not too close. Possess each other, yet be understanding. Have patience with

391

each other, for storms will come, but they will pass quickly."

Laurel sighed loudly. "Unlike this ceremony."

Lily hoped he would hurry things up; Jenny seemed to be turning paler by the moment. Perhaps she'd been too nervous to eat before the ceremony.

"Love should be the core of your marriage, love is the reason you are here. But it also will take dedication — to stay open to each other; to learn and to grow together even when this is not always so easy to do. It will take faith — to always be willing to go forward to tomorrow, never really knowing what tomorrow will bring. And it will take trust — to know in your hearts you want the best for each other."

"And it will take forever to get to the *I dos*," Laurel complained audibly.

The priest shot her a sharp look, but doggedly forged on. "Allow each other time to be an individual, respect each other's wishes as well as dreams. Selfishness — and impatience" — he directed another glare toward Laurel — "has no place in a lasting relationship. Happiness is what each of you should seek for the other. Ask less for yourself than you are willing to give. In every relationship, trust is of utmost important; never break that trust.

"Keeping all that in mind, John Angus, will you receive Jennifer as your wife? Will you pledge to her your love, faith, and tenderness, cherishing her with a husband's loyalty and devotion? Will you trust her not just with all your worldly goods, but with your heart, as well?"

Lily's eyes became misty as her father said, "I will," in a strong voice that wavered uncharacteristically with emotion. She reached out to Lark who, in turn, reached her other hand to Laurel.

John Angus turned toward Jenny and took her hand. "I, John Angus Stewart, promise to love you, comfort and encourage you, to be open and always honest with you, and stay with you as long as we both shall live. I promise to respect and honor you, to be your confidant, always ready to share your hopes, dreams, and secrets. And I swear, by all that is holy and the love you've blessed me with, that I will never, ever break your trust."

Tears had begun streaming silently down Jenny's face.

Seeming oblivious to her distress, the priest turned to the bride. "Jennifer, John Angus has sworn his fidelity and faith to you for all time. Do you likewise —"

"No! I can't! Not like this!" She tore her hand from John Angus's, picked up her long blue skirt, and to the amazement of all those gathered, began running down the aisle. "Don't move, John," she called back over her shoulder. "I'll be right back."

With that, she raced out of the chapel.

35

Confused murmurs followed the runaway bride like a buzzing swarm of bees. Missy, apparently unable to decide whether the escape counted as an official recessional or not, began loudly piping "Scotland the Brave." Caught up in the moment, Freedom barked.

"Damn. I'd better go after her," Lily said.

"She said she'd be right back," Lark said.

"If I were Dad, I sure wouldn't hold my breath," Laurel said.

"You're so cynical," Lark complained.

"And you're amazingly naïve for a woman who sang for the royal princes last month."

"Could you two please knock it off?" Lily asked. She closed her eyes briefly. "Laurel, you keep everyone in their seats. Lark, you take care of Daddy." Who was the color of putty and looked as if he were about to fall flat on his face. "I'll go after the runaway bride."

Lily caught up with Jenny at, of all places, the Firefly Falls Gallery.

"I think you have some splainin' to do, Jenny."

"Oh, quit being cute and just open the damn door."

Lily reached into the hanging pot of red cascade petunias hanging outside the door. She'd no sooner handed Jenny the spare key than Ian and Brady showed up.

"I thought things might be more interesting here," Ian said, as they all followed Jenny into the gallery. She went straight for the display of her dolls, and chose a red-haired one dressed like a Highland dancer.

"Do you have a pair of scissors?" she asked. Before Lily could answer, she said, "Never mind, this will do," snatched Brady's staghorn-handled dirk from its leather sheath, and used the blade to slash open the doll's back.

"Oh, my God," Lily gasped, as she stared down at the sparkling jeweled brooch Jenny extracted from the cotton batting.

"I take it that's not a replica," Ian said.

"No, it's the real one."

"Are you saying the one my father held up the other night was fake?"

"No." Tears welled up in Jenny's baby-blue eyes again as she shook her head. "That one was real. I switched them after he went to sleep."

"But why?"

"I'm sorry, Lily." Jenny took the handkerchief Ian held out to her, and dabbed away the moisture on her cheeks. "But I think John Angus deserves to hear the answer first."

No one spoke on the short trek back up the hill to the castle. Ian and Brady stayed a bit behind, filming the events as Jennifer took that long, slow walk back up the aisle in absolute silence. Conversation had dropped off like a stone in the well the moment she'd appeared in the chapel doorway.

"I'm so sorry, John. I thought I could go through with this. But I can't," she said.

"Go through with what?" John Angus said, still obviously confused. "Getting married? If you need more time, darling —"

"That's not it." She held out her hand, palm up. "This is yours."

"Well, of course it is." His mouth slammed closed as comprehension dawned. "If you have the brooch, then the one I have in my pocket to give you after the ceremony —"

"Is fake," Laurel guessed. She folded her arms across her chest and shot her sisters an "I told you so" look.

"But why would you feel the need to steal it?" John asked. "I was going to give you the real one, Jenny dear."

"And you'll never know how guilty that's been making me feel. When I first came to town to steal it —"

"You came to Highland Falls to steal my Brooch of Lorn?"

"Oh, dear," Lily heard her grandmother, who was seated in the first pew beside Molly Moodie, murmur.

"Yes, but —"

"So all those things you said to me, about

loving me, about wanting to marry me, were a lie?"

Jenny looked around, obviously uncomfortable. "John." She placed a hand on his sleeve; he snatched his arm away as if burned. "This is a personal matter. Perhaps we ought to go somewhere private to discuss it."

"It's not personal when you leave me at the altar in front of God and all my friends," he shot back, his earlier shock overcome by his anger. "It's not personal when you steal something that rightfully belongs to the Stewarts."

"It belonged to The Bruce."

"True. And had it not been stolen by the MacDougalls in battle, it would have passed down to the Stewarts through The Bruce's daughter Marjorie to her son, Robert Stewart, the first Stewart king."

"And what a miserable lot they were," Ian heard Duncan, sitting beside Annie, mutter.

"Did you never wonder," Jenny asked, "how Robert Bruce came to have the brooch in the first place?"

It was the first time in her life Lily had seen her father struck speechless. "How would a person know such a thing as that? The first record of the brooch is when it was taken from the king in his retreat from Dalree."

"It was given to him at his coronation," Jenny said, with such assurance Lily was almost forced to believe her, "by Isabel, countess of Buchan."

"I don't know how you'd be knowing that, but it makes sense," John Angus allowed. "She was a strong supporter of Robert. Didn't she run away from her husband to ensure The Bruce was crowned by a MacDuff, who'd been granted the hereditary right to crown all Scotland's kings?"

"Yes, and her husband was a Comyn. Your ancestor's murder of the Red Comyn was what put The Bruce on the throne, but Isabel's husband had commissioned the brooch to be made as a coronation gift for the Red Comyn."

"Are you claiming the brooch belongs to the damn Comyns?" John Angus demanded. "And how would you know such a tale?"

The pretty flowered coronet went askew as Jenny shook her head. "I know it because the Comyn name evolved into Cumming. I happen to be a Cumming on my mother's side, and my cousin Donald has compiled the evidence."

"Donald?" Lily asked.

All heads turned toward the banker, who was seated on the aisle in the third row of the bride's side. Which, now that Lily thought about it, she should have found a bit odd, since except for seeing them dancing at the Tartan Ball, she hadn't even realized Donald and Jenny knew each other.

"Donald Forbes?" John Angus boomed out.

Donald squared his shoulders and jutted out his chin. "My full name is Donald Cumming Forbes. My mother was a Cumming."

Ian had come up the aisle, still filming the scene.

" 'While in the wood there is a tree, a Cumming will deceitful be,' " Molly quoted the old Scots proverb.

"Oh, for heaven's sake." Annie exhaled a long breath, stood up, and looked down at her elderly roommate. "Wouldn't you be a fine one to be going on about deception, Duncan MacDougall?"

"MacDougall?" Duncan blustered, jumping to his feet as well. Deciding that nothing would surprise her at this point, Lily wouldn't have been surprised if Ian's grandfather leaped up on the altar and started doing a Highland fling. "I don't know what ye'd be talking about. I'm a Moodie woman, as me plaid skirt plainly shows —"

"You're a MacDougall man." Annie reached out unerringly and whipped off the wig, revealing a head as bald as an eight-ball. "And while I remember you as a bonny man when you wore your MacDougall kilt, even I can see that you look bloody ridiculous in a skirt."

"You're a thieving MacDougall?" John Angus's attention was momentarily distracted by his clan's longtime enemy. "Come here as a spy to steal the brooch!"

"Aye, I did come here for that purpose," Duncan shouted back. "But only after me grandson refused to go through with the plan." He shot a censorious look at Ian, who shrugged and kept his camera running. "But then I realized that even if I could find the bluidy damn thing, taking it wouldn't get me what I wanted most."

He placed a hand over his heart and looked almost plaintive. "I love ye, Annie. I loved ye when ye were Annie MacFie, and God help me, I love you as Annie Stewart. And I'd be willing to do anything to make this deception up to you."

As if wanting to make him squirm a bit, Annie took a time to respond. "I don't know, Duncan. It was quite an untrustworthy thing you did. It'll take some time to made amends."

"However long, I'm not going to give up trying."

"That's probably true," Ian said. "My grandfather's nothing if not tenacious."

"So it seems." Annie shook her head and studied Duncan. Although her vision was impaired, there were few people who could see into a person's heart as well as she could. "I've owed you an apology for sixty years. It seems we both have a great deal to say to each other." She glanced around. "In private."

"In private," he agreed. "Wherever you want. Whenever you want."

"I was thinking Scotland might be a nice place to begin. As soon as I see my son married off to his bride."

"Scotland?" Duncan's eyes widened. "Would ye be saying —"

"I'm an old woman who wants to see my home one more time before I die. Take me back to the Highlands, Duncan. Then we'll talk about where we'll spend however many more years we're gifted with."

"Would ye be saying that you're willing to give me a second chance to prove myself to you, Annie?"

Her smile gave him her answer first. "I'm saying that if you're willing to forgive me for my sixty-year-old transgression, I'm willing to forgive you a little misunderstanding about a silly piece of ancient jewelry that's certainly not worth feuding over."

"It's priceless!" Donald corrected sharply. "And it's ours."

"Not yours," Jenny corrected. She appeared to have regained her composure during the little detour with Annie and Duncan. "It's ours." She lifted a hand to John Angus's bearded cheek. "Like Duncan, and, it appears, Ian" — she glanced over at him — "my reason for coming here was not exactly honest. But I never told you a lie, John. Not once."

"Not even when you claimed to love me?"

"Especially then." She met his atypically uncertain look with a level one of her own.

"I think I'm going to cry," Lark murmured.

"Me, too," Lily sniffled.

"You're both so softhearted," Laurel complained, though her own eyes looked suspiciously moist.

"Well?" John Angus turned to the priest. "What are you waiting for, man? My bride and I have a honeymoon trip booked to Inverness, and I'm not getting any younger."

36

Ian was packing to leave when Lily knocked on the door to the tower room.

"Come on in." His tone was less than inviting.

"I've been looking for you."

"Well, now you've found me."

"Are you angry at me?" she asked.

"Of course not." He threw another sweater into the suitcase, not bothering to fold it.

"You disappeared right after the wedding."

Since it wasn't a question, Ian didn't bother to answer.

She came up beside him, picked a black T-shirt from the mattress, and silently handed it to him.

"That's a lie," he ground out as hunger and frustration thundered through him. He threw the shirt into the bag and slammed it shut. "I *am* angry." He trapped her between the bedpost and his body. "I'm angry at you for being who you are. *What* you are." His fingers curled around her slender shoulders, but Ian managed to resist the unruly urge to shake her. "I'm mad as hell that you made me fall in love with you when my guard was down."

"Someone should have warned you that I'm sneaky that way," she said mildly.

"Dammit, didn't you hear me? I said I bloody love you!"

"I think everyone in Highland Falls probably heard you."

"I didn't want to fall in love. I had a bloody life before coming here. I want to get back to it. I don't want to stay here in this small town, where the high point of the year is these stupid games."

"They're not stupid."

"No." Frustrated beyond measure and knowing he was handling this all wrong, he released her and plowed his hands through his hair. "Of course they're not stupid. They're grand. But they're just not what I want. Maybe someday, but not now."

"You've been open about that from the beginning, Ian. We made an agreement that we'd simply sleep with each other for as long as you were here in Highland Falls."

"It's not just about sex, dammit. It's never been just about sex."

"No." He thought he saw a little smile tease at the corner of her delectable mouth, the mouth he'd become addicted to. "It hasn't."

"I love you. And you bloody well love me." His hands took hold of her again, moving down her arms, gripping her tightly by the wrists. "You can't deny it."

"I wouldn't try."

Ian was becoming more frustrated by the moment. How the hell could she stay calm, when every atom in his body was tangled into painful knots?

"Yet you never said it. Not once. Not even after we made love." He'd waited, last night. All night. But she, the most outspoken person he'd ever met, had never said a word.

"We made a deal," she reminded him again. "I'm a woman of my word, Ian. A Highland fling, that's what we agreed to have. And when it was over, you'd go on your way to your next adventure, while I stayed here running my little gallery and taking care of my family."

"You belong here in Highland Falls."

"I do. And I plan to spend my old age here, if it pleases my husband, as well. But a famous filmmaker whose opinion I value very much says he believes I have talent."

"You do. In fact, I sent some of the rehearsal tape out last week, and we got offers from PBS and the History Channel this morning. I figure we'll let them bid each other up for a few days, then let one of them win."

"That's wonderful! Did you say *we?*"

"Your work sold the story as much as mine. I went with the theme of the clans being extended families, connecting people with their pasts. And with each other."

"I can't wait to tell everyone!" Her eyes lit up with the first flash of emotion he'd witnessed since she'd come into the room. "And to think, if it hadn't been for your grandfather, I might never have discovered I've a flair for film-making. Which brings me to what I came up here to tell you: I've come to a decision."

"Oh?"

"Now that I've had a taste of what I can do, I'd like to try taking it further. There's this island I've heard about. A matriarchal land that's never known war, which NATO wants to use as a bombing range."

Ian stared at her. He'd worked through all the possible scenarios of this farewell scene, but he'd bloody never expected this. "That's my story."

"Really?" She tilted her head and lifted a challenging brow, which reminded him she was much more complex than the perky former cheerleader who sold Scottish souvenirs in her small-town mountain gallery. "I don't believe you've shot any tape there. And it only stands to reason that as a woman, I'd have better rapport with the native population."

"I can't believe this. You're actually going to steal my project?"

"Well, it's occurred to me that it's probably time our families stopped the feuding. I know you've worked alone in the past, but I think we made a good team."

"An excellent team," he agreed. "But I'm not interested in training you how to do my job, then having you take off on your own."

"Funny you should mention that." She

reached into the back pocket of the snug pink jeans she'd changed into after the wedding, and pulled out a piece of paper that she held out to him.

He skimmed the single page. "This is a contract."

"For a collaboration," she agreed. "Brady said you prefer to work on a handshake, but Laurel thought I ought to make it official."

"There's no length of time stated."

"That's because the term's negotiable. I was thinking of maybe fifty years — for starters."

"Add a lifetime renewable option to that, and you've got yourself a partner."

The answer was shining in her eyes, and Lily flung her arms around his neck and went up on her toes to seal the deal.

"My bags are packed and down in the great hall," she said, when the long mind-reeling kiss finally ended.

His spontaneous laugh was rich and bold as he scooped his own bag off the bed.

As they walked hand in hand toward their destiny, Lily knew that of all the adventures she and Ian would have together, being in love would always be, hands down, the grandest adventure of all.

Dear Reader,

One of the best things about being a writer is the opportunity to create worlds and populate them with people I enjoy spending time with. In Out of the Mist, *fact and fiction became so blended, I feel the need to sort them out a bit.*

The story of Robert the Bruce's coronation is historical fact; controversy continues to swirl about whether the stone that sat beneath the coronation throne in Westminster Abbey from 1296 to 1996 (when Queen Elizabeth II "loaned" it back to Scotland), is actually the real Stone of Destiny upon which all Scots kings had been crowned until Edward I's raid on Scone Abbey.

The Brooch of Lorn does exist. For the sake of my story, I had Robert the Bruce wearing it at his coronation, but the other tales of its travels are documented up until the 1945 theft, which was totally fictional. It was last seen in public in 1956, and there have been claims that while it's a very important piece of Highland art, it's not the original brooch taken from the king in battle, but a copy created in the fifteenth century. I'll leave that for the experts to decide.

Brady's Rangers did indeed have a soldier-photographer, and Staff Sergeant Phil Stern's wonderful World War II photos provided the inspiration for Lily's grandfather, James.

The synchronized fireflies are true, as well; I merely used creative license to move them from the Great Smoky Mountains National Park to Highland Falls.

I do hope you enjoyed your visit to Highland Falls, and will return for Lark's and Laurel's stories.

Happy Reading!
JoAnn Ross

About the Author

JoAnn Ross has published more than 75 novels, has been published in 26 countries, and is a member of the Romance Writers of America's Honor Roll of bestselling authors. She has won several writing awards, including being named Storyteller of the Year by *Romantic Times*. Her work has been excerpted in *Cosmopolitan* and featured by the Doubleday and Literary Guild book clubs.

She lives with her husband and dog in eastern Tennessee and is inspired daily by the majesty of the Great Smoky Mountains, where she set her Stewart Sisters trilogy.

Visit JoAnn on the Web to subscribe to an electronic newsletter, at www.joannross.com

The employees of Thorndike Press hope you have enjoyed this Large Print book. All our Thorndike and Wheeler Large Print titles are designed for easy reading, and all our books are made to last. Other Thorndike Press Large Print books are available at your library, through selected bookstores, or directly from us.

For information about titles, please call:

(800) 223-1244

or visit our Web site at:

www.gale.com/thorndike
www.gale.com/wheeler

To share your comments, please write:

Publisher
Thorndike Press
295 Kennedy Memorial Drive
Waterville, ME   04901